MW00639254

Love You Always

By

Amanda Stogsdill

Amanda Stogsdill

Copyright©2023 by Amanda Stogsdill
Published by AJ Creative Writing Coach & Editor LLC

"Love You Always"

AJ Creative Writing Coach & Editor LLC

ISBN: ISBN: 978-1-0882-4508-8

Author: Amanda Stogsdill
Editor: April Johnson

Publishing & Editor

AJ Creative Writing Coach & Editor LLC
Website: ajcreativewrites.com
Email: info@ajcreativewrites.com
Phone: (877)647-0179
Saint Louis, MO

Love You Always

The Diary of Leah

DICTATED BY ESTHER

Table of Contents

1939 PART I

1940 PART II

1941 PART III

1942 PART IV

1943 PART V

1944 PART VI

1945 PART VII

1965 PART VIII

ACKNOWLEDGMENT

BIBLIOGRAPHY

The shrill train whistle blows one last time. Mama and Papa shout their goodbyes from the platform. I hear the other kids crying and shouting goodbyes to their parents.

Will we see Mama and Papa again? I wonder.
Beside me, my sister, Leah, touches my arm. She says, "Esther, they've disappeared. You can stop waving now."

Suddenly, I feel the train move forward as it pulls away, moving faster and faster.

Following our usual blessing last night, our parents reminded us again that we were embarking on an adventure to a place called England! They called it an "adventure," but I'm not exactly sure if it will be. We can't stay in Berlin because of Hitler and his Nazi soldiers. So, our only option is to go away until it is safe to return.

It had been a terrible morning for all of us. Try to be brave, I thought. Like Mama said, "It's an adventure!" Mama cried as she packed and repacked our cases. After saying goodbye, Leah and I were pushed onto the train with the other kids.

I held Leah's arm to keep my balance while walking to the back. I felt the floor rumbling under my feet. We're now sitting in the last seat; the wooden train seat is uncomfortable.
Leah says all the other cable cars are full.

I'm sitting on the end, and every time the train turns a corner, I feel like I'm going to slide onto the floor.

The kids around us are talking about how excited they are to arrive in England and to meet the new families waiting for us. I ask Leah if she knows anything about the family we're going to live with, but she doesn't.

One girl near us cries for a long time.

Singing to her seems to help a little. She's five and traveling alone.
Leah says we've stopped for water. Some of the kids stand up. I hear
groans from some of them; I know how they feel-my back aches, too!
Like I said, the train is very uncomfortable. We've been traveling for
hours.

"Can I stop writing, Esther?" Leah begs. "It's difficult to write on a moving
train, and my hand is stiff. Anyway, I said you could share my diary with
me for the beginning of the journey, not all of it!"
Night Leah

Friday, September 1

We sleep leaning against each other as the train passes through towns
and villages. I should say everyone's asleep except me. Like Mama and
Papa said, we're going on an adventure.

In the evening, Esther wanted to take her doll
Minna out of her case, but they're sealed. I told her not to worry.
Minna will be safe inside until we arrive; she could play with her then.

Some of the others wonder who will be there to meet us when we arrive.
Before we left home, Esther said, "It will be strange being with new
families, but exciting, too." Will there be other kids? How will the new
parents be? I wondered.

One of the girls on the train tried to teach us some English since we only
speak German. We tried to learn words like school, I, eat, and family.
We couldn't concentrate because it was extremely noisy, but it is a relief
to know one of us speaks English. That will be useful when we arrive in
England.

Esther Again Monday, September 4

After departing from the train, we traveled for three days on a boat,
which was very cramped. It was an extreme challenge to breathe, and
most of us got seasick. The journey was terrifying! All I could hear was
water splashing and men's voices shouting in a different language. The
boat rocked, sometimes, it was smooth, but when the sea was rough, the
boat felt like it would tip over. Our cases slid across the deck as we all

held on to one another. The wind made awful howling sounds too. I'm glad we weren't above deck. Finally, the sea calmed, and we were able to move around. We tried to wash ourselves with water from a bucket.

We smelled terrible, and our clothes were filthy.
When we entered the bathroom, we tried not to breathe because of the smell. At night, I heard kids crying and some calling out for their parents in their sleep.

Now we're on another train to England. I hope things get better for us once we arrive, but we still need to know where we are staying or who will care for us. When we got on the train, some of us were able to change into clean clothes, which was a relief. The whistle is blowing, and it's so loud my ears are ringing. But that means we're finally stopping.

Leah
September 4, Late Night

I still can't believe it.
Esther and I are separated. An English family took me first.

When the train stopped, we gathered our suitcases and stepped off onto the platform at the train station. The noise and smells hit us like a wave. There were crowds of people, traffic beyond the station, and lots of smoke. I held Esther's hand tighter than usual, afraid she'd be pushed or lost in the crowd. We stopped and lined up with the other children.

People stared at us, lined up one by one. Some kids went with families in twos and threes. After what seemed like a long time, it was our turn.

"Leah, come with me," a woman ordered, pointing at me. I followed her to a family with two daughters. "These are your new foster parents and their daughters. You will live with them while you're here." I just stared at her blankly.

I called Esther's name. I attempted to ask whether my sister would join me, but they didn't answer. I pointed to Esther, but I was led away by the mother of my foster family.

The younger girl and her father smiled at me, but the older girl didn't. When I looked back, Esther was crying. I saw two brothers being taken by a man. Esther tried calling me, but I couldn't hear. I started to run after her, but I was pulled back by my foster mother.

3

Her grip was extremely strong; she tore my coat.

We rode in their car through the town to a farmhouse. Out my window, I saw a barn, henhouse, and outhouse. When I stepped out of the car, my stomach fluttered, and I thought I might throw up. I followed them into the house but was too exhausted to notice much inside. The mother immediately pointed to the stairs, so I didn't have a lot of time to look around.
I'm sleeping in the attic.

I know this isn't what Mama and Papa imagined.
The attic is small, with a bed against the wall, hooks for my clothes, and bare walls. I'm writing this by moonlight. Better sleep now. Who knows what tomorrow will be?

Tuesday, September 5

(This morning, a loud knock woke me. I was dreaming of our family back in Berlin before Hitler's violence. In my dream, I was attending school. Esther and I both learned piano and helped with the housework. Mama and Papa were bakers. We had Shabbat every Friday night, and I spent time riding my bike with friends.

The mother entered my room and threw clothes at me. I showed her my suitcase, but she kicked it under the bed and pointed to the clothes she had brought.

She said something to me in English that I didn't understand. I put on my dress, which is too big, shoes, and a bonnet. I left the nightdress she brought folded on my pillow. I will wear it tonight.

Outside my tiny window, I have a view of a stone wall, and inside is a vegetable garden. To the right, I see hills and tall trees.

I said our morning blessing, Modeh Ani, praying for Esther, too.
More later, diary, I must go downstairs.)

I stumble down the stairs to the kitchen. My too big shoes almost tripped me on each step.

"She's ugly!" The older girl cries, pointing at me.
Whatever she just said must have been mean because she isn't smiling. She and her sister are wearing dresses, too, but their dresses are pretty

4

and clean.

Their kitchen is huge, with a pantry, wood-burning stove, sink, and table in the center of the room. I see a smaller room off the kitchen.
Plates of food sit at each place setting at the table. The oldest daughter sits between the father and me when the father comes in and sits down. In one hand, she grasps my hand, and in the other, she holds her father's hand. He begins speaking with his head bowed, eyes closed.

"Thank you for bringing Leah to us. May she be useful!" Then, everybody says, "Amen."
He said my name.
That I understood, but why? Was that an English prayer? I say our Hebrew meal prayer to myself.

"Eat, Leah!" The mother says, pointing to my plate. The mother gestures to my chair, at the very end of the table, furthest from the stove.

I look down at my plate and begin to eat bread, butter, eggs, and potatoes, even though everything's on the same plate. The Torah commands that meat and dairy be separate in everything from preparing to eating.

"She's not eating her bacon, Mum!" The older sister says, pointing at my plate.

"Jane, leave her alone." The father is eating now. "She's upset. She was separated from her sister, remember?"

"That blind girl shouldn't have come," Their mother says, "I can't imagine who would have agreed to take her."

I wish I understood what everyone is saying. Everyone's staring at me, but I don't say anything.

"She'll have to learn English quickly. Sarah, take her to the garden. Start teaching her English while we clean up." The younger sister nods to me.

We go outside, but the older daughter stays inside and helps her mother.

In the garden, we pick vegetables, dropping them into a basket.
"My name is Sarah." She points to herself, repeating her name.
"Sarah," I repeat. I tell her my name and Esther's. She tells me the English names of the vegetables.

"Carrots, onions, potatoes, peas," I repeat them. The newly introduced words sound strange on my tongue.

She also teaches me the names of her sister, father, and mother.
An hour later, our basket is full, and we return to the house.
"She knows them, Mum."

The mother points to the vegetables, testing me. I slowly say their names.

"She learns quickly, that one."

I know they're talking about me. I don't know if I should be proud that I learned some words or angry that the mother's making me repeat everything! I understand why she's doing it, but I still feel embarrassed, especially with everyone watching.

"Can we play now?" Sarah asks.
"No, you can't.
Sewing for you three."

Mum has all three of us sit in a room off the kitchen, and we sew for what seems like hours. Sarah and I sew buttons on clothes while Jane and Mum work on a quilt. There's almost no talking. Sarah tries to talk to me, but Mum says, "Be quiet, or you can't listen to Children's Hour!" Whenever Mum talks, her voice rises; she glares at Sarah.

Later that night, Dad comes in for dinner. He prays in English again—Ham with potatoes and gravy, chocolate ice cream for dessert. I wish I could tell Mum I can't have everything in one meal like this. Definitely not a Kashrut meal!

She gestures for me and Jane to clear away the dishes. I start to wash the dairy dishes when Jane throws the ham platter in.
With a lot of pointing, I explain that the dishes have to be washed separately. Mum shakes her head NO. Jane takes my spot at the sink while Mum supervises.

"That girl needs to learn to eat English food!" Mum comments.
"I agree, dear.

She'll have to learn everything else, too." Dad says. He and Sarah sit at the table, and Dad listens to her read.

"Can she play with me sometimes?" Sarah repeats.

6

"Maybe tomorrow.

Now, finish that page, young lady." Mum and Dad look at me, and not for the first time today, I wish I understood.
Finally, everything's put away, and the kitchen is clean. At the table, Sarah and Dad finish reading. Mum commands us to go to bed. I'm exhausted!

(I'm back in the attic.
It's dark now, so I write while the moon shines through my window. I know the names of vegetables and my "new family." I have to call them Mum, Dad, Jane, and Sarah. Where is Esther? Is she safe?)
I finish, undress, then lie down on the unbearably stiff bed. I feel overwhelmed and very homesick. I start to cry.

"What's that noise?" I look up and see Jane sneering at me. "Mum wants you now."

Shivering, I get out of bed. Mum meets me at the bottom of the stairs.

"She's been crying, Mum!" Jane says.
I blink, confused.
"I wanted to tell you to be grateful from now on. Be grateful for the clothes you wear and the food you eat. You'll be safe with us. Now, you may go."

I start to leave, but Jane speaks again.
"Say thank you, Mum." She says.
"Thank you, Mum," I say each word, hoping I'm pronouncing everything correctly, even more confused! I look into Mum's cold black eyes once more before heading back up the stairs.

(More to write; back in bed, I think about this strange family. Why was I called downstairs to say, "Thank you?" Perhaps, now I can sleep.) * *
Finally, exhausted, I do.

7

(Morning
"Leah, wake up!"
I sat up and looked out my tiny window at the dark sky. Sarah entered, dressed in a buttoned dress and hat.

"Mum says wear this." Another old dress for me. This one is similar, with buttons down the back, and flowers in the front. "I'll help you."
Sarah buttoned the dress while I slipped on the same shoes as before.
"Church today!" Sarah informed me.

I've been here for a few days now, and it's still horrible. I have to eat strange food, learn English, and work on their farm, even during Shabbat! The other day, Dad showed me how to milk their cows! I actually felt sorry for them, being prodded like that. It was kind of disgusting watching the milk flow into the pail.

It wouldn't be so bad if everyone treated me nicely, but Jane and Mum don't. Dad answered my question when I asked him what he does before every meal.

"It's called praying! Thanking G-d for the food we have and being grateful for being alive." So, a prayer before every meal. At least I'm used to that. We pray before meals too.

And still, no word about Esther; Mum claims she doesn't know where she was taken. Well, better go down!)

"Did you hear me, Leah?" Mum squeezes my shoulder, making me jump. I almost spill my milk. "What did I say?"
"I don't know," I answer.

"I asked if you know what this is?" She hands me a leather book, very faded. I open it and see English writing which I can't read.
"What is it?" I ask.

"The family Bible," Dad says, coming in from the barn. Mum gives him a "hurry up" look. He washes, then heads upstairs. He returns wearing a suit, and we walk to church after eating.

The church is huge, with wooden benches on both sides of an aisle that stretches from the front to the back. Everyone is dressed in their finest clothes. Some women have flowers on their hats.

The songs are strange, played on an instrument I've never seen or heard. Everyone seems to know them, so I pretend to sing along since Mum and Dad expect it. Then, we sit, and Mum hands me the big book.

"I can't," I point to the words, shaking my head.
"I know, just hold it." She whispers. I turn the pages like everyone else.

The man standing in front speaks for a long time.
I miss our synagogue back home, where I knew everyone. The rabbi chants in Hebrew, his voice rising and falling as he reads the Torah. This man's voice drones on and on like it will never end. But finally, it's over.

"Leah, say hello to Mrs. Evans," Dad whispers.
"Hello, Mrs. Evans." I smile. The woman wearing the brown dress doesn't smile back.

"She remembered." Mum and Dad smile. I'm relieved to have done something right.

"Do you help your family?" Mrs. Evans asks.
"Yes, I do, every day," I say slowly, pronouncing each word carefully.

"Very well." Mrs. Evans finally smiles. Then I see her. The girl stands behind Mrs. Evans, staring at the floor. Two English girls beside her have similar expressions to their mother's.
"We're better than you," their expressions say.
"Anne!" The girl looks up at the sharp word.

"What do you say to them?" Mrs. Evans points at Mum and me.
Anne looks confused, then says, "Hello, Miss." Mum smiles. Then, she spots me.

"Hello, what name?" She whispers. Mrs. Evans glares.
"It's "'What's your name?" Ignorant child!" She hisses. "Try again."
She does; this time, she receives Mrs. Evans's approving smile. Her daughters giggle.

9

"Better."

I look around to see Sarah and Jane talking to their friends. I look for Esther but don't see her anywhere. I see other children like me, all staying close to their families, not even talking to one another. I start to walk over to a little boy standing by his family, but Dad stops me.
"We're leaving, Leah." Leaving means going, I think. So, I head towards the door.

"Wait, say goodbye first," Mum says. I assume she means to Mrs. Evans and Anne. I say it, and Mum nods. "Very good, you're learning English well!"

"I wish mine learned quickly, like yours," Mrs. Evans says. "I gave her a proper English name, but she won't speak to me."

"Leah was the same when she first arrived," Dad adds, "She wouldn't say a word, but now she speaks without being told."

"Yes," Mum agrees. "She'll start learning the alphabet and arithmetic soon."

I know they're talking about me, but the words are jumbled. Start what?

Finally, we leave.
I felt like I was on display while in there, only for their amusement.
Sunday lunch is quiet.

Mum sits stiffly, Jane and Sarah not even whispering.

"Good girl, you ate everything!" Dad praises me. I want to explain that Jewish people don't eat meat like that because I can't explain the Kashrut laws properly in English. I like everything else on my plate, though.

Mum takes me into the parlor, where the dreaded pencil and paper sit on a table. (That's the room we sew in.) I sit without being told, and Mum stands in front of me. She always stands when she instructs us. "A," she says, printing it.

My head is spinning as we work through the alphabet! Sarah and Jane talk as they clear the table, but their English is too fast for me to make out more than a word or two.

They go to their rooms, Mum ordering them to read.
Thump. I jump, and Mum thumps the table again.

10

"Pay attention, child." Her eyes snap whenever she's angry with anyone, especially me.

"X Y Z." She prints, and I slowly copy them.
"Better." She says, before taking the paper. She examines each letter, making corrections. "Tomorrow, we'll review it again and maybe add some numbers."

"Mum, it's past dinnertime," Jane complains. Thank you, Jane! I'm relieved she came in when she did. I need a break.

"Leah made mistakes." Mum explains, "So, dinner is late!" I thought she said I was doing better. I think to myself.

(It's night, I'm writing everything I can remember in the cold attic. Will Anne and I be friends?

Oh, Mama, thank you for our song. I'll hold on to it until we're together again! And I wish you'd told us where Esther was going. Do you know where she is?

I'll plan to write every day, but if my days are as busy as today, I'll probably be too exhausted.)

Sunday, September 17

I was right! Mum and Dad keep me busy with writing, arithmetic, and spelling in the evenings and doing daily chores. Laundry is the worst, but I never did like that chore! Remember Mama? You scolded us when Esther and I squeezed the soap out of our underclothes and got water everywhere? Mum does the same with Sarah and me, but she's not you.

It's still fairly warm outside, so our clothes are pinned on the clothesline. Pinning is the one part about laundry the three of us like. We race to see who can pin the most on one section of the line.

I enjoy being with Sarah because she doesn't laugh at my mistakes. We try to play when she returns from school, but Mum won't always allow it.

My least favorite chore is feeding chickens! They fly toward me when they see me coming, and the feeding bucket spills everywhere.
One day, Mum watched it happen; I was given extra English lessons that

night. "That'll teach you not to waste again!" She shouted.

Anyway, Sarah told me the chickens' names. She and Mum's favorite is Henrietta. Jane named her when she was younger. Mum promises she'll never eat her!

The lesson taught me that there's more than one word for "fast." Speaking English is harder than I realized. I wish there were fewer words that are spelled the same but have different meanings. For example, the word "watch" means something you wear on your wrist to tell time, and "watch" also means looking at someone while they do something, like "Watch me." Or the word "Pay" means buying something with money, or "Pay" as in "Pay attention!" Mum says that to me often.

Today after church, I learned that today is called Sun-day and tomorrow is called Mon-day. And the strange instrument is an organ—no sign of Anne this morning.

I found out what Jane and Sarah were reading last week-their Bible. Mum and Dad want me to read it, too. That's why Mum and I are reading Genesis, "This will help you learn our Bible," Mum says. I know; I just wrote English words.

Back to Writing in German

I managed to play with Sarah yesterday. Dad gave permission while Mum was out. It was dolls, of course. Her room has a dolls' corner with little dishes, clothes, and a doll house! They all have names, too. When we play, sadly, I think about how Esther would really like her!
I also hate bathing here. I'm always made to go last, so there's no hot water left. There isn't much soap left, either!

The English people have a man in power, Winston Churchill, whose speeches talk about being against Hitler.

My foster family listens to his speeches on the radio. Sarah says sometimes he speaks from London. Dad told me that on September 3rd, Britain declared war on Germany.

Sarah explained that Children's Hour is "A radio programme for kids, with talking animals and stories." We listen to that, as well.

English food tastes awful! At least, the things in cans. I've only been to the local shops once, and lots of things are sold there in tins, like fruit and salmon. I'm glad my family grows their own vegetables.

I can't believe I just wrote "My family." The only people I like here are Dad and Sarah.

Jane is bossy, like Mum. She sometimes orders Sarah or me to do chores she doesn't want to do. Dad heard her last night and made her do her chore. I heard her complain to Mum, but I couldn't hear how Mum answered.

Hopefully, Esther and I will return home when this is finished, if I can find her!

Home. What will it be like? Will you be there? Will our neighbors? The nights when Germany was showered with broken glass, you and Papa whispered about something. I know now you were talking about sending us away. I hope we all have homes to return to!

Dad told me about the Prime Minister here, Neville Chamberlain. A few years ago, he met with Hitler three times to try to prevent Britain from entering war with Germany. Those meetings weren't successful. As I said, Britain's involved now.

If only I could find Esther! Whenever I ask, no one knows where she is. If anyone knows anything, they're not telling me.

I know this diary entry is all over the place, but this week's been chaotic.

One last thing, Mama! I am not sure why I didn't think of this before. I'll write you a letter. I doubt you'll be reading this diary anytime soon.

Now I'm all caught up. I need sleep. Jane says I have a busy day tomorrow.

Monday, September 18, After Dinner

I should have suspected something was strange this morning when Jane gave me a new dress to wear!

No secondhand dress this time-it was a new dress. In fact, everything I wore today was brand-new. I discovered why at breakfast.
"School today!" Mum announced cheerfully.

Mouth open, I stared at her, shocked. I haven't been to school since

Hitler's Nazis took over, with their signs saying where we could and couldn't enter. They took away our jobs, schools, and our homes. Before Hitler gained Nazis, he'd speak on the radio about his hatred of anyone not "Pure German." Now, the Nazis are burning homes of anyone who isn't "Pure," by their standards.

Nazis even have their own symbol: a swastika on their uniforms and banners. I explained to Esther it looked like a cross with sharp pins coming out of it.

Anyway, I was terrified and had butterflies in my stomach as we walked to school, arriving just as the bell rang. The schoolhouse was divided into two rooms by a curtain – younger children on the left and the older students on the right.

I recognized the other evacuees. We sat with the younger ones.
Our teacher Miss Simmons said that she wanted to "Keep an eye on us and check our progress." I think that means she wanted to see how we're doing.

Those English lessons my family gave me proved to be helpful.

By the end of today, she told me I "Did well for a beginner." She looked overwhelmed, trying to teach the English kids, plus us (the evacuees.) I actually felt sorry for Miss. When she asked if I wrote in a diary in English, I lied.

"I don't have a diary." She told us to start one and to show them to her every Friday.

Some can write a little English. Others are learning the alphabet. Anne wasn't there; perhaps she'll come tomorrow!
At dinner, Mum and Dad questioned me about school. "Did you enjoy your lunch?"

Forcing a smile, I said yes. Actually, I hated the meat, but the bread and cheese were delicious. I must try to explain what Kashrut food is.
"What did Miss Simmons give you for homework?" The longer the sentences, the more I must concentrate on their meaning. When I told Mum about my English diary, she thought it was a brilliant idea. Sarah offered to help; Mum scowled. "We'll start after dinner!"

Dad wanted to know the names of my friends. I told him I sat next to a girl named Helen and there were other German kids there.

When I inquired about Anne, he said Mrs. Evans's children were taught at home. "That family doesn't speak much except in church."

When dinner was over, dishes were done, and the kitchen cleaned, Mum and I worked on my English diary. I had to write about my good family, church, and how grateful I am to be in England.

Mostly lies, of course. I thought I'd be able to invent things, but so far, with Mum watching, I couldn't.

(Now, I'm caught up. Staring up at the moonlight, I write what I please. I might have to write a false diary in English, but no one can prevent me from keeping this diary in German!)

Friday, September 22, Night

I think Miss suspects something. When she read my diary, she asked, "Did you write this yourself?"
"Yes," I answered.

"Is this how you really feel, Leah?"

I nodded, but I could see she didn't believe me. She gave us our spelling test, and I missed the word 'wory.' "Two R's, not one!"

So far, school's interesting. I enjoy writing, counting to twenty in English, and getting acquainted with the other German kids.

A six-year-old named Daniel lives with another English family in town. He doesn't say much, but Miss is patient with him. She helps him when she's not teaching other lessons. His big eyes are sad, and he seems frightened of loud noises; he hasn't smiled or laughed so far. Another is a little girl named Eva, who doesn't say much either but seems content.

If I wasn't with the other girls at recess, I'd say hello. Jane and Sarah make sure I'm always with them. Other evacuees seem to stick with their "siblings" if they have any.

We play hopscotch, tag, and sometimes jump rope. Like at home, games are simple to learn. We don't need to speak English!

On Tuesday, Miss called on me to read. "Face the class and speak clearly."

I was terrified.

Wiping my hands on my blouse, I thought to myself, what if I mess up? One of the girls whispered to her friend, and they giggled. When I finished, Miss addressed the class.

"I hope you won't be as rude when it's your friends standing here?" I misread a couple of sentences, but Miss said, "It's OKAY. You're learning." Another boy named Leron went next; he made mistakes, too. Helen's brother Andrew pulled Eva's hair during recess.
He was assigned extra arithmetic as a punishment.

The food is becoming bearable. I miss your Kugel and dumplings, Mama. Esther and I used to help by rolling and filling them.
I also miss making Passover cookies.

When I tried to explain how to prepare Kashrut (Leron explained it's Kosher in English) food, Mum scowled. She replied, "We're not Jewish. You will eat like us and get used to our food."

Mum and Dad insist we all blackout the windows every night. That means covering all the windows, so "The enemy can't find us." Our neighbors do the same.
I've written your letter.

I'll try and post it on my own, Mum won't try and steal it. She can't read it, anyway, but I'm not taking any chances. I hope it reaches you.

Sunday, September 24, Night

Church again today.
After the service, I saw Anne, but we couldn't speak. Mrs. Evans still criticizes her English.

"May I teach her?" I asked.

She looked surprised and replied, "No, thank you, dear. You're German. She needs to learn from my girls."
"Please!" I begged.

"Let's go, Leah." Sarah pulled me outside. I glanced over my shoulder and saw Anne mouthing something, but I was too far away. I couldn't understand what she was saying. Mrs. Evans's daughters looked miserable this morning.

"Do you know why Mrs. Evans's daughters aren't in school?" I asked Sarah.

"Don't know. They all keep to themselves. We see them at church and while shopping only, like Dad said."
"Where's Mr. Evans?" I asked. Sarah said she's never seen him, but she's heard people talk about him.

"He stays inside their house. He was injured at work somehow!" Still, why can't Anne attend school? I wondered sadly.

Dad says "injured" means hurt or wounded. I wonder how that happened?

Sunday, October, Night

What a day! After church, Mum had me memorize Bible verses from the Old Testament. Then Dad came in from the barn and ordered Sarah and I upstairs.

All we heard was, "So, how's Leah progressing?" We couldn't hear Mum's answer, but I don't think it was what Dad wanted to hear. Soon, both stepped outside. We saw them from Sarah's window.
Sarah and I looked at each other.

"Are Mum and Dad angry because you're not reading the New Testament yet?" Sarah asked me. I told her I wasn't sure, but Mum wanted me to learn the entire English Bible. I wanted to say, "I understand it in Hebrew!"

After evening chores, we listened to the radio. Mum insisted "It's to improve Leah's English and to help her understand what's happening in Britain." Like it or not, we all listen most nights.

Tonight, Winston Churchill spoke to Britain about the Soviet Union's invasion of Poland.

(The Soviet Union is a place far away; they are trying to stay out of this war.) British ones are attacking German submarines. The English government says to prepare for a three-year war. I suppose I better get used to this English family! A few days ago, Dad caught me sneaking outside to meet the postman, he didn't throw away your letter! Instead, he said he'd post it for me.

The first week in October was busy. In school, Leron and I are progressing in English; when we finish our lessons, we assist other evacuees with theirs.

Miss is delighted that everyone's improving. "The more English you children learn, the sooner you can join the older children," she tells us almost every day. So, the pressure is on for us to learn quickly.
Daniel likes his English family; I wish I could say the same about mine!

He told me they have a Siddur at their house, just for him. He likes reading the prayers. They allow him to pray quietly in Hebrew, even in church.

Eva is doing great. She lives with a Jewish family and has a younger sibling who isn't in school. She enjoys being the big sister. But like the rest of us, she misses her real family.

The only bad thing that has happened recently was Mum "forgot" to give me lunch for three days. Sarah and Helen shared theirs; I don't think Jane noticed.

The other night, we listened to the radio.
"We took you in just in time," Jane remarked. "When did you leave again?"

"September the first," I said.

"Didn't Hitler bomb your part of Germany that day?" She asked.
I looked at her, startled. "What do you mean?"

"Jane, it was Poland that was invaded, not Berlin," Dad said sternly. "Germany wanted to take back the territory they lost during the previous war."

"Apologize for your tone."
"I was only saying she should be grateful she's here instead of over there,"

18

Jane answered.

I wanted to say, "At least you know your family's safe." I stayed silent, though.

She and Mum are alike. They're constantly reminding me to be grateful. Today, for afternoon tea, Mum handed each of us a chocolate bar she'd bought in town. Before she gave me the candy, I had to say, "Thank you, Mum."

"You wouldn't get this in Germany," she said cruelly. Dad didn't say anything. I think he agrees with her about everything.

Even though this week's been busy, I always say Modeh Ani every morning and Shema every night; I don't want to forget how to say either of them. No matter what Mum does, I'm still Jewish.

I have to be patient but waiting for a reply from you isn't easy.
Monday October 9, Evening

"Daniel made a mistake at school today," Jane announced during dinner. Tonight's dinner was chicken and vegetables with chocolate cake. I was given a smaller portion without cake.
"What was it?" Dad asked.

"Miss told him to stand and recite his arithmetic, and he said "five" in German!" She looked gleeful.
"Leah, what happened next?"
"He fixed the mistake, then apologized."
"They both stayed in during recess," Sarah added.
"To help him with English," I explained.

I didn't tell them that Daniel talks about his family in Germany during these short lessons. His mother and three brothers have disappeared.

Miss allows us to speak in German to each other! It's wonderful we can talk to one another, but I wish we could do it more often. None of the others have joined us.

I did speak to Leron walking home. Like Eva, he lives with a Jewish family.

I'm very jealous. I wish I could live with their families or Daniel's! I've thought about showing Leron this diary, but I can't unless he keeps it a secret.

Mum gave me a piece of hard bread for lunch. Sarah and Jane had bread, too, plus cheese and an apple.

Friday, October 13, After Dinner

There's some daylight!

Miss Simmons likes my English diary more each time I bring it to school. I mostly write about things on the BBC (British Broadcasting Corporation.) When Leron asked her how long we have to keep writing, she replied, "Until I tell you to stop." We all nodded unhappily. We do this because we have to, not because we want to. Eva's and Daniel's diaries were also read. I appreciate that Miss never reads our diaries out loud.

Recess was horrible for Leron! One of the boys called him "Jew boy."

When Miss asked who'd done it, no one blabbed. (I was inside with Daniel, Sarah told me!)

Still no word of Esther's or your whereabouts. Are you even alive? I'll say a special prayer for you all tonight. I've thought about asking Miss if she can help.

Sunday, October 15, Afternoon

I slipped up to my attic to write, tired of moonlight writing!
The Reverend greeted me today for the first time.
"Leah, do you like church?" He asked.
Of course, I said yes.

"Tell Reverend your favorite hymn." Mum prompted.
Everyone stood around talking; someone tapped my shoulder.
"Leah?"

It was Anne, by herself.
"Mrs. Evans's outside!" She said, "Can we talk?"
We sat on an empty pew.

"What is it, Anne?" I asked.
"I want school," she said.

Speaking quickly in German, I explained Mrs. Evans's reasons for not allowing Anne in school.

"Yes, she told me. But ... talk to her?" She asked in broken English.
I promised her I'd try but told her not to be too hopeful. Luckily, Sarah found us before Mrs.

Evans noticed us talking, we left in time. I still don't know how or where I can talk to Mrs. Evans besides church, but like I said, I'll try.
One more thing, her real name is...
Someone's coming; finish later.

Same night... Late
Back to moonlight writing. It was Jane calling me. Good thing she didn't come into the room.

Anne's name is Atalia. In German, she whispered to me, "I wish Mrs. Evans hadn't changed my name."

Like all the evacuees, her family hasn't written. Do any of our families even know where we're living?

Monday, October 16, Night

Hitler's army seems more powerful every day. We heard about a German bomb that destroyed three Royal Navy ships on the radio. No wonder people hate us!

I spoke to Miss after school today, and she said she'd try to find where Esther is, but "Don't get too hopeful. This will take time." Still no word from you, either Mama.

Helen was punished. She was talking during someone's recitation.
When it ended, Helen stood in the Cold Corner. She stood there until the bell rang, two hours.

"Let me see your hands." Miss touched them, then said she could leave.

"What happened?" I asked.
Helen replied, "It's just a corner of the wall that's always cold. If your hands become really cold, she lets you leave."

"When I was in school, my teacher just had us write lines," I said.
"Still no letter from your family?" She asked sympathetically.

"No," Jane answered, "Her sister's blind, so she can't write letters. And their parents are in Germany, so still no letter from them." Up ahead, Eva and her parents were talking. We'd reached Helen's house. Eva waved and continued to her house.

Tuesday, October 17, Early Evening

The weather's colder today.
I had to wear Jane's old coat and gloves.
The leaves are falling off the trees, becoming crunchy piles on the ground. Esther and I loved jumping in leaf piles.

The stove in school was smoky. The desks were arranged so we could be as near the stove as possible. Leron and Andrew brought in extra wood without being asked.

We studied Geography all afternoon, naming places in England.
Unfortunately, during our lesson, one of the girls yelled, "You Germans need to return to Germany." Miss tried calming her, but she kept shouting, demanding to know what the Germans would bomb next. I wanted to point out we don't like Hitler, either.
For me, spelling is less difficult now. This morning, we had a spelling bee.

Miss had us line up with the English kids. Andrew didn't look thrilled. She called out words and kept score on the board.
Daniel's started speaking in class without prompting and playing during recess. (Miss gave him and Eva words to spell, and they usually play together.)

Before bed, I asked Mum for another blanket, but she refused. Someone must have listened because there's one outside my door today.

I'm grateful for it even though it's a bit ragged.

Evening
It was Sarah's old blanket, of course, going to be tossed in the scrap bag. Thank you, Sarah! Hopefully, Mum won't notice. Sarah wanted to give me another pillow, but that probably would have been noticed.

Friday, October 20, Morning Before School

Mum noticed, after all. She asked Sarah about "the other blanket in her room." Sarah lied, saying she'd already given Mum that one to be thrown away.

She hasn't questioned me or come up here.
Later, the same night...

I am writing by moonlight again! I will keep this short.
School was interesting today. Miss gave us evacuees a surprise arithmetic test.

She'll let us know our results on Monday.
Recess was uneventful! Thank G-d, there was no "taunting from other students." In class, the English kids didn't laugh at us for once.

We're going into town today. We need sugar, bacon, and tea. I need another notebook for school.

Later in the afternoon...
Driving into town was fantastic. I love looking at everything out the car window. Since petrol is being rationed, driving is a big deal. Dad says people can only use their cars when they absolutely must. The leaves have already changed colors again. There were so many people hurrying by, everybody seemed busy. We parked outside one of the shops and went in.

The shop was crowded with people, but I spotted Mrs. Evans down the aisle.

"May I get the sugar?" I asked. This was my opportunity to talk to Mrs. Evans. Dad nodded yes. I walked up to her and said, "Hi, Mrs. Evans, it's Leah."

Surprised at my English or maybe my presence, she almost dropped her sugar. "May Anne please come to school with us?" I figured if I just asked her, she might give in.

"Why?" she asked.
"Her English hasn't improved, Miss. Maybe she could learn with a teacher and me," I said.

I waited, praying she'd say yes.
Finally, she said she'd think about it but not to pester her again.
I walked back up to Dad, my spirits sinking.

Mum, Sarah, and Jane brought more items to us, including the notebooks. We paid and left.
On the drive home, I told them about my conversation with Mrs. Evans.

"She was right to tell you to go away," Jane said, in her know-it-all voice.

"They keep to themselves, you know, so leave them alone." Dad said

24

Mrs. Evans rarely changes her mind about anything! I sighed and gazed out the window at the bare trees.

Later, Mum found the blanket. When I returned from feeding the chickens, Mum demanded to know how that blanket ended up in the attic. She'd gone up to look for something. When I told her, I wasn't sure she believed me. Sarah and Jane were still outside!

Monday, October 30, Evening

Today, as promised, Miss returned our test results. I missed four arithmetic problems. Leron and Daniel missed some, too. I don't think any of us had a perfect score. Miss said these tests showed how much we'd learned. Will there be more?

As punishment for giving me the blanket, Sarah's pocket money has to go to the church's offerings.

That might not seem like a punishment, but Sarah and Jane only get extra money once a month. Dad says that may stop soon, so they need to "Make the most of it."

After dinner, I quietly asked Dad if he knew where Esther was. "No, dear. Everything takes time, though. Try to be patient for a response. It may take a while longer."

"Maybe she'll write you!" Sarah suggested.
"Of course, Sarah," Jane smirked, "I'd love to see a letter written by a blind girl."

I almost hit her with the cooking pot that I was drying. Esther can't write, but if she wanted to send a message, I'm sure she'd find a way.
"You're right, Jane," Mum added, sitting at the table, knitting. "Her sister's useless!" I was so furious I ran upstairs without finishing my chores. Esther, useless?
She certainly isn't! Mum doesn't even know her.

It's just agony, all this endless waiting for answers.
Meanwhile, the BBC reported Mr. Churchill and others were on a warship that didn't explode when it was attacked by the Germans yesterday. I understand why most children here call us "enemies." If we're enemies, why did families accept us?

(*Writing before breakfast*

In my cold attic room, still in bed, I say Modeh Ani. Shivering, I get dressed. At my window, my breath steams on the glass as I try to see out. Faint light trying to shine through. The window won't budge. It's frozen shut. "Come on, Leah, I need you." I hear Mum's voice calling up to me. Big groan. I must go down. At least it'll be warmer down there.)

Later, the same night...,
School was predictable. Andrew tripped a younger boy at recess. He's assigned extra work as a punishment.

Of course, he tripped one of the evacuees. He claimed it was an accident. An English girl told Miss she spotted his foot slide out when the boy passed. Why does he hate us? I'm surprised he hasn't taunted me.

Helen and I received good marks on our homework. I couldn't see Jane's, but Sarah showed me hers, which was also excellent.

Miss heard some of us read after recess. Leron recited history and made no mistakes in the recitation or his English pronunciation! Next, Eva read. She messed up a few times, and some English girls laughed.

She cried because of it, and I was furious. When the bell rang, those girls were asked to stay after! Eva's parents were coming to the door when Helen and I left.

During dinner, I told Mum and Dad what had occurred, since they always asked about my day.

"She should try harder tomorrow," That was Mum's heartless answer.
"Who's her family?" Dad asked.

"The family with the flowers in their garden and the barking dog," Sarah said. I looked puzzled. What was she talking about?

26

"Oh, that Jewish family!" Mum said disapprovingly, "She won't be coming here! You may invite Helen, though."

When Sarah and I snatched a few minutes alone in her room after dinner, she explained more.

"Eva's family lives past Helen's house. They have a barking dog and a little girl."

"I know, Eva told me. I know she likes her family," I said.
Even so, why did I have to live in a town with strange neighbors?

Monday, November 20

We've been bottling fruit all morning, and we're finally finished!
The kitchen became crowded, with us kids and Mum working in there until the preserve jars lined the pantry shelves! Now, we have fillings for tarts and pies to last for months.

It's begun snowing really hard, and school was canceled last week. Not really, we still have lessons because Mum still insists, we all have daily Bible study. I have to write in my school diary. I'm writing it without her help now. I only wish she wouldn't read it.

The cows and horses stay in the barn. I pray the cows' milk won't become our butter and cheese, but it probably will. I'm very relieved I don't live on a pig farm like Helen. She can hear squealing pigs from her bedroom when they are being slaughtered. She has nightmares because of it, and she lives there!

Now that we are staying home, Mum not feeding me is finally noticed by Dad. All he said was, "Leah, aren't you eating?" This morning, he asked her why I only got one piece of dry toast. Mum's response even made Jane glance up.

"She deserves it. If she behaves, she'll get more." I was speechless. I do everything I'm told. I'm even learning their language. What more does she want?

"Leah, wake up now!" I hear Mum's shrill voice calling to me. I peer out my window, and it's still dark. What does she want?)

The same evening, groaning, I got up, dressed, then stumbled sleepily to the kitchen.
"You have to help me.

Here, take this!" She handed me a knife and showed me how to chop almonds.

"What are we making?" I mumbled.
"Christmas pudding. Now be careful! Everything must be perfect."
Next, something called candied peel had to be chopped.
"Leah, what are you doing?" Mum cried.

"What?" I looked down. The peel was almost shredded. Mum grabbed my knife and showed me how to chop the peel.
"Better!" she said.

I glanced out the kitchen window while working and saw the sun coming up.

"Stop!" She commanded, "For now." Smiling sweetly, she added, "Complete your chores, then you may eat." Sarah came in, then we went to the henhouse.

"You're up very early!" she said as she began scattering feed for the chickens.

"Making the Christmas pudding!" I sighed. "Why does it have to be done now, anyway?"

"It takes a long time for everything to get mixed together." "Why are you doing it? Jane always did it before." She looked curious.
"Don't know. Mum just called me this morning!" I replied.

28

Sarah laughed as I ducked to avoid a chicken. Crouching, I scattered feed, then ran to the nest. Swiftly, we gathered eggs, then paused to pick straw from our hair.

"Any news of your sister's whereabouts?" She asked quietly.
Sighing in irritation, I told her I was still waiting! She looked sympathetic.

"I miss my friends at school. But I like this snow, too," Sarah said, to change the subject.

"I can't wait to go back to school," I said as I plucked a piece of straw from my dress.

"Can we play dolls after you're finished with the pudding?" She asked.
"I hope so. Your dolls, Bertha and Sally, must have their dinner."

"You two, hurry up." A voice shouted. Turning, we saw Dad in the doorway.
"We will!" We answered in unison.

"Leah, Mum says to fetch apples from the cellar, then you can eat."
After he'd gone, we gathered the baskets and returned to the house. Sarah gave Mum the eggs, I fetched apples. When I entered the kitchen, everyone was eating.

"There you are." Mum scolded, "Hurry, peel and chop that."
"Mum, she hasn't eaten," Sarah spoke up. She looked puzzled, "Dad said she could eat."

"Shhh, finish your toast. You, the apples." She pointed to me. Stifling a groan, I peeled and chopped. My stomach growled. I glanced hungrily at the platter of toast on the table.

"Dad, can I go into town with you?" Jane pleaded.

"No, help your Mum!" He commanded. Jane knew better than to argue.

"Take this!" Mum said, handing him a list and kissing his cheek. He left quickly. As he opened the door, I saw fresh snow falling, not to mention being hit with frigid air! "Cold, Leah?" Mum smiled thinly.
I nodded.

"Girls, into the parlor!" Mum ordered Sarah and Jane. "Wash those, girl."

She pointed again, this time to the stack of dirty dishes—and still, no breakfast.

As I scrubbed the last plate, I asked. "May I eat now?"
"Soon. Grate this nutmeg first!" How much more? I thought. This seems a lot of work for pudding.

Around lunchtime, Mum finally told me to stop. With a sigh of relief, I took off my apron and hung it up. My hands were sore.
"Parlor!" She ordered again.

"But-` I started.
She glared, and I obeyed. I watched longingly as Mum sliced cold meat for sandwiches.

"Sarah, Jane... lunch!" She called, "And wash your hands." They appeared in the kitchen with their sewing, Mum inspected their work. They washed and sat down.

"Finish your quilt, girl." Mum closed the door firmly behind her. Glumly, I sat on the sofa with quilt pieces.
As I sewed, I could barely hear their voices in the kitchen. I crept to the door and listened.
"Can she please eat?" Begged Sarah.
"Of course, when she's finished her work!" Mum replied calmly. Jane laughed.

"Jane, hurry. Your father should be on his way back by now."
I returned to the sofa.

My head hurt, and my stomach growled in protest.

Would this day ever end? At least at school, I usually ate lunch! I thought angrily.

Dad returned and asked Jane and Sarah to put away the groceries and tend to the horses.

His voice carried, I didn't need to eavesdrop now.

"Everyone's anxious about the Germans. If they keep attacking our ships, supplies can't get through!"

"We'll manage!" Mum walked across the kitchen. "Like last time."

"Where's Leah?" Dad interrupted. Mum called me in. After talking to Dad, all three of us hurried through our chores. The wind had picked up, but thankfully, there wasn't any more snow.

Finally, dinner was served.

Will I eat? I wondered. Racing in from the cold, we washed, and Dad prayed.

"Here's yours." Mum slid a plate in front of me. One potato, one piece of bread! I looked around at the others, but they didn't seem to notice.

"Eat!" Mum whispered, "You must be hungry." I stabbed the potato, wishing I was somewhere else. I ate it without complaining. After I tidied up, I was allowed to go to bed.

(I finish writing. Outside, the wind howls, my attic is freezing! No moon tonight!
Will tomorrow be as bad?)

Saturday, December 2, After Dinner

This morning, Mum called me again to help her. This time, I was given a slice of buttered toast before we started, thankfully. We ground more nutmeg, and we broke the bread into tiny crumbs.
I mixed the ingredients I'd chopped yesterday together. I added raisins, eggs, breadcrumbs, flour, and some type of sugar; Mum threw in brandy.

We'd just finished stirring when the rest of the family came in; I did chores while everyone else had breakfast. As they ate, I grated butter into another bowl, stirred pudding into that bowl, and added the remaining butter. This time, they all took turns stirring the pudding. Everyone ate lunch except me.

The afternoon was spent reading our schoolbooks and the Bible. "Leah, memorize these six verses, or you won't eat!"
Dinner was potato soup.

I must have pleased Mum because my portion was smaller than everyone else's. I wondered why Dad's so oblivious.

We worked on the dratted pudding again. I buttered one large bowl, put grease paper in the bottom, tipped the pudding into that bowl, and covered it with more paper, but not "too tight, loose!" Mum commanded. After being tied with a string, it's wrapped in more paper, tied with more string.

"The pudding expands!" Jane explained. "The strings hold it together." I placed it in our cellar. Three guesses as to what I'll be doing tomorrow...

Sunday, December 3, Late Night

Well, day three of working on the pudding. Today was easier, though! I ate with the family—porridge with sausage! I somehow managed to swallow it. Then, I put the pudding on the stove to boil.
"Eight hours, Leah.

Don't forget! Set the timer!" Mum warned.

We read, sewed, and took care of the animals for the rest of the day. I anxiously watched the pudding.

After boiling, Mum lifted it out of the copper pot, letting it cool on the counter. After dinner, of which (I didn't eat with the family again), I unwrapped it only to wrap and tie it over again. It's in our cellar until Christmas. What a miserable three days! Glad it's only done once a year!

Friday, December 15, After Dinner

"Will we have a tree?" Sarah asked a couple nights ago.
"Yes, we'll see!" Dad answered.

Later in her room, I asked her about it.
"For Christmas," she said. "We decorate it, and presents are placed under it on Christmas morning!" (I'd heard of Christmas from our friends at home, and now, I'll get to experience it!)

Monday, December 25, Christmas Night

Once again, I was summoned to the kitchen before dawn!
"We're making the sauce. Follow my instructions," Mum ordered.
I mixed brandy, more sugar, butter, ginger, and something called orange zest in a bowl. I placed it on the cold shelf. Like before, we did chores and had breakfast. She let me eat with the family this time.

Then it was time for church. On the walk, I stopped and took a breath of crisp, cold air.

"Leah, what are you doing?" Dad called, "Hurry up!"
The wind blew just then, so I had to run into it to keep up. Our boots crunched on the ice as we walked single file down a slippery hill.
Helen's family met us along the way.
Andrew actually said, "Merry Christmas" to me.

We had a special morning church service, with the Reverend reading the story of Jesus' birth. Thanks to Mum's Bible lessons, I knew a little of it and had to follow along.

We all said a prayer for the servicemen overseas. I prayed for our loved ones, especially Esther, wherever she is. I'm slowly adjusting to this English church.

I heard babies babbling and feet stomping.

I saw I wasn't the only one rubbing my hands together for warmth.
The other "evacuees," as some call us, managed to talk after church. We all miss celebrating Hanukkah this year. Next year, we won't celebrate any holidays with our families if Hitler has his way. Mr. Churchill was right-it's going to be a long war for everyone.
Kids were excited when leaving because, "It's snowing, look! Can I play?"

Fresh snow was indeed falling.
Our footprints were clear.

Looking back, I saw many more prints, all fresh. Walking back was like a game, with people trying not to walk in each other's prints.
And we have a tree! I don't know where Dad got it, but somehow, it appeared last week. We've been decorating for days. I brought down boxes of ornaments to hang, and Dad found tinsel. Of course, the presents were under the tree this morning, just like Sarah said. My pile was smaller than theirs, but I wasn't surprised.

Mum and Dad gave us new clothes as gifts. Finally, I have an actual new dress.

Sarah and Jane each opened new shoes; green for Jane and pink for Sarah. Sarah's biggest present was a new doll with real shoes. "Your last one, Sarah!" Mum said. Sarah nodded but looked sulky.
Dad gave us something even better, our own diaries! He wants us to

write our thoughts about what's to come. I just hope he won't ever ask to read mine.

Christmas dinner was some kind of roasted bird in gravy, boiled potatoes, and vegetables. While we ate, the pudding boiled again. Dad carried it in with delight. The sauce we'd made was poured over the top. Then, Dad lit it with a match. It was beautiful! And it was delicious. I should have known since I worked so hard on it.

The King gave his Christmas broadcast today like Dad says he does every year. Like the Reverend in church, he gave comfort to the people fighting overseas and wished everyone a peaceful Christmas.
As we washed the Christmas china, Sarah, Jane, and I heard them talking.

"You spent precious money on paper?" Mum asked Dad.

"Leah has to keep a diary for school. Why shouldn't they all keep one? They can look back on these times when the war is over and perhaps share them with their children. Leah and the other evacuees need these diaries more than most," he said.

"I know. One of the other foster mothers was telling me that her child cries every night!" Mum said. I think I know who that is, I thought sadly. I'm surprised Mum cares.

"Hitler's army's getting more controlling every day!" Dad said.
The three of us fell into silence in the kitchen. We all stopped working and looked at one another, not knowing what to say. So, they are aware of Hitler's terror. A little, anyway. Do they know about my family, too?

(Still no letter, by the way). Well, a new year is coming, like it or not.

Esther 1939

Standing on the platform, I cry as the strange people take Leah away. Around me, more kids are taken by new parents. I didn't know we wouldn't be together! I almost wish we had stayed in Berlin, but then Hitler's voice plays inside my head. He hates people who don't look like him. When he talked, crowds of people cheered.

Since I don't have a diary, I'll have to remember everything from now on.

A hand taps my shoulder.
"Esther?" A female voice asks me.
But I don't speak English yet, so I can't answer.
"You're coming with me, darling, to school. Don't be afraid!" She takes me by the hand and gently leads me along. I hear kids calling goodbye. I try to answer, but I'm being hurried along, then we slow down as we leave the station.

I get in the back of a car with the woman, and a man is in the front seat.
"My name is Mrs. Davis," she says softly.
"I'm William!" The man's voice says from the front, deep and gentle.
"You're Esther, I presume." But I can't answer.

"You're going to a special school with other blind girls!" He says, I don't understand completely, but Mrs. Davis pats my hand lovingly.
We drive for a long time, and I fall asleep. I hear bits and pieces of their conversation as I drift in and out.

"Poor thing. The lady who separated them said they took her sister first!" Mrs. Davis says.

"Does she understand English besides her name?" The man asks.
"Can't tell, William.

I'm not expecting her to speak, not for a while. But this school was the only place for her. You know how strict those rules are! All that paperwork and good medicals.

With her little bit of schooling, it's a miracle she was able to get on that train at all."

I'm awake, listening to their soft voices. I'm not afraid. I have no idea where I'm going, but hopefully, it won't be too bad. Will it? I know the word school, from learning it on the train. Mama and Papa always wanted me to go.

Before we left, they told us to obey our new families and that we'd see them soon. I could tell they were just trying to be calm for us.
When the car stops, I hear the wind and birds chirping.
"Esther, we're here!"

The door opens. I grab my suitcase, and the man helps me out of the car.

"Let me, Miss." The man takes my case. My legs turn to mush as we walk across the grass and up four wide steps. I take two steps on each one.

"Come in, dear." Mrs. Davis leads me inside a building with a stone floor, and I see light coming from somewhere.
Our shoes echo when we walk up more stairs, down a long hall, and into a room.

"Girls, Esther's here. Come say hello." I wish I knew more English words! Esther is all I understand.
Suddenly, I hear many voices at once.
"Hi, I'm Catherine."
"I'm Mary!"
"I'm Hannah."
"My name's Kathleen."
"I'm Lydia; nice to meet you."
As the girls say their names, my head is spinning; how will I ever remember all their names? Then, suddenly, my legs really become mush under me, and I almost fall, so the woman makes me sit.
She pushes me down onto a bed. Then my head hits a pillow. Almost immediately, I'm asleep again.

The next morning, I wake to people talking over me. "Is she awake yet? I want to play," I hear a young voice say.
"Mary, leave her alone." Someone instructs.

I open my eyes, listening to the girls' voices. I can tell Mary is younger than the other girl.
I slowly sit up.

"I'm Mary, remember? Do you have a sister? I do. Do you have pets? We have horses and dogs."
"Mary, stop chattering! She just woke up." Another woman's voice.
"Good morning, I'm Kathleen. Mary and I will talk to you later," Kathleen says. I can tell she's pulling Mary away from me.
A bell rings, making me jump. Someone claps and the girls start to leave; I think I hear tapping.

"Mrs. Davis will be here shortly." The other woman speaks slowly, but I still can't understand. I feel around to find my suitcase on the floor. Opening it, I pull out the clothes Mama packed.

"Good, you're up!" Suddenly, a woman knocks and enters.

"Wonderful, you're dressed as well! I'm Mrs. Davis, remember? I brought you here. How are you?"

I start to cry because I'm overwhelmed, and she gently holds my hand. "Poor darling!" she says. After a while, I stop.
"Use this." A handkerchief is placed in my hands. "Are you hungry?"
I don't answer. Why is she talking to me?

"Let's go to breakfast." "The other woman here was Mother Anderson. You'll meet her again tonight."

I need to use the toilet, but I can't tell her. She must have guessed because we go into a room with everything I need. She helps me find everything.

After that, we walk down another hall, down more stairs, into what must be a big room because I can hear girls' voices echoing. They stand as we come in, and I hear wood scraping against the floor; it must be chairs.

"Girls, this is Esther." They say something to me together, then sit again.

"Sit here." Mrs. Davis says and takes me to a table, and I slide onto a bench. So that's what I heard. A plate is put in front of me. I smell toast and eggs. I pick up my fork and eat. I guess I was really hungry because I finish quickly.

"Well done." Mrs. Davis is eating beside me. "Now, we wait."
All this time, the girls talk and laugh, but the words run together. Some voices are tiny, like little kids, others are deeper, and there are older people here, too.

A man comes along the table, picking up the plates and silverware. When he comes to me, he touches my shoulder and says my name. "I'm John," he says.

"I know your dishes are washed separately," I don't answer.
Another bell rings, benches scrape, and girls leave.
"Let's go to your first class," says Mrs. Davis.
She leads me to a quiet room.

How will I ever find my way around here? So many halls and doors.
"Esther!" I think that's Mary's voice.

"Yes, we're here." Mrs. Davis says calmly. She leads me to a table. I reach out to feel a chair. "Go ahead, sit." The table is like a circle, and it wobbles a little.

"Esther, this is Hannah, Mary, Kathleen, Catherine, Lydia, and Amy." I recognize the names from last night.

"She can sit by me. I'll show her what to do!" Mary says excitedly.
"Mary, no talking. You were a beginner once too."

"Sorry, Miss," Mary says quietly.
"Esther, this is for you." I feel something long and straight being put in my hands. "This is your white cane." Mrs. Davis takes my hand, and I stand up. She shows me how to put my right hand on the handle and stick it out straight.

"Miss, let me show her, please?" One of the girls speaks and stands.
"Yes, Lydia, you're about her height, so go ahead."

The girl tells me her name again. Standing beside me, she takes my hand. We start to walk. The stick doesn't do anything; It just drags along the floor. Lydia stops suddenly. The stick hits something hard.
"Take it and swing it in front of you to see what's in your way," she says. She shows me how to move my arm from the left side of my body, then back to the right, wide at first, until the stick hits the hard thing again. I reach out until I find a wooden chair. I wonder how did Lydia know the chair was there?
As we slowly walk around the room, Lydia drops my hand. I tap the stick from left to right but find nothing. Then we turn, and the stick hits another thing, soft, like cloth. My face brushes up against it, too. Reaching out like before, I feel coat sleeves. I feel a coat hanging on a wooden peg. Then past the coat, the stick bangs against something wooden—the door.

"Well done!" Mrs.   Davis's voice sounds happy, but I still can't understand the words. The girls clap. Smiling, I make my slow way around the other side, tapping the stick with Lydia beside me. I bump into chairs, so Lydia again shows me how the stick stops me from running into things. The stick finds another object, like the chair and door.

I feel a tall wooden thing with shelves. I feel along the shelves and find items with paper.

Books, maybe? I didn't know blind people could read! Touching the outside cover, I wonder how this is possible. I start to take one of the books out but then stop.

"Yes, Esther, you can take it." This is Mrs. Davis across the room.
Lydia helps me lift the heavy book, and we sit on the floor. I can hear
Mrs. Davis talking and something making funny little clicking noises.
There's rustling, like when Leah turned pages in her books.
"Esther, open it!" Whatever she said, Lydia seems excited. Lydia places
the book on my lap, and I open it.

What are these strange bumps all over the page? I turn the page and
find more bumps there, too. I suddenly feel very happy, and I can't wait
to find out what these funny bumps are. In fact, each page is covered
with lines of bumps.

"Well, what do you think?" Lydia asks. I can't answer. "Miss, I forgot.
She doesn't understand our words yet."
"English, Lydia!" Mrs. Davis says.

I understand those words.
"I...
But... I can't finish, can't say how happy I am. Touching the book, I say,
"Tanakh?" I think about how I've always wanted to read that!
"No." Mrs. Davis says, standing beside us now.

I can tell she's standing because her voice sounds higher up. "Sorry." I'm
disappointed. Finding the bookshelf, I touch each book and ask again,
and I hear the same answer.
"No, Esther." I'm heartbroken!

"What's the Tana?" Lydia says incorrectly-she can't pronounce "Tanakh"
yet.

I'm happy I am no longer the only one struggling with a different
language.

"The Hebrew Bible!" Mrs. Davis explains.

"Let's stop for now," she says. She leads me to a chair at the table. I sit
quietly until another bell rings. The girls leave, tapping their sticks. Mrs.
Davis leads me to another room.

In there is another teacher, with the same girls, I think. I know Lydia's
voice now.

"I'm Miss Walters, and this is the Sewing room," the new teacher says.

"Here, take this." She hands me a box of different-sized beads, a needle, and thread.

I begin to thread the needle. "Very good!" She says. I can't understand, but she sounds pleased. Stringing beads is easy. It's something we did at home before Mama taught us sewing.
Because I don't have to talk, I can daydream.
I imagine I'm back home, baking bread in the kitchen or playing piano with Leah. I wish she were here.

"Esther, did you hear me?" The teacher's voice is angry. She taps my shoulder.

I say the first word that comes to me, "Leah."
"No, Esther. I asked you, what bead comes next?"
I can't understand her.

What? I guess I look confused because she apologizes. She puts my hand back in the box. I guess she wants me to pick up another bead. I feel the almost full string; the square and round beads slide back and forth. I pick another round one.

"Good!" She moves on. Beads strung, I tie the end and wait. "Wonderful, Esther." She seems to like it.

The girls leave when the bell rings, but the teacher stops me. "Your name?"

When I answer, she says, "Very good. Other girls' names?" What? I don't understand that question, even though she uses less words when asking me.

"Miss Walters, she can't understand you!" Lydia answers.
"Of course. See you tomorrow," Miss Walters says.

Next lunch. Oyster stew! When I realize what it is, I try to explain why I can't have it. (in Our faith, we're forbidden to eat shellfish!) Someone gives me a bowl of vegetables.

"I'm sorry, Esther!" A woman says, "I'm Mrs. Porter. Miss Leigh and I are learning, too." I can't understand all that! I think, irritated.
After lunch, Lydia takes me to another room. We sit at a long table. I feel something soft like paper. It's not bumps, but whatever it is, it feels curvy. When I push on it, nothing happens.
"Let's see what you know." A woman grabs my hand. "Find the ocean."

What did you say, I think.

"Miss Pryce, she can't speak English," Lydia says.
"Oh, why didn't anyone tell me." She moves on.

I feel the soft stuff again and notice how some of it is pointed, other parts are curvy, and all are different shapes. The soft stuff is stuck on thick paper, with glue, maybe?

"Esther, that's her name." Mary's voice, I think, "She arrived yesterday."

"Well, try and listen," the teacher sighs. "Lydia, look-I mean, feel that? What are those?"
"Mountains, Miss."

That evening, I meet the other lady again. I don't remember her name.

"I'm Mother Anderson," she says to me. "But you call me Mother for now."

Another new word, but I practice it until she's happy. "I'll be here every morning when you wake up and every evening before you go to bed. "Kathleen, show Esther where her clothes are kept!" Mother Anderson says.

Kathleen takes my hand and walks away, but Mother says, "No, Esther, you need this." She hands me my case, and Kathleen leads me across the room to a long chest of drawers. She opens one on the bottom.

"Put your underclothes in here," she says, but I don't understand. She opens my case to show me. We both feel the clothes until she finds something.

"This!" She says and hands me a pair of stockings. Taking my hand, she helps me put them in the drawer. I understand now. I find all the stockings, socks, and underwear and put them in.

"Good!" Mother says, "Now dresses." We hang my dresses on hooks in a long closet.

"Very good. Next, show her where the washroom is, please." We went out the door into the hall and into the room I was in this morning.

I want to tell her I'd been here before, but all I can say is, "Mrs..." because I can't remember how to say her name.

"You mean Mother!" Kathleen answers. No, that's not right! I wish I knew more English. I sigh, frustrated.

We explore, Kathleen showing me where our towels are hung near the long row of sinks. She shows me the toilets and the bath too. "We use it every Saturday," she says. I don't answer, but she keeps talking.

"Sometimes, it's noisy in here... and wet!" Mother has to remind Amy, Mary, Catherine, and Hannah not to splash." She laughs, and I laugh too. I can't understand anything, but I think I like her.

Before getting into bed, I finally take my doll Minna out of the case. She was at the very bottom. I brush her hair and put her on my pillow. I can smell Mama's perfume on everything. I hope her scent lasts forever.

I try to sleep, but of course, I can't. I try reciting the Shema, but that just makes me more homesick and lonelier. The clock in the hall chimes ten times. I can't count in English yet, but I can still count the chimes.

I must've fallen asleep because I suddenly feel a hand awaken me. "Esther, it's Kathleen. Wake up." Kathleen showed me around yesterday. I slowly get out of bed.

"Kathleen?" I hope I said her name right.
"Yes, Esther?" I want to ask her where the closet is. Her hand finds my arm, then my shoulder.

I start panicking.

I don't know the words for clothes or dress. I touch my nightdress, hoping she'll understand.

"Mother, Esther needs something." Mother comes over. I touch my nightdress again. Then, my hand touches Kathleen's dress.
"I think she wants her dress?" Kathleen says.

"Oh, yes, over here!" Mother says, and we walk across the room, past the others getting dressed. I hear Mother telling one of the girls something. Then, I remember the dresser. We find my clothes, and I get dressed.

"Now that you're dressed, Esther, let's make your bed." Mother takes me over to my bed, showing me how to fold the sheet until I do it all by myself.

"Good, well done." "Now everybody's dressed, and beds made. Time for breakfast." But I don't know what she said.

She claps, and we line up.

A bell rings, and I hear the sticks tapping as everyone leaves. Mother guides me to the table. "Sit next to Mary."
Breakfast is something sticky and sweet. Mother gives me a spoon to eat with.

After breakfast, Lydia takes me to Mrs. Davis's room.
I hear girls talking.

What will they show me today? I'm excited. This room is full of wonderful things. I sit next to Mary again.
"Esther, say A," Mrs. Davis says.

Some letters sound almost like German, but then they become harder to pronounce. After several mistakes, Mary interrupts. "Miss, please let me show her." She begins to sing, "A, B, C, D, E, F G." I hear giggles. I'm not sure from who. "Enough, let Mary try." Mary takes me to a corner, and we begin again.

Today is Friday. So far, I'm learning how to use the cane, and I'm learning English words every day.

Mama and Papa said we'd be living with good people. They've been right. Kathleen and Lydia are my age, and Mary, Hannah, Catherine, and Amy are younger, around six or seven years old. Some older girls stay in another dormitory. They call us "the little girls."

After breakfast, I'm in the reading room with Mrs. Davis, and she hands me a long metal thing with little squares cut into it. The object can open and shut. When it opens, I feel pins; two on the left and two on the right. Mrs. Davis hands me a piece of thick paper. She shows me how to put the paper between the two pieces of metal. I hear a click when it closes.

"This is a slate." Then, she hands me a small round object with a tip at the end.

"That's a stylus." "Put the stylus into one of the little holes." I feel the point of the stylus, press into the paper. I can press more than one-time in each hole.
"The hole is full."

She tells me to turn the whole slate over and open it. When I do, on the left side of the paper, I feel six bumps, like in the books.

"What is this?" I ask.

"Braille, you read it with your fingers," Amy says.
"How many dots are there, Esther?"

I slowly count, "Eins, tsvy, drei, vier, fúnf, sechs" in German.
"That's funny!" Catherine laughs.

"Very good. Can you please count in English now?" Mrs. Davis asks.
That's harder, but I slowly count to six. "Catherine, she was counting in
German before. Please, remember she's learning and be kind. No
laughing, please." "Esther, start on this side." She places my hand on the
right side of the paper.

I fill the paper with four rows of six dots. After each line, I move the
stylus down to the next row. Next, Mrs. Davis shows me how to lift the
paper off the top pins and move it, so the bottom holes of the paper are
on the top pins. Before I close it, I see the blank spot between the four
pins.

I close it and make more rows with six dots. I'm not sure if all the dots
are there, but I don't think Mrs. Davis will mind.
"Well done."

"Can I make letters now?" I ask.
"Yes, let's start with A," she says.

It's my second week here, and I'm back in the reading room, finish
writing the alphabet in English. I've always wanted to read and write!
"Can I write to my sister?" I hope I've said everything correctly.
"You have a sister?" Mary asks. "What's her name?"

"Not now; finish your sentences first!" Then, Mrs. Davis says to me,
"We'll see. You need to learn more, Braille." I can't wait!
Sewing's next; I'm still stringing beads. Miss says this may be my last time
doing this.
Geography after lunch.

Miss Pryce says, "Can she speak English yet?"
"Yes, Miss," I say very slowly.
"Well, that's a relief. Feel this? It's a map."
I slowly say this new word.

Most of the girls here are nice, just not some of the older ones.
Every evening, all of us have to walk around outside. Mother calls it

exercise.

This evening, Mary and I walk past the flower garden.
"Hello, girls." A man says, "I'm John. You must be Esther."
"I am. Nice to meet you." I think I recognize his voice from before.
"How are the roses today?" Mary wants to know. She asks questions about everything every day.
"Beautiful.
Smell?" he offers.

We move closer to smell the flowers. I touch each flower, careful not to touch the thorns. There are so many flowers. I walk along, my hand on the edge of the flower bed, surprised at its length. I hear Mary and John talking on the other side.
I can't understand them.

"John, I think I've heard you, can't remember!" I say in broken English.

"You have. I also help Mrs. Porter in the kitchen. When you're lining up, we set the tables. Afterward, we all clear away and wash up." John answers.

"William and I also work around the school, repairing broken things in your dormitories."

"I know William." Mary is still on the other side. "I was lost one day, and he showed me where to go."

"Who told you what food I can eat?" I attempt to ask.
"Mrs. Porter knows Jewish shopkeepers," he says warmly.

"Can I meet them?" I'm excited. I say something in German. "Do they talk like me?" He says he'll ask her.

"That's the bell!" Mary says. I know the bells, too. "We have to get back. Come on, Esther."

We hear voices as the older girls walk by.

"Look, there's that German girl and her little friend. "Where are your parents? "Can you read?" Do they have Braille in your country?"
"Susan, that's not fair," Mary's voice is furious. "She's new, and you're mean."

"Don't answer them!" John replies. "That's very rude, girls. Apologize, please."

45

They stop walking.

The other girl laughs and says, "She can't understand us, anyway. And besides, we don't have to listen to you. You're just the gardener." She sounds very bossy.

"Yes, I can," I say slowly. "I don't know where Mama and Papa are." The girls giggle and walk away.

We say goodbye to John and head back up the steps to Mother, who is waiting by the door. John follows because he whispers something to her when we pass.

Now, in bed, I begin to feel anxious. What if they can't find Leah? I don't even know who took her.

Then, I remember the piano which I heard yesterday.
Using my cane, I was walking down the hall with Lydia. I stopped when I heard something.
Was that music?
"That's a piano!" I said suddenly.
"Yes, that's right.
It's a piano," Lydia replied.

"It's pretty.
Can I play?" I asked. Lydia said the girls were playing now, but maybe tomorrow. And after Geography today, we played.

The piano was smooth, with the same keys as ours back home. The teacher entered, saying, "You must be Esther."

"Yes, Miss." I've learned that's the polite thing to say to a teacher here.

"I'm Mrs. Blake. Can you play?" I said yes, and I slid onto the bench. Memories filled my head. I'm back home. Leah and I walk to Fraulein Gerta's house. She's our neighbor, two houses down. We begin playing right away, me by listening to Leah, Leah learning with sheet music. Fraulein Gerta explained that music is made of symbols called notes. The notes tell people reading sheet music what to play.

Since I couldn't read it, I had to listen and remember the music.
"Stop now." Mrs. Blake said to me.

Suddenly, I realized where I was. I heard the song I was playing. Mrs. Blake touched my hands.

"You're playing very well. Where did you learn?" She asked.
"Home," I answered, hoping that was right.
"Sorry, who was your teacher?" She asked slowly.

"Fraulein Gerta!" I said excitedly, remembering her.
"How old were you when you started?"

"Six. Leah was five. We practiced at a neighbor's. Mama gave her bread when we went over there." I said in German.

"You must speak English here. Say it again, please."
"Sorry, Miss.

I forgot." I told her what I could muster up in English.
"Well, you're not a beginner, and you can play here. What was the name of the song you just played?" I told her the name of the German song.
"Can I read music?" I asked. She said there's Braille sheet music, but I'll have to learn more Braille first.

Leaving the music room with Lydia, I felt like flying back home and telling Mama and Papa everything.

Today's Saturday, we have breakfast, then do our morning chores.
"Today, Lydia, Hannah, and Mary will dust. Kathleen and Esther, clean the windows! Catherine and Amy, sweep!" We're told.
We do this quickly, trying not to step on each other's feet. Mother knits.

Once, she came over, saying, "Stop. Like this." I guess she takes Amy's hand and pushes the broom under the bed. "All the way in the back!"
"Hannah, that wardrobe door is still dusty."

Lunch is next.

"What's this?" I think it's potatoes, peas, and some meat.
"Sausage and mash!" Amy says with her mouth full, so I can't understand her. Mary tells me. I drop my fork with a clatter. "Mother, I can't eat that." I show her the sausage.

"Esther, I'm sorry. I'll get Mrs. Porter." Mrs. Porter gives me another plate without sausage. She promises it won't happen again, and we finish eating.

"Mother, why can't she have sausage?" Mary asks. "It's good."

"She's Jewish. They can't eat pigs or cows." I'm glad Mother explained. I don't know how.

47

After lunch, we have free time. "You can sew, read, or play piano." We're told. I want to write to Leah, but I don't know where she's at! I want to say.

Kathleen and I go to Mrs. Davis's room. I find a small book and try to read. The words are easy.
"Sun, flower, go, stop?" I read aloud.

"Very good!" Kathleen claps. "Try the next page by yourself." We read our books silently.
Suddenly, I hear the dinner bell.

"How many pages do you have left?" She takes it from me. "Five more pages. Maybe you can finish tomorrow."

After a cauliflower and fish dinner, I'm walking with the older girl, Susan. She's the mean one that Mary and I met in the garden the other day.
"Do you know why you're here?" Because your parents couldn't keep you!" She says.
"I know," I say quietly.
"You do?" She's surprised. I tell her about our journey.

"Yes, but do you know how you came to be here at this school?"
"No. Our parents said that we'd go to England. Families would take care of us" I say. I want to tell her all we needed was our pictures, school, and medical reports. I think about that.

I've never been to school before, not really. When I was six, Leah and I went to school together. I learned counting and spelling. The teacher was nice; and let me listen in class. At home, Papa would test me on what I'd learned each day.

When I turned seven, it was harder because everyone was writing more. The teacher asked me questions in class and wrote my answers for me.

This was during recess, so my classmates didn't hear. When I finished that year, I helped Mama and Papa in their bakery. Now, I wonder, how did Mama make sure I was on that train if I didn't have school reports?

Susan tells me her mother worked for one of the groups that put us with our families. She was pleased with my piano playing, housework, and what schooling I'd had. But that wasn't enough. Her mother had to promise that I'd be useful until I left.

48

"That's what this school does," Susan explains.
"We learn to be useful? Does that mean we work hard?"

She laughs, but not in a pleasant way. "It means we'll get jobs and earn a living when we leave school. We won't be a burden to our families." We walk in silence, passing girls being told to walk and not skip by Mother Anderson. I hear their voices and start to say something to them, but Susan pulls me away.

"That's Amy, Hannah, Mary, and Catherine" I say. I want to join them, but she doesn't answer me.

"Hurry up! We're nearly done!" She says, yanking me in one direction.

We stop, and Susan walks away. I'm suddenly lost! I know I'm far away from the other girls. I search around with my cane and find nothing.

"Is anyone here?" I call in German.
"What did you say?" I turn, and a man touches my shoulder. I step back. "Esther, it's me, John."
"Where am I?" I ask slowly.

"The steps aren't far," he says. He takes me to them. There's something strange about the way he walks, but I'm not sure what. We sit and wait; Mother returns with the other girls. "Thank you, John!" She says to him.

"You're welcome, Mother Anderson. She was lost." We go in together. "Susan left me," I say.
"Yes, she's horrible!" Mary says, "She did that to me, too. She doesn't like walking with new girls."
"She said I'm slow," I add.
"Where did she leave you?" Catherine asks.
 "By the steps!" I reply.

Mary says, "She left me by a tree. I thought I'd have to find my own way back. John helped me, too.
It was raining with loud thunder."

"All right, washroom time. And no messes." Right, Catherine?"
"Yes, Mother!" Catherine says.
We take turns bathing.

"Hannah, enough dawdling, remove that dress!" Mother scolds.
I suppose remove means to take off, because she does, then climbs in.

Mother assists by showing her what to do. Next, it's Lydia's turn, but she doesn't need help. Then, Catherine climbs in.

"The water's not very warm anymore." She washes quickly.

I hear Mother saying, "Go back. You missed your feet."

"Sorry, I dropped the soap!" She says and starts to cry.

"It's all right, love, let's find it." They look in the bath, then the floor.

"Here it is," Kathleen says, "It skated close to one of the toilets."

I don't know what skating is, but everyone laughs.

Mother says, "Thank you, now finish, please." This time the soap stays in the bath. Next, Mary and Kathleen take their turns. Mother helps Mary wash her long hair.

"Esther, your turn!" she says to me.

"She's such a show-off," Hannah whispers, but I can still hear, "Little Miss Perfect."

"Use this. It's a flannel!" Mother hands me a cloth and the soap. I rub some on the cloth. I wash everywhere, not skipping my feet.

Catherine was right. The water is freezing!

Then, Mother hands me something for my hair. It smells awful. "Don't forget the back." After everyone's finished, we dry ourselves and put on nightdresses. I finally ask Kathleen a question I've been thinking about.

"You can see the soap?"

"Yes, I can see bright colors, and the soap is blue!"

We brush our teeth, trying not to splash too much water. The older girls enter when we finish. They're giggling about something.

"What's that sound?" I whisper.

"My keys. I'm Mother Matthews. Are you Esther?" I turn around, and a woman is behind me.

"Yes, how do you know me?" I ask.

"You're the only one here with an accent like that!" She laughs. "You still can't speak English like us, can you? No, you still sound German!"

"Mother!" Mary screams suddenly, "Look!" But she's washing her hands, so I guess she doesn't see. "There's a slimy thing in my hair!"

"A little bug," Mother replies, pulling it out. When she asks who did it, no one speaks. Mother Matthews is quiet. "What about you, Susan?

50

Anna? Or Julia?"

Mother Anderson asks, naming the other girls, too.
"Why them? Your girls aren't angels, you know." Mother Matthews sounds mad, and she laughs again.

"You're right. Now though, this washroom has gotten too crowded. Girls, come with me."

Back in our dormitory, she asks us again, and we give her the same answer.

"Very well," She sighs, "I'll speak to her." I guess she means Mother Matthews.

"What does "I sound 'German'" mean?" I ask.

"Your voice, how you talk. You're German. When you speak English, you still talk differently," she explains.
"Will I always sound German?" I ask. Mother answers, probably so.
As the days pass, everything becomes easier for me. Wake up bell, dress, prayers. (I whisper mine in Hebrew.) Breakfast bell, classes, lunch. After lunch, there are more classes, dinner, a walk, evening chores or play, prayers, and finally, a bedtime bell. Every evening, we all have chores, like sweeping or dusting our dormitory.

Hannah doesn't like doing anything herself. She always says, "I never do this at home."

Mary tries to help her, but Mother won't let her. So, Hannah yells and stamps her feet, but Mother scolds her.
"Put your shoes on.

Brush your hair. You're not at home." Try again!" She says to Hannah.

Kathleen doesn't need Mother's assistance. She sometimes helps Amy and Mary fold their clothes. Mary hates cleaning and the smell of the polish. We all hate different chores.

On Saturday, we practice piano, write letters, do handicrafts, like beadwork, or just talk.

There are other kinds of chores too.
We care for our own small vegetable garden. Mrs. Porter cooks with the vegetables from our garden in our meals or she trades, meaning she gets something in exchange for them.

We had orange juice for breakfast one day. Someone asked her where she got it, and she said she traded it for our vegetables.

On Sunday, everyone walks to church. It's different from a synagogue. The Bible and songs are in English. It was strange listening to the English words.

I've been here for two weeks. It's Saturday night, and it's raining. Soft at first, then louder. Suddenly, we hear loud booming thunder and flashing lightning.

Catherine starts crying, "I can see it" she says.

So, I sing, "Summ, Summ, Summ." I finish, and everyone claps.
"What does that mean?" Hannah asks rudely. "That's not an English song."
I tell her I don't know the English words. "That's one of me and Leah's favorite songs to sing!" "Can you sing a song?" I ask.

"Ring Around the Roses!" Mary calls out. We dance in a circle, and they sing, "Ring around the roses, a pocket full of...

"Girls, you know the bedtime bell's about to ring. Nightdresses and prayers, immediately!" Mother calls.
"But, Mother," I say, "We are not done singing. Can we please sing all of it?"

Amy gasps, but Mother answers, "Esther, since you asked nicely, you may finish. Then to bed, all of you."

"Mother, she should be punished!" Hannah cries.

"She won't be." Mother replies, "She's still learning. Now, finish!"

"Pocket full of posies. Ashes, ashes, we all fall down!" We fall to the floor, giggling, getting in each other's way when we stand up.
"What's posies?" I ask.

"Flowers!" Mother answers.
We say our prayers, and I say the Shema prayer out loud for the first time.

"What's that? I've never heard those funny words before!" Hannah pretends to whisper loudly.

"Be quiet," Lydia whispers angrily.

"Girls, you can both be quiet unless you want extra chores tomorrow!"

Mother uses her stern voice. "It's called Hebrew." We finish.
Mother continues, "And, Hannah, try undressing yourself tonight." I think it's strange how she's been here longer than me and still can't or won't dress herself.

"I thought your prayer was beautiful!" Kathleen says, "What does it mean?"

"I don't know the English words to that one!" I say sadly.
"Silence, girls!" The bell rings, and we fall asleep quickly.

Walking to breakfast the next morning, we pass the older girls. We hear their canes first, then, "Here comes the Charity girl!" One calls.
"Stop that!" Lydia shouts back. "She's new!"

"Lydia, keep walking, hurry!" Mother Anderson stops to wait for her. "What's Charity Girl'?" I ask.

"You...!" Lydia whispers. "Anna was calling you a "Charity Girl" because you're not from England, I think."

We're outside after church—the air is colder, and the wind is blowing. We walk through crunchy leaves on the ground. We're not jumping in them, though, like Leah and I used to do.

Instead, we're watering and weeding the garden. Hannah complains that her hands hurt, but Mother does her work just like the rest of us.
"I never do this at home. We have a gardener!" She reminds us.
"Last night, you said you saw lightning. How?" I ask Catherine.
"I can only see bright lights. I sort of remember my Mum's face and hair. She said I was ill when I was little. When I got better, I was blind. My eyes don't work like they used to anymore."

I was silent. I didn't know people could become blind. I was born that way.

Across from me, I hear, "My sister's got long hair," Amy laughs. "Sometimes, she lets me brush it."

"My little sister has short hair," Mary says, "But mine takes ages to dry. Mum won't let it get cut. She wants it braided."

"I'll show you sometime. When you're older, I can show you how to pin it." Mother says. Mary seems to like that idea.

"Finished, Mother!" Hannah groans, "Can I go in now?"
"No, you may not. We still have work to do!" Mother replies.

Watering is next, we try not to splash any on our clothes.

We return our tools to the shed when the dinner bell rings. Walking back, John passes us. He and William were working in the flower garden.

"Where have the weeds gone?" He jokes. We laugh and say they're far away.

One morning, we wake up really cold. Then, I remember that it's November. I've been so busy, the weeks have flown by. Shivering, we go through our morning routine and hurry to breakfast. Hannah still won't make her bed unless Mother scolds.

We almost missed the breakfast bell because she took so long.

I know my way around pretty well since we all have to use our canes.

Outside the dining hall, we usually line up until it's ready.
We sit, and food is served on our plates.

"Esther, here's yours!" When they finish serving, we all eat together. The teachers and the other staff have their own table.

When John and Miss Leigh clear the plates away, everyone at our table says, "Thank you." Except Hannah. She angrily whispers, "John, hurry up. You're slow."
"I'm going as quickly as I can, Miss!" He answers.
Mother reminds her, "What do you say, Hannah?" Sounding angry, like Papa when Leah and I were caught doing something wrong. She stands beside Hannah's chair.
Hannah mumbles, "Thank you!"
"What else?" Mother prompts. Hannah apologizes, but I don't think she means it.

After breakfast is another Braille lesson with Mrs. Davis.
I'm learning numbers and sentences.

Writing on the slate is hard, if I make a mistake, I can't fix it until I turn the paper over. Sometimes, I reverse what I'm writing and have to start over. After writing, we take turns reading aloud. It's a story about animals. When my turn comes, I slowly read so I can say all the words perfectly.

"No," Kathleen stops me, "The word is 'treetops.'" I have to start over. Amy messes up, as well.

"It's an F, not a D. Try again." Mrs. Davis says.

Next is one of my favorite classes: sewing. I like learning English words for things I do at home. Miss Walters was proud when she saw I wasn't a beginner, just like Mrs. Blake was when I played the piano.

When we are in our dormitory, Hannah hates doing things herself. In class today, I try to help her, but she yells, "Go away. I don't need your help." Mary does, though. I help thread her needle.

We're sewing buttons on shirts. I try not to rush, but this is too easy. "Finished?" Miss Walters comes over.

"Yes, can I do something harder?" I ask, hopefully.
"Can you knit?" When I answer yes, she says, "Make something for me."

She hands me knitting needles and yarn. I make a dress for Minna. "Catherine, very good. Hannah, your thread's tangled. Let me help." "This is too hard!" Hannah stamps her foot.

"Stop that. If you practice, it'll get easier." "Lydia, that button's too close to the first one." Kathleen, excellent, all six as well!" Miss Walters says.

It's my turn again.
"Wonderful, too." She takes the dress from me, examining it. Handing it back, she says, "This dress even has buttonholes.
Well done!"

"No fair!" Lydia calls out, "How are you that fast?"
"I'm quick, my Mama says. My sister Leah sews fast, too."
At lunch, Catherine talks about her Mum. "My Mum sews. She makes quilts."
"Who cares!" Hannah bangs her cup down, "My Mum buys our quilts."

"What colors does she use?" Lydia asks, ignoring Hannah. Her elbow brushes mine.

"All colors. She likes to make the sun and the moon."

"How?" I didn't know you could put real things in your quilts," I ask.
"She sews with different squares. I don't know how she puts the colors

55

together, but people love them!" Catherine says.

"Amy, what's that?" Miss Pryce says too loudly. She feels the table.
"Nothing's here.

Where is it? It's just paper, Miss." I feel paper in front of me, too.
"Of course, you blind children can't see that. Here are the maps you use."

Finally, it's our last class, piano. I'm still playing without music.

Lydia shows me her Braille music, and it doesn't feel easy.
The dots are mixed up.

They don't feel like letters or numbers.
Leah wouldn't even be able to read it. I think she'd like Mrs. Blake, though.

What is she doing now? I wonder. Is she playing the piano? Maybe she's in school? I hope her family is nice.

"Esther, did you hear me?" Mrs. Blake interrupts.

"No, I was thinking about Leah, how she liked playing."

"Well, love, try again. Both hands, and sing." Mrs. Blake tells me this is called a scale, and it's sung in English.

Now I'm called "Charity girl" by the older girls almost every day. Susan and Anna are the worst. Julia sometimes talks to us. We still only see them in the washroom or halls. Luckily, I'm always with someone. Never alone. After that bug joke, they haven't tried anything else.

We also listen to the radio, so we know there's fighting going on between countries. We've heard about how the Germans are fighting with Poland and Britain. That's how this war started when Germany attacked Poland. Amy tells me children from England have been moved from their homes in the city and are living with new families in the countryside. Her next-door neighbor has a brother and sister living with her.
"They left in case of bombings," She whispers on our walk, "I guess everyone's afraid of Hitler!" I'm glad we're not in the city.

A much happier radio programme is called Children's Hour. In Toytown, talking animals live together and get into trouble. Catherine likes Larry the Lamb character.

It's Friday night.

I can hear heavy rain hitting the windows.

"Why don't you play hide-and-seek?" Mother has me be It.
I start to count, "Eins, tsvy..."

"English, Esther." Mother says, "Please start over."
Sighing, I do! I hear giggles when I reach twenty. I start to find everyone.

Catherine hides under her bed, Kathleen in the closet. I search the whole dormitory but can't find the others.
"They're not all here. Try outside!" Mother says.
"The garden?" I'm not sure what she means by outside.

"Sorry, Esther, I meant, look outside this room," she says. The first place I go to is to the washroom. "Please be in here!" I say out loud.

"Well, if it isn't the Charity girl?" Anna laughs loudly. I tell her I'm looking for my friends. "Not here!" She says quickly.

I search the whole room, but they are not here. I tell Mother, and she tells me to search the hallway. The next door is unlocked, so I step through to listen, but all I hear is the clock. My cane hits an empty chair. My leg bangs against a dresser; then I find a bed. Kneeling down, I feel around and pull someone's hair.

"Ouch! Finally, Esther." Lydia crawls out, "I almost fell asleep waiting."

"Where am I?" I ask.
"Mother's room.
Who's left?" She asks.

I find a door I've never seen before.

"Mother Matthew's dormitory! Not there!" I find another door. "That's Mother Matthew's room. They're not there either," she says. We knock on their dormitory door, anyway.

We hear someone say, "Hello!" It's Julia. I'm relieved. We tell her what we're playing, and she swears our friends aren't here.

She offers to come along, but Mother Matthews, of course, won't let her.

Together, Lydia and I find Amy and Hannah in the music room. Mary is the last one hiding. Hannah comes with me to help. Please, don't be nasty tonight, I plead to myself.

It wasn't bad walking with the others. Now, we go to the dining hall. The halls are dark, and it's funny not seeing any electric light. The only sounds are our voices, tapping canes, and our shoes.

Outside, we hear the loud rain and sometimes thunder.

"Stop jumping, silly.
It's just thunder!" Hannah hisses.

"I don't know when I'll hear it!" I explain.

We speak softly, but our voices sound loud. Nobody's around, silence.

Walking down the stairs, I hear every loud step.

Hannah tries a door, but it's locked. We find another door.
"Try this one, Esther. I've never opened this one. It's unlocked." She's excited.

I open it, and my shoes squeak. A light comes on.

"Girls, what are you doing?" It's Miss Leigh.

"Sorry, Miss!" Hannah whispers. Mrs. Porter is awake, too. We tell them why we're there, and Miss Leigh says to try the reading room. "We tried the classrooms."

"Well, she's not in the other bedroom. That's a rule here. Hannah, you know better. And the outside door's locked, so she must be inside, somewhere."

We start walking back to the dormitory, and I'm angry now. We find Mary sitting on one of the windowsills. I never even thought to look there.

"You hid well." Mother is happy! "Now, hurry, bedtime bell."

"Mary is good. She hid in a difficult spot," Hannah says, "I had trouble finding her."

As we get ready, I wait for Hannah to tell everyone about our adventure. She does everything herself tonight, no arguing. "Excellent, Hannah!" Mother says.

The next morning after breakfast, Mother greets us with, "Esther, Hannah, come with me. You lot, go in, and be quiet." We stand outside the door. "Why didn't you two tell me what happened last night? Esther, you are first."

"I thought Hannah would. It was her idea!"

"No, Esther opened that door. I told her who it was, but she didn't listen." Hannah whines.

"Very well. I'll let you know your real punishments tomorrow." Next time, I better hear about it from you immediately!" Mother warns.
"What's immediately?" I ask.

"It means after it happens. Instead, Miss Leigh told me at breakfast. I was ashamed! And she's right. You knew better, Hannah."
We have to stay in our dormitory all day. I read, not speaking much, but Hannah complaining because "Esther opened the door!" Our meals are brought up by John.

"Mother, our library is small," Lydia complains. She slams the door. After scolding her, Mother asks what she means. "They don't have the book I want. Mrs. Davis told me not every book is in Braille."
"Yes, she's right, love. It takes a long time to Braille a book."

It's Sunday, after church.
Mother gives us our punishment
.
We have extra cleaning and scrubbing the long hall outside the dormitories. Mother gives us our bucket and rags and goes back inside. I clean one end, and Hannah starts at the other end. We stop for lunch, and our hands and knees are sore.

Mother looks at our work.
"Good, you can stop now."
After lunch, we finish.

I hate you, I thought, as we brought our buckets to the kitchen. "I missed piano." It's my turn to whine a bit. Miss Leigh just takes my bucket.

"I missed talking to Mummy." I turn to Hannah.
"What do you mean?"
"My Mummy. She always calls on Sunday," she says.
"Next time, you'll remember that before you do anything like that again."

When John takes her bucket, she says he hurt her hand. "Mother Anderson says you may eat with the others tomorrow." With his hands

59

on our backs, he pushes us out the door.

We go to bed exhausted, not speaking much.

One night, I turn to the window and can't sleep. "It's almost Hanukkah," I think.

I must've said it out loud because Kathleen whispers, "What's Hanukkah?"

"Once, a long time ago, there was fighting between Jews and the Greeks who wanted the Jews to pray like them. When it was over, the Jewish people tried to light the candles in the temple, but there was only oil for one night. But it burned for eight nights," I say. Next, I explain that a menorah holds nine candles, and the shamash (the big candle) lights all the others. "One on the first night, two on the second, until the eighth night, when we light them all."

I hear yawning.
They're all awake now.

"What else happens?" Mary whispers.
"We sing songs and play games," I tell them.
"That's not fair! Father Christmas only comes once a year!" Amy whispers.

"Whose Father Christmas?" I ask.
"Girls!" We all sit up, hearing Mother Anderson in the doorway. "Go to sleep at once. Esther, you may finish your story tomorrow." She leaves, and we slowly fall asleep. Amy promises to tell me who Father Christmas is tomorrow.

It's the first week in December, with everyone excited about going home and for Father Christmas to arrive.

It's been snowing, so our walks are more difficult. Our shoes are covered in snow, and we sometimes slip, but that was the same back home, too.

On Sunday, Mother starts reading to us. It's a story about a horse and his mother.

"Why did you stop?" Mary asks.

"That's the end of a chapter. One chapter a week, how does that sound?"

We think that's a great idea.

"That was nice.
Where did you get it?" Mary asks.

Mother's sitting next to her.
"I had it sent from home. Our library doesn't have it, so I thought you might enjoy it." We fall asleep, talking about this new book.

I wish I knew where Leah is, but Mrs. Davis hasn't heard anything. Then, I remember what Susan had said.

The next Saturday, I find Susan in the sewing room. "Please, I need help," I say to her. Her knitting needles click, but she doesn't answer. I start to ask again.

"I heard you. Now let me finish this row first." She snaps. I sit and wait. Finally, she asks, "What do you want?"

I tell her about Leah and ask if her mother can find out where she lives.

"I might be able to, but we're in a war, and Mum is busy providing meals to factory workers right now."

Later we're listening to Mother read the story when she gets to the part where the horse has to go to live with another farmer. I start crying.

"What is it?" Amy's hand touches my arm.
Sniffling, I can't speak.

"Is it your sister again?" Hannah's on my other side.
Her shoulder pushes mine hard.
"Yes!" I say.

I'm quiet the rest of the night.

Catherine and I wake Christmas morning to find packages at the ends of our beds. The others are celebrating at home.
Should I open mine?

"Go ahead, Esther," Mother says. "They're for you." There are Braille labels on them. I eagerly look for Leah's name, but there's nothing. Then, very disappointed, I find a new coat from Mother Anderson and a packet of writing paper from Mrs. Davis. We give Mother Anderson a crocheted baby blanket she can send to her niece.

After breakfast, where we read about a baby named Jesus being born in a stable, I head to the Music room.

I play my songs from home for a while, feeling incredibly lonely. What is Leah doing now? I wonder. I hit the high keys softly, one at a time, then the low keys, very loudly! I feel the keys' sounds vibrate right through me.

"You're practicing!" I hear someone say. I turn, and William enters. I don't know him very well, but he speaks to me when we see each other.

"Not practicing, just playing," I say. I hear squeaking at the window. He says he's cleaning it.

"You're very good.
I hear you, girls, sometimes. What were you playing? It sounded angry."

"I miss my sister Leah!" I answer in German. There, I said it. He doesn't say anything. He just continues cleaning the windows. "She's gone. I don't know where she is at. So are Mama and Papa. They're in Germany, where Hitler is. When we left, Mama said we had to get away from him because he doesn't like Jews!" "I miss baking Challah bread, singing and playing piano with Leah, and listening to the Torah being read. It's not in Braille yet. I wish it were so I could read it myself."

I've stopped pounding the keys.

"You miss your family very much. You must always remember the happy times with them. Don't forget the songs and prayers!" He stops speaking.

I gasp. "You speak German and English?" I whisper, "You understand me?"

I can't believe what I'm hearing. Suddenly we hear a knock. We both turn as we hear Mother's voice. "I knew you'd be in here, Esther. William, when you're finished here, could you go to Mother Matthew's dormitory? She says it's urgent."

To me, she says, "Now, let's go back to our dormitory. I know a game you might enjoy." I don't feel like using my cane, so I take Mother's arm, and she guides me back.

She was right, the game is fun, singing and clapping, getting faster and faster. Catherine and I are laughing by the end.

Christmas dinner is wonderful! Turkey with potatoes and carrots.

Mother Anderson says this might be our last good Christmas dinner for a long while, so we should enjoy it. While we talk and share our presents, everyone figures out that we've all gotten the same thing from Mrs. Davis.

After Christmas pudding, Mrs. Davis explains. "I'm sure everyone's wondering why I gave you all the writing paper. It's for your letters. Even the younger ones, I'd like them to write something every day.
These next years are going to be harder for everyone because of the war."

There's silence, then Catherine asks, "Will my Mummy see it?"
"If you want to show her, you may."

"Why do we have to write anything?" An older girl asks, "The war is in Europe, not here."

"Haven't you been listening to the radio? Our Prime Minister wants us to be prepared."

You wouldn't be saying that if you'd heard Hitler say the things he'd said. I couldn't understand everything, but Mama said he hates Jews.
Then, Leah saw signs telling us where we could and couldn't go. Soon she couldn't go to school anymore.

After that, we listen to the King's Christmas message. He lives in Buckingham Palace, in London, with his family. He talks about the courageous servicemen overseas and ends with a poem about G-d's love.

I ask Mother what courageous means? "Brave,
doing something you think is right, even when nobody agrees with you. Servicemen are soldiers fighting for their country like people are doing now.

Overseas means countries far away."

In bed, I think about bravery. Mama and Papa were brave to send us away with the other children. I hope we might see our family and friends again.

We're brave, too, going to a new country to live. I'm still very homesick, but I like it here. And William speaks German, which gives me comfort!

Before I fall asleep, I think to myself that "Everything's different from the celebrations at home, but it's still nice. I wonder what next year will be like."

"Ration books!" Sarah exclaimed. "We'll starve!"

"You shouldn't be surprised, young lady. Weren't you listening when it was announced in September?" Sarah shrugged.

"Look in the pantry and cellar. We live better than most people." Dad said, and stood, then paced across the kitchen. "And yes, everyone has one. They must be registered with our shopkeepers. Do you want the army and the navy to starve? Brave men and women are helping to fight Hitler, so we have to do what we can." We were quiet then, staring at the coupon books in front of us. I looked inside and was sort of relieved because ham and bacon were no longer going to be on our table as often.

"If only America would help," Mum added.

"Why isn't President Roosevelt sending his Armies?" Sarah asked. Dad explained, "Churchill pleaded for America to fight against the Nazis and everything they stand for, but they won't even take evacuees, not as many as Britain has." So, that sort of explains Mum's endless "Be grateful" speeches; if America wouldn't take us, and if Britain hadn't either, Esther and I, along with thousands of other children, would probably be killed by now! The thought leaves me speechless.

Tuesday, February 20 Evening,
I'm Bleeding!

This morning, I woke up with blood on my sheets. Girls at school told me about their monthlies happening. I saw the supplies Mama packed. I think I know how to use them. This means extra laundry and hoping nothing bleeds through.

When I told Mum, all she said was, "Good, use the towels your mother packed."

Still no school and no letters. I'm starting to fear that you or Esther is dead.

Meanwhile, Dad's tried to dig a path from the house to the outhouse and barn, so it's easier to walk through the snow. Walking through snowdrifts to milk the cows or feed the chickens is exhausting and numbs your hands, but chores have to be done, no matter the weather. We all have gloves, scarves, and coats, but the wind seems to blow right through our layers.

My clothes are Jane's old clothes, of course. Some coat buttons are missing from my coat, and the gloves have holes. I have to warm my hands after each trip outside. The scarf is threadbare. Worst are the shoes. They're big and fill quickly with snow. Sarah tried stuffing them with paper, but it didn't help.

Monday, March 11
Night

Snow still falls outside, and we've entered our fifth month with no school. Mum's still teaching us.

It would be all right if she didn't constantly fill my head with their stories from the English Bible; we're almost to the New Testament.
Sarah and Jane have to participate, too, but they know everything already. Dad says it's good for when we return to church services.
She's been teaching us the different Kings and Queens of England, especially Queen Victoria.

"She ruled for sixty-three years.

I have pictures of her." We learned that she had nine children; her son Edward was the grandfather of the current King of England. When Prince Albert died, her grief lasted the rest of her life. She was named Empress of India in 1874.

I was not impressed with the picture Mum showed us. She could have gotten it anywhere.

Besides, there's been endless knitting, crocheting blankets for soldiers, and baking—some baked goods for us, others to sell. Since sugar is rationed, I doubt we'll be doing much baking after this.
When I asked if we could make Challah, Mum refused. "To waste flour on foreign bread like that!" She snapped. When I tried explaining what it was, she hissed, "We don't worship like that; haven't I taught you anything?"

"What?" Dad asked loudly. He'd been listening, I guess. He pulled her into the parlor and ordered us upstairs. "Thanks a lot, Leah." Sarah was furious with me. "Now, they'll be angry for a week."

"I only wanted to do Shabbat!" I said, blinking back tears, "Our family always does it." I'd ran up here, to my attic, furious.

It isn't just the baking part that's important, but the two covered loaves of bread symbolize the Manna the Israelites took with them through the desert. Every Friday, they're blessed during the Shabbat dinner.

The recent news in Europe helps lift our spirits; British men were on board a German tanker, rescued by a British Navy ship in Norwegian waters, where Dad says there isn't fighting, and one of Hitler's planes was shot down over Scotland.

Now, the bad news: Hitler's Nazis invaded Denmark and Norway. He must want Europe under his control.
My attic is freezing!

Mum still won't let me light a fire because we have to save wood. I shouldn't complain because all the bedrooms are cold now; the only fire is in the kitchen stove or sometimes in the parlor. We stay downstairs as much as possible where it's warmer.
The most depressing thing is, this snow means no post, so no news of Esther or you, Mama.

I wonder how the Evanses are. Mum was talking about sending them some food, but Dad pointed out how bad an idea that was.

"Too much snow, and besides, you know how she is about charity," he said.

"Maybe she'd accept it for Mr. Evans and her children then." Mum looked thoughtful. Still, Dad refused. I offered to go so that I could see Atalia. Again, he refused. Double depressing.

There's a puddle on my floor! My roof leaked. It must have rained during the night.

I think we're all tired of being cooped up inside. Everyone's snapping at each other over the simplest things. Sarah and Jane bicker about chores, Mum and Dad worry about how we'll eat. Mum was saying something about skipping meals. They went into the parlor to talk, but we could still hear them through the kitchen door.

Our meals are mostly bottled vegetables from the garden. We use the coupons in the shops. We get a certain amount of each, but we still have to pay. Mum couldn't find bacon, so it was vegetable turnovers for dinner the other night.

Later Today,
When I told Mum about my leak, she thrust newspapers at me! I couldn't believe it!

Anyway, Mum tried to buy apples, but they were sold out. Dad wanted apple pie for his birthday, but he had to settle for jam and scones instead. I went with her. The shop was crowded with women and children queuing for food.

Many small children were impatient, and Mums were saying, "Be still. We have to wait." Many left empty-handed.

Saturday, March 16,
Morning

(I awoke to loud thunder; out my window, I see a gray sky without rain.)

Afternoon I slipped up here to write, only place for privacy. When I entered, I glared at the puddle in the corner. When I told Mum, she said, "Here." More useless newspapers! Wiping up the water, I screamed silently.

Back to my crazy day: During lunch we had an unusual conversation. "Miss Simmons explained that India's fighting with us!" Sarah announced.

"Really!" Mum sat back, "Did she explain how those people fought with us last time as well?" I replied that she had.

"After this war, they'll get what they want, unlike last time." With a clatter, Dad set his cutlery down, "It was a bloody mess."

"The Indians died of that sickness-the Spanish Flu!" Jane interrupted.

"But it's a poor country that had famine or disease anyway."

"Only because Britain taxed farmers for their crops." Sarah jumped in.

"Stop this nonsense." Mum raised her voice, warning in her eyes, "That country's powerless without us. Right now, you kids have chores."

Rain was coming down heavily by then. Groaning, we trudged out into the downpour. My too-small coat barely covered me. My hair became drenched before reaching the barn. As for my shoes, they slipped and sank into the soft, sticky mud!

Our chores were finished, and we raced to the house, hearing thunder rumbling above us. Glancing down at my caked shoes, I removed them, placing them beside Sarah and Jane's shoes. "I'll wash them later!" Sarah offered."

Certainly not! You're not the girl's maid!" Mum's sharp voice rang out behind us. "Now, get in at once!"

Inside, I overheard Dad remarking, "Shouldn't Leah have a new coat by now?"

"No! She'll get it when I decide she needs it." Mum replied coldly.

"Our girls receive new coats every year. Leah deserves another."

"She isn't our child," Mum's voice rose, "She never will be."

Now, I can think about what Mum said. How is India powerless? Because it's under British rule?

That coat discussion was infuriating and hurtful. This family didn't have to foster me!

After dinner, Jane and I washed up. As we left for bed, Dad winked at me.

Sarah returned my clean shoes. "At least you'll be dry tomorrow." She grinned. Glancing up, I noticed the repaired roof.

Finally, on the first day of school since our long winter break Miss spent the winter in London with her sister, who just had a baby.

Today, she explained a bit more about rationing. "Rationing is different there, they don't have farms; instead, they have small gardens, and meat is rationed everywhere.

I'm sure your parents told you, it's hard for everyone, especially those fighting overseas. Farmers will have to grow extra crops. Who's heard of the Women's Land Army?"

Several kids raised their hands.

"We have two Land Girls working on our farm!"
An older girl called out.

Helen's family has some, too.

More kids told similar stories.

Some have dads, cousins, or brothers fighting in the Royal Air Force, navy, or another military. Some mothers here are factory workers or nurses.

"Since Dad's away, Mum has to work in a factory!" A boy said. Miss looked moved. "After what you've all told me, can I count on you to help?" She asked.

We all said yes.

I heard kids complaining about their lunches, though. "Bread, Margarine or 'Spam!" have been common lunches.
At least we still have our pint of milk. Today, I even had lunch.

During recess, Leron, Eva, and Daniel said they had Kosher coupons. I'm so jealous. For the rest of the afternoon, I thought about why Mum denies me everything having to do with my beliefs. Even ration coupons.

Thursday, April 4

This afternoon, in class, I asked Miss Simmons about India. We were discussing our Allies. "Isn't India part of Britain?"

"Yes, it has been for centuries now. The English government feels that the country's people can't govern on their own."

"My parents said the English are there to prevent violence. Some savages took to the streets," a boy said.

I gasped! That term sounded so cold and heartless. I also wondered where his family learned that information.

"Enough!" Miss glared sternly around the room at us.

"First, they're called Indians or Natives. Second, they took to the streets because they're fed up with their country not being independent. India wants its freedom."

That same boy wouldn't let the subject drop.

"My parents say the British are superior to those people. They need us to keep some of the unruly brutes in line."

"Since you know so much, you can explain to the class what you mean," Miss ordered, looking him in the eye.
"Stand up."

The boy obeyed with a smug expression on his face. "Begin!"

"The English Empire is powerful. When our government formed the North India Company in 1630, those merchants were hoping to become wealthy. The savages were jealous. Some powerful leaders tried to assassinate the English Viceroy." They failed, so our people took over. Those farmers failed to grow corn for the merchants. They starved for a while. To make them hate us even more, a few years ago, some religious blokes couldn't agree on whether India should be split or left alone.

Now that we're at war with Hitler, those people should defend their homeland."
"Very well.

That was the poorest recitation I've heard this year. It was very inaccurate. Your homework-write a paper with the correct information!"
I bit back a satisfied smile. "That's what happens when you think you know everything!" I thought.
Everyone else laughed, enjoying their friend's humiliation.

Jane had the pleasure of telling Mum after dinner. She commented, "His parents should learn their history."

Sunday, April 7
Night

Finally, I got to spend a weekend at Leron's. His family is wonderful. We spoke in German, mostly about our real families. Comparing diaries was funny.

His family isn't as obsessed with Churchill as mine. Music instead of news on their radio. We listened to a man named Sandy play the organ and read letters from families to their soldiers. I actually cried!

Best of all was observing Shabbat. The prayers and blessings all brought back memories. I almost cried during the services when the rabbi recited the prayers.

Talking to people afterward, it was like being at home. They spoke to me and said they were happy I was there.

We had a traditional dinner in the usual way. Friday night, Leron's Dad read from the Kiddush, the candles were lit by his Mum, and the bread was blessed.

Yesterday, we read and played games. It was great practicing Hebrew again. At the end of the weekend, his mother invited me back, I asked if I could bring Atalia, and she agreed.

When I returned, I saw most of the lights were out. Good, I thought, she won't question me.

"Not so fast, young lady! Come here." Mum commanded, as usual.

Great, I sighed.
Here come the questions. Mum and Dad were sitting in the parlor. She was knitting. He was reading.

"Well, what did you do?" She looked furious.

"Studied," I replied quickly.

"What did you talk about?" She asked.

"Our families," I was irritated. Why should she care what we said?

"We had dinner."

"Of course, you did! Did you enjoy it?" She snapped.

"Very much!" I said, smiling, looking right at her. "His Mum is a good cook."

"I see." Mum stared right back, "Well, you're staying here." I know that. I thought. You don't have to tell me.

"Mum, can you look at my window? It's stuck." Saved by Sarah. I don't know how long she'd been there. She winked at me as they went upstairs. Mum whispered angrily about, "Girls who don't stay in bed." Dad was still sitting in his chair, reading the paper. He never even looked up!

Monday, May 13
Evening

Winston Churchill is our new Prime Minister. Miss told us about one of his speeches today. He has formed a new administration with a war cabinet and Parliament. His aim is victory at all costs. The speech ended by saying Britain must be united against Hitler. His Armies have invaded Holland, Belgium, and France. It ended with, "We must go forward together."

School is almost over, which means exams are soon. I was talking with the others, and we're all nervous because everything is going to be in English. Eva's worried she'll forget everything when the day comes to take the tests.

One more thing: "I have a writing assignment for you!" Miss announced. Not another diary, I thought. The other German kids weren't pleased, either.

Eva raised her hand. "But Miss, I write every day." "That is our assignment." We, evacuees, murmured in agreement.

"This is for you all.
I want you to write to Princess Elizabeth." Some of the class burst out laughing. Miss Simmons raised her voice. "Grammar will count. Pretend she's a relative you haven't seen. What would you tell her?"

"How hungry everyone is." A boy called out. Miss frowned.
"Something they don't know." A girl spoke up. "Will she read them?" Miss shook her head from side to side. "Then why bother?"

"Because it's important for you to write about your experiences. It's an assignment at the same time." She then told us the letters could be any length we chose and, like our diaries, would be reviewed weekly. And they wouldn't be read out loud.

Sunday, May 19, Night
No Atalia in Church Today

One of Mrs. Evanses' daughters told us, "Dad's not well, she's looking after him."

"What's wrong?" Dad looked at Mrs. Evans, knowing how touchy she is. But she surprised us. "He has had some sleepless nights, but he's getting better. He's eating more, too."

"What a relief!" Mum actually beamed. "Will we see him anytime soon?"

Wrong thing to say. Mrs. Evans returned to her usual self and said, "No, come on, girls." She hurried out the door, one daughter holding her hand, the other trailing behind. Mum sighed and wiped her eyes. I couldn't believe Mum was crying!

We heard another speech by Churchill, this one asking that the people who aren't fighting to provide more weapons because Britain must win the war.

Side by side, Britain, and France fight unaided. (Dad said unaided means without help.)

At least Churchill sympathizes with the Jews, Hitler's victims. That's what the people of Europe are, victims! Because of their beloved Fúhrer, families are being torn apart, and countries are being invaded.

Mama, you told me to be brave, but now it seems impossible, especially with no word from Esther or you. Mum is trying to change my beliefs. Some of the Christian Bible is the same (the books are in a different order), but the New Testament has many bizarre ideas, like Jesus being born, dying, and rising again. We're only in Mark's testament, so there's a long way to go. Enough for now. I will try to sleep.

Thursday, May 23
Evening

Exams are almost over.
We started with simple spelling and arithmetic, but everything was more difficult today. Naming places in England, drawing a map.

We have ours in the morning. The older kids are in the afternoon. So, no taunts.

Leaving is another matter.
We pass them, and trouble usually happens. Like today, we passed the others coming in, and one girl yelled, "Any results yet?" We all were relieved. We considered ourselves lucky that was all she said.

Saturday, May 26
Night

Dad says many ships have been destroyed in the battle of Norway. Allies are still fighting.

Exams are finally over. They weren't as bad as I'd feared.
If I don't pass, I'll still be with the little kids—me twelve and still learning with the six-year-olds. At least we get along.

Mum and I are still reading Mark. So far, every book of the New Testament ends with Jesus' death and rising from the dead. Today, the Reverend asked me questions about everything I'd read. Why do I have to pretend to believe what they believe in? And for how long?

As I've said, I'd prefer to be in a Jewish family! I suppose I'm stuck here. Wherever Esther is, I hope she isn't forced to read their Bible. Are any evacuees living with English Christian families given a choice?

I saw the Evans family without Atalia. I tried to ask the youngest girl where she was, but Mrs. Evans heard. "Lily, no talking. We're leaving." Taking her by her shoulder, they walked swiftly out, the older one following glumly behind. She looked back, then ran to catch up. Was she crying?

The British, Germans, and French are now fighting in Operation Dynamo in a place called Dunkirk, France. Sometimes, when I sneak up here to the attic and look out my window, I see planes flying. Their engines sound loud up here! Maybe they're going to Dunkirk.

Thursday June 6
Evening

Nine days of waiting.
Operation Dynamo is over.

In a speech on Wednesday, Mr. Churchill spoke about the English troops being rescued by boats and navy ships, making the journey across dangerous water and in stormy weather. The ships made trip after trip, bringing back men they'd rescued. He praised the Royal Air Force. British planes attacked German bombers. The French airmen protected their homeland. The wounded were taken across the sea by hospital ships, which were being threatened by Nazi bombs. He said the missing troops will return home. France and Belgium have now surrendered. (I was right, those planes were helping.)

That was the longest speech I've ever sat through. Sarah and Jane fidgeted, but Mum and Dad hung on his every word!

More news, Italy has declared war on France and England.
Norway is now under Nazi control.

The other day, Sarah, Jane, and I went to the cinema. The film was about a woman who marries a rich man, and the people who work in his house don't like her. He didn't want his new wife to wear his first wife's clothes, but his new wife didn't know it was her old dress. A doctor turned up to say his first wife didn't die in the way everybody thought! The film ended with the house on fire, but everyone got out. It was my first English film. I think I understood most of it.

When we returned, Mum and Dad wanted to know who'd sat next to us. "Friends from school!" Jane replied. That was sort of true.

Friday, June 14
Late Evening

Factory jobs are dangerous, too. You have to wear special equipment, and the pay and hours aren't exactly a walk in the park."

I looked around but wasn't surprised when I saw Mrs. Evans or Eva's Mums weren't present. "There's nothing wrong with it!" Another woman said, "All I was saying was I'm glad I can work from home." Needles clicked as they sewed silently.

"Where's Helen's Mum?" Jane asked. Nobody knew.

"I'm glad she's not here!" Another woman spoke up, "That boy of hers is bullying children!" I looked up. Daniel's Mum dropped her sewing.

"My daughter told me." That was Sally's Mum, I guess. The others looked sympathetic.

"It's nice of the church to raise money." Mum smiled, "And the soldiers will appreciate our donations."

"Do you have your shelter?" A woman asked Sally's Mum while sewing on buttons. She said it was delivered yesterday.

"We won't fit comfortably." Sally's Mum switched colors in the shirt she was sewing, "But, what can you do?"

"Pray that it's strong enough to stand a direct hit." A woman sitting on Sarah's left frowned, "If you ask me, nothing can stop those Germans." Several nodded in agreement. "I just wish Hitler would stop stalling. Not that I want bombs, but I can't stand this waiting."

"Well, I say all these warnings are nonsense! We're in the country. Hitler will only attack cities, seaports, and military areas."

A dark-haired woman smiled, "We have nothing to worry about."

"I disagree.

We can't just wait and see. We have to be prepared just the same." Daniel's Mum snipped her thread. She looked around the circle. A couple looked skeptical, but most nodded. "That's why all the parents evacuated their children last year, to keep them safe."

"The only evacuees we have are Jews." This one speaking had long hair, "Our school's full of them. It's a wonder Miss Simmons can teach our kids." I looked more closely but couldn't see whose Mum that was.

"Please, Miss, whose Mum are you?"

"Nobody's, child.
I just meant that our English children can't be taught with those foreign kids around."

"I agree. They should never have come here. I don't have one." This lady sniffed.
"Oh, sorry." She glanced at Mum. "You have one. How is she doing?" I was furious. I was sitting right there; she could have asked me. Mum said I was just fine.

"Have any of you heard that new song?" Daniel's Mum changed the subject, "I think Vera Lynn sings it beautifully." The talk continued, then the clock chimed after another hour. The ladies packed up their baskets, agreeing to meet at another house next week. We stretched and began putting away our work.

"Leah, let me see yours." Mum examined the socks I'd finished. "Well, good. Girls, you're next." After examining their work, we could finally leave.

Miserable up here, but I can't write anywhere else. Today, the Battle of Britain's begun.

"Everyone's listening to the radio until this is over!" Dad instructed us. Sarah and Jane started to protest but stopped when they saw Dad's scowl. "Yes, you two, and you will write every night."

Sunday, July 14
Night

While gathering eggs this morning, Sarah asked if I'd walk her to Helen's. "We'll see if you know how your Mum is?" After kitchen chores, Sarah asked her.

"Very well but study your Bibles first and be back in time for dinner." We rushed through our verses, recited them for Mum, and ran out of the house. We stifled our laughter as we passed Jane working in the garden.

"This is beautiful!" I gasped. With a pond at the bottom of a garden and an orchard, I almost envied her. Then, I reminded myself I hadn't met her parents yet.

"Look, Land Girls!" Sarah pointed to the barn. The door was open (probably for a breeze), and we saw two girls wearing trousers and boots sitting on hay bales.

"I wish we could wear trousers," I sighed. "Your Mum said no."

"I agree, doing chores in dresses is horrible. Hard to move!" Sarah said.

"You're here!" Helen ran to meet us, hair flying. "Come in. Lunch is ready." Her mother scolded her for not walking. She walked to the barn.

While we ate, the Land Girls told us about themselves. "We're from a big city that was bombed. We read about the job in the paper." They traveled by train, just like Esther and I. Helen and her brother talked about school.

Helen was about to run out with us, but her mother glared. "Helen, you still have your chores. You two can wait outside."

We explored while she washed up. The pigs in their pen were disgusting!
I thought chickens were messy. Sarah laughed, watching two piglets rolling in mud, but stopped when she was splattered.

"My dress!" She cried. "Mum will be so angry." Helen found us then, and she showed us the pond.

"Let's skip stones!" We had a stone-throwing contest. She won, her stone making the most ripples. Then, Andrew crept up behind her and pushed her into the pond. It was shallow, but her dress was drenched! She came up spluttering and furious. We helped get the mud out of her hair, and she ran after him.

He was in the barn, helping with the animals. She rubbed pig manure on his head. We escaped, laughing. Their mother came out then. Helen explained what had happened. "You two need to stop. I don't care who started it." Leah, Sarah, go home, please. Maybe next time, they'll be better behaved."

At home, we talked in Sarah's room. (Besides helping, she's never come up here!) We talked about having Helen come over.
Then, it was time for dinner and chores.

After dinner, we listened to a report of an actual air battle. It was frightening, all that noise.

Wednesday, August 21

Yet another speech by Churchill yesterday, he said that the enemy aircraft were destroyed, and pilots were killed or captured.
British pilots bomb Germany night after night. He talked about helping America and Canada, giving them navy and air facilities to use if they needed them. Facilities are places to be used for different kinds of battles.

"Do we have to listen to every one of his speeches?" I asked after it ended.

"That depends on everybody's diaries!" Dad said, looking up from his newspaper.

"Leah, when Mum says it's correct and perfect, then maybe we'll think about less speech time. Like I said, everyone must write."

"We already know how to speak and write English. We shouldn't have to listen!" Jane pouted.

"She needs it." Pointing at me, she ran from the room. We heard her door slam. Not hard, just loud enough to show she wasn't happy about our radio listening either.

Correct? What does that even mean? I doubt I'll ever be like them. I'm German, not English.

Anyway, this battle-filled summer shows no signs of easing up, just like the weather. Rain is followed by heat. Maybe September will be cooler.

Hitler's plan to attack Britain is causing people to be more cautious and prepared. Like the women said, people are setting up air raid shelters and buying blackout curtains and gas masks. Since Dad's the Warden, he says we need to be ready for bombs.

When I asked what a Warden does, Mum replied, "You'll see."

Everyone is trying to act normal, but the adults say, "We need to expect the worst, even out in the country." Could the Nazis attack here? Is that what they mean?

Thursday August 22

I ran into one of the Evans girls today, and she brushed past me with parcels in her arms. Some fell out of her arms onto the ground. "Wait!!" I shouted, "You dropped this."

She snatched them from me, eyes lowered. "How are you?" I asked.

"Why do you care?" Still not looking up, she started to walk away.

"Because my family wants to help. Please, let us." She shook her head

80

from side to side, turned, and practically raced away.

When I returned, Mum grabbed her groceries and sent me to the barn.

Dad and I fed and groomed the horses. They whinnied when I entered. We worked silently, only speaking when necessary. Mum rang the dinner bell, and Dad locked up.

"Thank you, Leah," he said. I was surprised since he's never thanked me before. We washed, then had dinner.

Thursday, September 5

Well, the British Air Force bombed Berlin; I hope our street wasn't damaged. Still no word from anyone.

We're doing air raid drills in school where we lie flat on the floor until we hear, "All Clear."

"What's the point?" Andrew burst out, "If we're hit, nothing can stop it."

"It's to protect you!" Miss said and looked exhausted, "I know some of you think these drills here and at home are silly but being safe is important.

Those shelters are steel, and underground, you're safe."

At home, we sleep downstairs, so we can easily run to our shelter, or I should say to the cellar.

This letter-writing project is proving to be successful. The letters aren't read, but some kids talk about them at recess, anyway.

"My sister's a QA! She tends soldiers' wounds." A girl called Nora announced proudly. We nodded politely; there were lots of nurses in the local hospitals and overseas. Eva asked her what QA meant.

"Queen Alexandra's Imperial Military Nursing Service!" She said importantly, "Mum said Queen Alexandra founded a nursing school many years ago. The nurses train for four years, then are sent where they are fighting. A Matron (head nurse) is in charge."

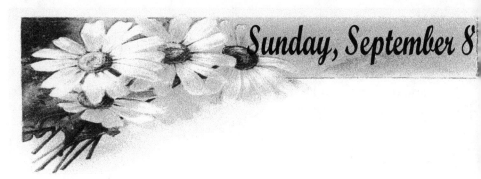

Well, it has happened! Bombs over London last night. When will he stop? I'm writing in the morning before school since we're downstairs every night. This is the only time I have some privacy.

I found out what a Warden does. Dad's job is to make sure everyone's house is invisible to the Germans. If not, they pay a fine (or money.) Of course, like everyone else in Britain, we have a "no lights on" house.

Every inch of the window is covered with curtains. Even up here. No candles, electric lights, or even dimmed street and car lights.

Dad's been reporting to us about our neighbors. We were studying when Dad told us the Evanses are really horrible about their kitchen light.

"I bang on their door, shouting, "If I can see you, so can those Germans."

"What does Mrs. Evans say?" I asked. "Leah, be quiet, and finish your arithmetic" Mum ordered!

"Nothing from anybody," Dad said. Then the light goes out.

"What about Mr. Evans?" Jane asked eagerly. Even Mum looked up with curiosity on her face. "Nothing from him, but I'm sure he was safe."

"He'll need carrying downstairs!" Mum said softly, "I suppose that's what that girl will do."

I winced. How dare she call Atalia "that girl!" Luckily, no one else noticed.

"Her daughters can help, too." Dad finished going over Sarah's homework.

"Have you seen Mr. Evans before?" Sarah's eyes were big.

"A few years after you were born." Now, finish before bed, all of you."

"Did you hear Anne?" I whispered when everyone had gone.

"No, darling, like I said, no one can be seen."

"I just thought she might've called out or something." He shook his head.

"Like I said, everyone must be quiet. Don't worry Anne is perfectly safe as long as she follows our rules." I'm not so sure.

Thursday, September 26, Night

There was fighting in West Africa. British, French, and Australian troops failed to capture the Port of Dakar from the Vichy French. Dad says the Vichy French are on the side of the enemy.

Still, bombs show no signs of stopping. London continues to be bombed! The radio reports are horrible. I wish we didn't listen to every single one, but Dad says we need to understand.

Helen's house is one of the more prepared ones. Except for her brother! He smokes in their back garden, so Dad has to walk around back almost every night to check. "Their parents need to be more watchful with him!" He scowled. "It will make my job easier if he'd only obey the rules."

"You know what boys are like!" Mum said as she added more wood to the stove. "We're all stretched thin as it is. Rationing, now this!"

"No wonder he hates drills in school!" Sarah added, "He's rude to Miss. He yelled about how they were a waste of time and walked out."

"School was almost over." Jane set her fork down, "But he was disrespectful to her."

"Miss Simmons' house is secure, too." Dad continued, "Andrew needs to obey her instructions."

"What about Eva's family?" I paused between bites. "Yes, Leah," Dad replied, "Their house is light free, as well."

Of course, school is still filled with drills and less playtime. Andrew returned with a written apology. His parents came by Friday. I guess to make certain to see if he was there.

Many of our classmates have relatives in cities where the Nazis could attack next.

Some relatives have evacuated. One girl's aunts are still in London. (It's the girl who yelled talking about us last year.)

"Whenever they hear the siren, they run quickly to the nearest shelter. It's crowded and noisy, but they've been lucky.
Sometimes, they sleep there."

"Where are their shelters?" A little boy asked. She explained they were in the tube stations, and other underground places where people can wait and not be seen.

Most are very angry with Germany, and I can't blame them. Some won't even speak to us anymore. Helen says hello sometimes. Other kids call her a traitor when she talks to us. Andrew thinks Dad is "The worst warden ever. I can't even smoke!"

I wanted to yell back, "You'll thank him later if we're hit, and you survive."

With everything going on, I can't ask Miss Simmons if she's heard from Esther.

Eva's and Daniel's parents still pick them up. I sometimes hear Eva's family talking whenever we pass each other.

Lately, our meals have come from our garden because Mum's afraid to go to the shops. And lots of tinned foods. Salmon and spam, or sausages. I still only eat if Mum allows it. Today, our lunch was tinned sausage and an apple. I got nothing for dinner. The family had vegetable soup.

Still, leaves fall, and the harvest is gathered. Animals need feeding. For now, must go, time to blackout the windows.

Children's Hour had a special guest yesterday: Princess Elizabeth. She talked about evacuated children. It was strange when she talked about us having adventures because I'm not having an adventure. Not a pleasant one, anyway. I think she meant what she said about all children having courage, though. For this broadcast, we all had to write down our thoughts. Mum and Dad actually checked.

Sunday November 10, Evening
More kids are telling stories at recess. Nora's friend, Bridget, has a sister who was involved with the Dunkirk rescue. The hospital ship she was traveling on took many patients; one had to have an amputation. When asked, Bridget explained the patient's leg was removed.

They were traveling with other military ships for protection. Even with the cross on the side of the ship, bombs still fell around them.
Several times, they were told to turn back and were delayed in returning the troops to England.

"We didn't receive her letter until it was over. Everything was delayed, but Mum was still relieved. She wept while reading it. We weren't sure where she was or even if she was safe. Dad wanted to send for her, but she won't leave the patients, no matter what."

Liverpool was hit last night. Dad says the reason docks are being targeted is to prevent British ships from coming in or out.
This means no supplies or equipment can get through to us or the people fighting overseas!

In fact, it's been a week of raining bombs. They fell on Coventry, Birmingham, Southampton, and Bristol. Thousands were killed or left homeless!

This afternoon, Nora shared news of her sister. "Where is she now?" Someone asked.

"North Africa, in the desert. Everything's packed on to lorries and driven out to the camp. Their equipment's primitive, canvas washbasins, sleeping in tents, with little water for drinking and washing."

"How are their meals cooked?" a girl asked. Nora explained that the stoves were fueled with paraffin oil, and their water had to be boiled before each use. "And it's not used for cooking. They eat in the mess tent. The stoves are for boiling water."

"What about their hospital?" I asked.

"Everything's in large tents. They use soapboxes for medicine cupboards, boxes for patients' lockers, things like that."

I wondered why Nora's sister would put those details in her letters. Perhaps she wanted Nora to know what life was really like. I hate to think what will be in those letters once the fighting begins.

Monday, December 2
Evening

Miss Simmons is anxious about her sister. She only mentioned her once. She pointed to an English city on the map and couldn't speak. A boy asked her one day if her sister would evacuate and come here, she said no. "My sister won't travel, even though it's for her own good."

In church, we pray for the dead and wounded. I read the English Bible on my own, mainly our Torah portion.

Monday, December 9
Night

Yesterday, a battle began in Libya, Egypt. The British and Indian armies are trying to push the Italians out.

Today, Miss Simmons surprised us. As the recess bell rang, we eagerly headed towards the door. "No. We're staying inside this afternoon. Lunch will be eaten at your desks." Puzzled, we resumed our seats and began eating our lunches.

The humiliated boy sat at his desk, head lowered. "Well, did you complete your assignment?" Miss Simmons tapped his head with her ruler. The whole class fell silent.

"Yes, Miss!" He mumbled, still not looking up.

"Very well! You may begin."

He rose, a paper clutched in his hand. "The British Raj was very powerful. The English merchants formed the East India Company in 1600. The people were growing wheat for the merchants. The English were taxing farmers on rent and crops.

Three religious leaders have debated India's splitting. The Indian National Congress is made up of Hindus and Muslims. There's Muhammad Jinnah, a Muslim leader, who recently proposed Muslims have their own nation—Pakistan. He believes Muslims should have their own state to worship freely.

Gandhi was the head of a peaceful resistance movement for a while until he was arrested. He wants an India where all religions can exist peacefully.

Another leader is Nehru, who supports Gandhi, but wants a modern nation with education and individual rights."

"Can you explain why these three leaders disagree about India's future?"

"Because the Indian National Congress is still debating this split. The Hindus and Muslims want independence, just in different ways."
Again, I wondered how he'd acquired his knowledge.

I hope I won't have to make that horrible pudding this year. What will Christmas be like?

Tuesday, December 10
Late Night

Well, it happened. We were sleeping downstairs when the siren wailed! We managed to get down the stairs without hurting ourselves. Mum held Sarah's hand; I was in the middle, and Jane had my other hand; she squeezed Dad's. Sitting on the cold, hard, floor, we waited. Sarah clutched her doll, Jane was silent. Mum and Dad were holding hands.

After what seemed like hours, the "All Clear" sounded. We walked upstairs and tried to sleep. Of course, I can't, so I write instead. No moonlight, so this might be difficult to read.

Wednesday, December 11

In school, everyone spoke about their similar experiences.

"Our Anderson shelter was crowded."

"Our dog kept barking."

"My sister cried for a long time."

Miss Simons spent the night in her shelter. "Just in case it happened again" she said. Everyone was restless, and not much work was done. We weren't even assigned homework.

Sunday, December 15

This year, no Christmas tree. I helped Mum wrap presents. Fewer this time, but she says, "Everyone should still be happy." I'm making Sarah a pink and white scarf.

But there is cheerful news. The Italians are out of Egypt. The British and Indian armies had to prevent them from reaching Tobruk (a city in Africa). Eventually, the Italians were driven out.

Less cheerful news, four nights in a row of bombing in Sheffield. Will they ever quit? We hate what those people have to go through when listening to the radio and dreading the sirens. It's awful for us, and we're not even there! Now, I'm grateful we listened.

Wednesday, December 25
Late afternoon Christmas Day

It was cold this morning when we got up early to walk to church. It was more crowded than usual. Everyone listened as the story of Jesus' birth was read, and carols were sung. I knew the words to the Sans Day carol and immensely enjoyed singing. A special prayer was said for the people killed in the Blitz and for their families.

Afterward, I found Anne (Atalia to me) talking to Daniel. I couldn't believe it. In German, we managed to whisper about our real families (wondering where they are) before Daniel's mother separated us. I saw her talking to Mrs. Evans. Atalia looked terrified, but Daniel's mother said, "Wonderful to finally meet you. We've heard a lot about you from Daniel." Even I was surprised. I didn't think Daniel had told them about her. His Mum whispered, "Please, keep talking. Don't forget your families."

Spotting Mrs. Evans, she said in her normal voice, "Merry Christmas! I hope you have a lovely day." Answering in English, we thanked her. Of course, Mr. Evans wasn't there. As usual, her daughters were silent. They didn't even smile when I wished them a Merry Christmas.

At home, we opened presents. Father Christmas came, bringing oranges, more writing paper, and doll clothes that looked like they were made from old curtains for Sarah. She liked her scarf from me. I now have another coat; I'm not sure if it's used since most of our clothes are made from old material. That kind of thing doesn't matter anymore.

Dinner was roast pork with potatoes and peas. The pork came from Helen's farm; Mum exchanged it for jam their mother wanted. Of course, I had to eat everything; nothing's wasted here! The pudding was apple crumble (finally, Dad had apples) with some sort of cream. When Dad made a face, Mum looked embarrassed. "No sugar, I used syrup."

Unfortunately, this Christmas is devastating for the people in Liverpool and Manchester! More bombs there.

On a lighter note, the King's Christmas broadcast was beautiful, wishing peace for all of us in the years to come. The way things are headed, I don't think next year will be very peaceful.

A new year. The snow is so thick on the ground our exercise is held indoors.

Mother has me and Catherine doing jumping jacks and running in our dormitory along the wall. Sometimes, we exercise with the older girls in the hall outside our dormitories. Mother Matthews has us in jump rope competitions and running to the end of the hall and back. Yes, we bump into each other, and our canes become tangled up.

The girls who went home for Christmas haven't returned, so it's very peaceful.

In sewing class, Catherine and I are learning to sew pockets.

We only see the older girls during exercise, meals, or in the washroom.

In Geography, Miss Pryce has Catherine and me naming places "Without looking, I mean, touching the map." As always, they have to be in order.

"You blind children should learn more quickly. The kids in my last school were much farther along by now."

"Miss, the lines are alike," Catherine explained one day. I silently agreed with her.

I say hello to William and John in the halls. Their other jobs include keeping the fires going, cleaning classrooms, and clearing snow. William and I talk when we're not busy. We can't talk long, but we always speak about my parents, which makes me happy.

One day, John returns with me to our dormitory to repair something. I notice one of his feet drags. When he leaves, I finally ask Mother about it. "Yes, he has one leg shorter than the other. Accident at birth!" She explains. "He's been here a few years."

90

We continue to read the story about the horse, Beauty. He's still living with his new owner and other horses. One is a mare called Ginger. She's mean-tempered because she was mistreated when she was a colt.

Catherine's been telling me more about her parents. "We live in a small house. Mummy stays home. Daddy works, but they can't look after me."

"So, you live here?" I ask.

"I like it here. I have my own bed, and we eat every day," she says.

"Who did you sleep with at home?"

"My two sisters. They kick and talk in their sleep!" She says happily.

"Leah and I shared a bed, too. She didn't kick, just stole the blankets. I was cold."

"Why aren't you two asleep yet?" When did Mother come in? I wonder.

"Try and sleep. Can't you hear the clock?"

"Ten chimes!" Catherine says, turning towards Mother's voice. "That's not very late."

"Very good, and yes, it is. Now don't make me come in again." We whisper some more anyway, then fall asleep. Outside, we can hear the howling wind.

We play with dolls, too. "Where's your doll?" I ask.

"I don't have one!" Catherine answers sadly.
So, I share Minna with her.

Mother shows us how to make doll furniture out of boxes and paper. We also sew doll clothes in our Sewing class.

The vegetables from our garden are all we eat, along with the little meat from our ration books. Butter and sugar are rationed, so no treats. I miss Mama's Babka. I have Kosher coupons. Mine are used for extra cheese, butter, and Kosher meat. Breakfast is eggs, pork sausages (not for me), toast, and sometimes porridge. Lunch and dinner are usually sandwiches or vegetable stew.

Worst of all, no news from Susan's mother. I have to patiently wait until after Christmas break. When I asked her about it, Susan just snapped, "Mum's still busy. Stop pestering me." Mrs. Davis said pestering means asking someone over and over again to do something.

Catherine says it's February; we're stuck inside all the time. Even when the snow melts a little, the temperature is too cold.
The fire in our dormitory keeps us warm at night; we wear warm clothes in class. Long stockings and sweaters. Mama packed my scarf, gloves, and coat for the outdoors. If we go out, I'll be able to wear them. Beauty's story keeps us amused in the evenings.

To avoid tangled canes, Mother Matthews now pairs a blind and partially sighted girl when we run.

It's after one of our exercise lessons, and William and I meet in the music room.

"Can you help me find Leah?" I blurt out.

"I'm not sure, love. With no information about where you were taken from, it might be impossible. Do you know anything about Leah's English family?" He asks.

I reply no, but I give him the date we were separated. He says he'll see what he can find with that.

It's now March. I'm very happy since the snow is finally melting.
The garden and paths around the school are muddy, but we can at least go outside. John and William are back in the garden, so there is less time for talking if we want privacy.

With Mrs. Davis, Catherine and I are writing longer sentences and doing difficult maths problems. We still have difficulty writing. We think there's enough room at the end of a line, but then have to start the word over again on the next one. With adding and subtracting, it's difficult to tell if it's a number. The number sign is only used at the beginning of a problem.

It's April; the girls are finally back! Tonight is like a big party, with everyone telling stories of their Christmases at home.

Hannah returns with new dresses and shoes. "Each dress is made of velvet!" She giggles. Next, she shows off her play dishes, a doll wearing a pretty coat, and real shoes. "We went to the Christmas pantomime, too. The dancing children were beautiful. We even saw Princess Elizabeth, I swear. My brother has his pony. My sister wears lipstick now. When I'm older, Mum said I will, too. For dinner, we had a goose, vegetables, potatoes, and of course, the pudding." Our butler lights it every Christmas." She stops for breath.

"That's not true," Mary cries, "Princess Elizabeth lives in a castle. You couldn't have seen her!"

"Well, she was there. I saw the back of her head!" Hannah insists. "My sister even said it was her!"

"You can't tell what someone looks like by looking at the back!" Kathleen interrupts, "I have trouble sometimes. So do most people with good sight."

"What about you, Esther?" Lydia cuts in. I'm relieved. I can't listen to Hannah anymore. I tell them about my Christmas spent here.

"You talked to William!" Hannah exclaims. "He works here. You give him orders and must not speak to him."

Mother overhears and firmly tells Hannah to come with her. "And, no telling stories, Hannah!" She warns.

He speaks German, too, I think to myself.

Kathleen shows us her pretty dresses and new shoes. "They're not very pretty without velvet." Hannah sniffs.

"Those are lovely clothes." Amy says.

Catherine fills everyone in on Beauty's adventures. Mother comes in many times after that, at first patiently, then angrily, finally ordering us to go to sleep because "You'll be tired tomorrow if you don't!" She snaps.

And she's right; we are exhausted today.

"Esther, turn your collar inside out!" Miss Walters repeats. "See, you pricked your finger."

"Lydia, that should be a plus sign, not a U." Mrs. Davis sighs.

At dinner, Amy spills her tea. Lydia helps clean it up, but Mrs. Davis isn't pleased. "Next time Mother Anderson gives you an order, please obey." We finish in silence.

For some reason, I feel like Hannah doesn't like me. She's now saying hurtful remarks about our family. Every time, I explain I'd rather be here than in Germany. When we walk to church, she says Jews like me don't believe in G-d. When I ask where she heard that, she answers, "Mum and nanny."

One day, in music class, we're listening to Mrs. Blake playing Bach when Hannah whispers something like, "Dad says the Germans want to kill us."

Mrs. Blake stops playing, and Kathleen says, "The composers we've been studying are German."

"Yes, Kathleen, that's right. Some of them were Jewish, too. Unfortunately, Germany is the enemy in war, just not in this class. They gave us beautiful music, don't forget that."

I try not to let Hannah's words get to me. I'm glad Mary and the others aren't like her. The rest of us enjoy playing with dolls together. I showed them Minna, and now she's played with a lot. It's more fun with everybody else here.

We pretend they're having tea with the tiny cups and saucers Hannah brought back.

"Real metal," Amy gasps.

"Yes," Mother explains, "Soon, there may not be any for toys. It's being used to make tanks and weapons for the war."

Hannah shares, but not nicely. "Mother makes me!" She whines one Saturday. "I never have to share my belongings at home. We have our own bedrooms! I won't share my doll, Catherine. You can play with Lydia's."

Someone asks what a tank is, and Mother says it's a really powerful truck made of thick steel. If the enemy shoots, the tanks are protected. So are the people driving them, I hope, I think to myself.

It's Sunday, we're listening to Mother read. "Beauty almost died!" Amy cries.

"I know. He became better, didn't he?" I ask.

"Yes!" Kathleen says. "But the fire was dangerous, too. Most of the horses got out safely."

"It was unfortunate." Mother stands, closing the book, "Now, bedtime." I ask Lydia what unfortunate means. She says it's when something bad

94

happens.

We're walking one evening when some of us overhear a conversation between Mrs. Blake and Miss Pryce. "Teaching those blind brats is hard. Besides, I shouldn't be here."

"My husband is fighting too, along with thousands of other men and women. You didn't have to agree to do this post, you know."

She sighs, "I know. I didn't think blind children would be harder to teach than sighted children. They have to feel the maps, and it takes longer for some of them to memorize their shapes."

"Everyone here struggles with something."

Catherine, Amy, and I walk on silently. We agreed not to tell the others. We weren't supposed to hear, after all.

It's now May. We have tests called exams coming up. Mine is Braille, and all are in English. It's terrifying because I have to remember how to write sentences and math problems. Mrs. Davis says she'll teach us a faster way to write Braille when we return.

We have our last reading before break. Everyone wants to hear another chapter, but Mother refuses. "When you come back, you'll hear more," she laughs.

"Who will Beauty live with next," Amy asks? "Someone nice, I hope."

Everyone leaves for the summer break. Catherine's parents come, say a quick hello, then leave.

I spend the summer with Miss Walters. Her house has two floors, with a sewing room. I learn more words every day, like weave and crochet.

I even have my own bedroom, with a window Miss Walters says looks out to the back garden. When it's open, I can reach down and feel climbing roses; sometimes, there's a cool breeze on my face.

This room used to be her daughter's, who's currently training to be a nurse. I explore the room on my first day and find a drawer full of crocheted doll clothes and handkerchiefs.

"Are these your daughters'?" I ask, showing her the clothes.

"Yes, she made them when she was little. She became a brilliant seamstress."

Brilliant seamstress.

Two new words I hear Miss Walters repeat a lot to me.

She says, "Keep sewing like this, and you'll be brilliant, like her."

I hear music on the radio. It's called 'Music While You Work.' "Why haven't I heard this before?" I ask one day.

"You're always in school when it's on the radio," she laughs.

The news from Europe is bad and good. There were men trapped on the beaches of a place called Dunkirk, France, and many died, but many were rescued, too. In the battle in the skies, many aircrafts were also shot down, but the English still won.

The weeks fly by between walks to the shops to buy new clothes and church. I learn many English hymns and some Bible verses. I miss our synagogue and our Torah. (In school, everyone reads the Braille Bible.) Since I've been here, I've been experiencing new things. Maybe, the more I learn, everything won't seem so strange.

Like the food it's not like the food back home, but it's something I have to learn to eat. Even though Miss Leigh and Mrs. Porter try to make it like Mama did, everything still tastes strange.

Now we're back in school; September has begun with bombs dropping on London. That's a big city in England! Bombs are like balls of fire that are dropped from airplanes. It's hard listening to that awful news, but we need to be prepared, too.

Like other schools, we're practicing air raid drills and putting blackout curtains on the windows. Mrs. Davis explains it's to stop the Germans from finding us. "No lights anywhere," she warns. We sleep in the dining hall near our cellar, just in case. If we hear the siren, we'll go there.

To stop us from worrying, Mother continues reading about Beauty.

"His owners are so cruel!" Catherine stamps her foot, "Why is he mistreated?"

"Different people treat their animals differently. Fortunately, the checkrein isn't used anymore."

"The lady was mean to Ginger!" I add, "So she kicked the groom."

"My brother uses a whip sometimes!" Hannah announces it like it's normal. "He says his horse doesn't obey." We gasp. I think that's horrible.

"Some of Beauty's owners were kind, like the squire!" Mother reminds us. "More next time." As usual, our conversation ended with the ringing of the bell.

Mrs. Davis kept her promise. She's teaching Hannah, Amy, Mary, me, and Catherine the quick way to write Braille. Instead of writing the whole word, we only need to write letters. "Almost every letter of the alphabet is a word!" Mrs. Davis explains. Lydia and Kathleen know most of it already.

October is a little colder now, we continue to walk every evening. The best thing about being outside is gathering leaves into piles and jumping in them. They crunch under our feet. Then we tumble into a pile, giggling. When they see us playing, the older girls call out, "There are the little children." Kathleen always calls back, "We're just playing."

It's Friday, and Julia wanders over. She surprisingly plays with us, scattering leaves in our hair. She calls us leaf princesses!

When we grow tired, we compare lessons. "We have a typing course as well!" Julia says.

"What's typing?" Mary shyly asks.

"It's a machine that prints letters onto paper when you press a key. The worst thing is we can't correct our mistakes." She sighs.

When we return, Mother Anderson swiftly checks our hair for stray leaves and dirt on our clothes.

I'm walking with Hannah on Saturday when we pass William and John working in the flower garden. "Hello!" I smile, remembering to speak English since John and Hannah are nearby.

We talk about gardening, and John tells us about his summer. Then William asks, "How was your summer, Hannah?"

"Miss Hannah!" She says loudly, "My summer was absolutely perfect. We attended the cinema, ballet, and opera."

"What's the opera and ballet?" I already know about the cinema.

"You need to wear fancy dresses to go, the opera has beautiful singers and music, and ballet is dancing. If I sit close, I can see a little."

"Sounds wonderful," William stopped shoveling, "Your family seems like an exciting one. Do you always visit those places?"

"Yes, I started going last year," she says.

"We all do fun things. My sister has ballet lessons, and my brother rides horses." She takes a breath.

"Mother Anderson says you're doing well," John answers quietly.

"Sometimes, we hear you, girls, practicing piano."

"I guess!" She mumbles, "Let's go, Esther. They have work to do." She grabs my hand and pulls me back to the school.

Sewing is getting slightly harder, too. "We're knitting sleeves today. Esther, Catherine, help Lydia and Hannah." As we begin, Kathleen asks when we can make dresses. "When you complete sleeves, backs, and other parts of a dress. Then, we'll complete one together." Miss Walters says.

"Amy, look! That shape isn't a mountain, is it?" Miss Pryce shouts.

"No, it's curvy."

"That's called a river. Which one, please."

"Esther, you tell us. In English." When I reply, she growls, "You're improving."

It's the thirteenth. We're listening to Children's Hour when the man announces that Princess Elizabeth is about to give a speech. This must be the Princess that Hannah thought she saw. The room grows even more quiet as she begins.

When she talks about the evacuated children and their wonderful adventures, I start crying. I am having an adventure. I'm learning so much and making friends. She finishes by saying G-d will take care of us, then she and her sister say good night.

"Did the princesses really have to go away?" Catherine whispers.

"Yes," Mother Anderson replies, "They were sent to Windsor Castle."

"Where do the King and Queen live?" I ask.

"In their palace in London," she replies.

"Will they see their Mummy and Daddy again?" Mary's question makes me feel homesick again.

"I'm sure the King and Queen hope to see the princesses soon, just like your parents want to see you," mother says.

We spend the rest of the evening talking about our families. Mary talks about her brothers and sisters, who always chase each other through the house until their Mum yells at them to stop. Her parents work in a big factory, making airplanes.

Catherine is next. All she says is her family lives in a small house, and she has two sisters.

"What does your father do?" Mother asks.

"He works in a factory, too."

Then, it's my turn. Before I can speak, Hannah groans, "Not your sister again."

"You know where your family is? I don't!" I explain for the hundredth time. "I don't want to forget them."

"Go on, love." Mother squeezes my hand. "And the rest of you, be silent! Please."

I take a deep breath and start talking. "I live in Berlin with my Mama, Papa, and sister, Leah." Hannah sighs again, but I keep going, "We live above a bakery, and my parents work there. I helped them when Leah was in school."

"You've never been to school?" Mary is surprised. "I've been coming here since I was six!"

"I tried when I was six, but I didn't know Braille then, so I had to listen."

Then, I tell them about our piano lessons. I talked about Leah's friends and how we played piano together. Sometimes, Leah would play without me at a friend's house.

Kathleen speaks next, "Mrs. Porter gives you different meals sometimes."

"Yes, but they're not like Mama's!" Everyone laughs, and we talk about

99

our favorite meals for a while.

"Why did you come here?" Catherine asks.

"Because" Mother starts to answer for me, "Their parents knew they'd be safe here in England. Good parents want to do what's best for their children. They knew we could educate Esther while she was here."

I tell them a little about the awful Nazis with their horrible rules. "Our neighbor said we couldn't practice piano anymore. She was afraid she'd be in trouble for teaching Jews in her house. Leah couldn't ride her bike or go to school. Our parents lost their jobs. So, we came here on a train with other kids. Leah was taken first, and I don't know where. Then, Mrs. Davis brought me here."

"Mother, you didn't tell us that!" Amy blurts out. "You just said a new girl named Esther was coming."

"All right, Amy, you're next!" Mother continues.

"My Dad's a fisherman!" Amy says proudly. "He takes his green boat out on the sea and doesn't come back until dark. When he isn't fishing, we go down to the beach and build sandcastles." This summer, he went on a special trip."

"Where?" Catherine interrupts, "Did he travel alone?"

"Yes," Amy replies quietly, "He wouldn't talk about it, but Mum was very happy when he returned home. When he came in, she knocked her hair over and started crying. She and Dad laughed and cried for a long time. He was away for many days.

My sister said that one day she saw a whole bunch of boats and ships leaving at once. I heard their whistles blowing when I was outside." Now, every time we ask about it, we're told to go to our rooms." She is angry now. "Why wouldn't they tell us anything?"

"Because" Mother answers, "It was a grown-up conversation between your parents. When you're older, they may explain it in more detail."

Hannah, Kathleen, and Lydia take turns, and then it's bedtime.

Tonight, I clutch Minna tighter than usual. I'm still wide awake. Will I ever see Leah again? The Nazis are terrifying; will we ever return home?

It's November now, it's beginning to snow. This is exciting for us as we play jokes on each other using the snow. Mother Anderson hates it when we "mess up the dormitory with that stuff," as she says. She doesn't understand the fun part, trying to figure out who did what! Today, Mary and Kathleen even put snow in the washroom bath "To trick the older girls" since it's their night to bathe. Trying not to laugh too loudly, we listen for their screams. Mother is wondering why we're so quiet tonight.

"May we come in?" Mother Matthews's keys are in her hand. We stop what we're doing and listen. "Very amusing!" Her voice is quiet, but we hear every word.

"I agree with you!" Mother Anderson says, standing beside her. "Girls, that was a horrible trick. They could've fallen. Luckily, they weren't hurt."

"One of the staff was filling the bath when we discovered your surprise. The whole tub has to be cleaned and refilled. Will they be punished?" Mother Matthews asks in a demanding way.

"Yes, but first, an apology. Bring them in!" Mother says. The older girls enter silently. We each say sorry, then they leave.

"That went well!" Kathleen says sarcastically, "They were supposed to find the snow!" Mother is in the washroom.

"How did she know it was us?" Mary asks, "We were silent!"

"Silly, we're the only other girls here," Hannah says furiously, "See what you did? Now we are all in trouble!"

The bell rings, and Mother returns. "Be silent. The room is clear of snow. Bedtime, now."

"Why do I have to be punished?" Hannah whines, "I didn't do it."

"No, but everybody's being punished just the same. If you didn't do it, you knew about it. I'll think of something. No talking tonight!" Mother orders. Once we're in bed, she slams our door loudly.

It's breakfast time. We get our punishment. "Your punishments are extra work from Mrs.
Davis, and cleaning." Mother announces.

In class, we had to write an apology letter to each of the girls. We didn't finish them, so we have that to do, in addition to more grade-two Braille homework. Cleaning begins after piano playing

"You'll clean Mother Matthew's dormitory!" We're told. We silently get to work, as Mother Matthews watches us. "You, little girl, don't miss that corner." She says to Amy.

"Yes, Mother." Amy scrubs quietly.

"And you, German girl, polish the mantle again. It's dusty."

She keeps critiquing our cleaning for two hours until she finally dismisses us. "You may go enjoy your dinner!" She says with a laugh.

Our slightly cold dinner is waiting in our dormitory. Mother looks at our hands for bleeding but says nothing. "Sit and eat!" She orders.

December Brings More Snow
For Christmas, We Have a Small Tree to Decorate

There was a snowstorm a few days ago, and a tree fell near the school.

William and John sawed off the top so it could fit in the dining hall. Everyone made decorations out of leftover scraps, paper, and fabric. Everyone's looking forward to Christmas.

Besides snow, bombs are falling. And not just in London, but other cities, too. I hope the countryside isn't hit.

Still, no word from Leah, Susan said she asked her mother, but that was last year! So, I go to Mrs. Davis instead. "I will try to phone Susan's mother, but don't get your hopes up. I don't know if records were kept on where your children were placed," she says. So, impatiently, I wait.

A few days before Christmas, we're awakened by this long, loud siren; we know what it means. We line up and go quickly, single file, down the steep stairs to the cellar. We've practiced, so we don't bump into each other, but this is the real thing. I hear Mother Matthews and her girls in front. It's smelly and crowded, but at least it's safe.

Mrs. Davis counts everyone's heads to make sure we're all here. The siren continues for a long time, starting out soft, then louder. Finally, it stops. Waiting in the dark, we listen for the "All Clear" signal. We're silent, and all I hear is breathing. I wonder where William and John are.

"This floor is cold!" Amy whispers.

"Shhh!" Mother whispers back, "Listen."

We sit for what seems like hours. Finally, we hear it-a single long sound! The "All Clear." Laughing and crying with relief, we slowly go back up the dark, steep stairs into the dining hall. When we're upstairs, I hear John talking to Mrs. Davis.

William must be nearby. Miss Pryce exclaims, "What a relief! I was afraid we'd be hit."

Mother Matthews tells the older girls to get settled. "That goes for you lot over here!" Mother calls to us.

Obviously, we can't sleep. The teachers have to remind us to get some rest because even though they will start later than usual tomorrow, we will still have class and the teachers don't want us to be tired for our lessons.

Well, it's Christmas Day! Catherine is very happy because she says, "Father Christmas came." I guess she was worried he wouldn't come. The presents are more practical this year, clothes, but there's small toys, too. Mother is trying to be cheerful for us. Mary shows me handmade doll clothes her Mum made from scraps. Amy has two new pairs of gloves. Kathleen opens a scarf that's red, "Like your coat," Mother points out. We all have new socks from Mother. We give her a knitted blanket.

"Thank you, girls. Now, let's go to breakfast."

At breakfast, we hear some of the older girls talking about fancy dresses and how they'd love to have boys see them in their new dresses, even though there aren't any boys around. "Why can't we see boys?" One complains, "My sisters do. They go to dances all the time." Mother Matthews says something about boys being at a different school.

When he collects my plate, William whispers, "Have a wonderful day."

"What did he want?" Catherine asks.

"He told me to have a wonderful day!" We also read the Christmas story from the Bible, like last year. This year, some of the girls read also.

After breakfast, we split up. Amy and I practice piano. We practice Braille music, and she teaches me the words to Joy to the World. Mrs. Walters looks in.

"Having fun? Very nice, by the way."

"It's a little fast," I answer.

103

Christmas dinner is shepherd's pie, which is a pastry filled with vegetables, and mashed potatoes covered in gravy. The others have meat in theirs. Most of us think it's delicious, but Anna complains, "It's not as nice as last year's meal!"

Mrs. Davis taps her water glass and stands. The chatter stops. She lectures about our good fortune. We're in the countryside, so we can grow our own vegetables, raise our own meat, and keep chickens for eggs to sell. Cities are being bombed nightly, people not knowing if their homes will be standing when it's over. She tells us we should be grateful for these things and our safety.

She sits, we finish our meal in silence. Well, most of us. At the next table, I hear the girls saying, "That's not fair. Why is she lecturing us? I just want pretty clothes and to be like other girls."

We listen to the King's Christmas broadcast, just like last year. Now, I can better understand everything. I feel kind of unhappy hearing him talk about the evacuated children and how hard it is being separated from our parents. He knows what it's like, I thought. We all suffer together. We must be united.

The day after Christmas! I receive the best Christmas present ever! Mrs. Davis calls me to her classroom after dinner. She tells me she spoke to Susan's mother and found the address of Leah's family. I want to jump for joy, but Mrs. Davis is still talking. "You can't see her, only write. You write in Braille, and someone can write underneath it in print."

"Can I phone her?" I ask. Mrs. Davis says we'll have to see. When I ask why it took Susan's mother so long to find Leah, she replies, "With her husband away and other children to care for, she was busy. Oh, please keep your letter to three pages or less." She adds.

I run back to the dormitory, not really using my cane, but I don't bump into anyone. I grab my slate and begin writing.

1941
Sunday, January 5, Evening

I can't believe it. I received a letter from Esther! When Mum gave it to me, she remarked, "Well, your sister can write, after all."

The return address listed is a school. I tear the letter open and notice

104

the paper is thick and covered with little dots with writing under them.

Along the right and left sides are little holes.

I cry as I read my sister's letter. I read about how she was taken to a school for blind children. She has learned to write in Braille (the dots), and uses something called a cane, which helps her get around by herself. Most importantly, she plays the piano again. I wish I could be there to meet her friends, share memories of home, and play piano, too. Everything seems perfect, except for Hannah and some of the older girls.

It ends with:

"Remember this song?

My refuge, my rock of Salvation." A friend helped me with the words.

Your favorite sister,

Esther

Laughing with joy, I put her letter in my suitcase. Sighing, I think, "I suppose I'll have to write in English now."

January 6

Dear Esther,

I cannot describe how I felt reading your first letter. Happy! Excited! We can write to each other! Well, here's mine...!

(I describe my family, school, church, and the friends I've made.)

I know how you feel about the Torah! But we all have to learn the English Bible now. They're more patient at your school, though. And, you have Kosher meals. At least Mrs. Porter and Mrs. Davis are trying to make you feel welcome.

That was an unusual conversation between Miss Pryce and Mrs. Blake. No wonder she's angry all the time. Be patient with her.

Anyway, Christmas was strange this year, because there weren't any treats, just clothes. Mum and Dad agreed that because of the blitz, we should give our Christmas money to a charity. Jane and Sarah grumbled, but we all gave to our local hospital.

I'm not sure what you know about the fighting going on so here's some news. It's not cheerful.

The first week of January, the English had already bombed airfields in Tobruk, North Africa. They didn't want the Italians to head there.

Speaking of war... A boy told how his Dad was in one of the planes that bombed that airfield. "He was involved in capturing the city." I wonder how much of his Dad's words he was putting in his assignment.

It's the twenty-fourth, and the English, Italians, and Australians had a battle there. All areas were captured by the British.

On to some happy news
We've been doing a lot of ice skating on our local pond; Leron taught most of us. On our first day, we all came home with drenched clothes. Jane was scolded for ruining her new coat. "I told you to save it for special occasions!" Mum shouted. Sarah and I ran to her room, trying not to burst out laughing. Jane, punished? Andrew wasn't there, so Eva enjoyed herself without worrying about being teased.

Here's another war story: Bridget told how her sister was aboard a hospital ship bound for Tobruk. There was an explosion, and bombs were dropped nearby. "Everyone had practiced drills, but this was real. There was damage to the ship, but no one was hurt or killed." Bridget explained, relieved. "When the nurses receive patients, they have to board them sometimes while fighting's happening." They're courageous out there on the sea. In one letter, she wrote about shells exploding in the water."

Some of us German kids celebrated Hanukkah this year. Daniel's parents said we could celebrate at their house. Obviously, I didn't tell Mum why I wanted to spend a week after school there, but she allowed it.

Leron's rabbi lent us his Menorah, and Eva's Mum gave us candles. Daniel's Dad learned Hebrew. It was very funny hearing an Englishman reading it.

Everything was beautiful, the flickering candlelight and hearing the familiar prayers.

The last night, Daniel's mother walked me home. "Come in and start your chores!" Mum ordered when I knocked. Daniel's Mum looked curiously at us but said nothing.

Daniel asked, "Can Leah come back next weekend, please?"

"Maybe, dear." Mum's smile was forced, "Now, get inside." Hand on my shoulder, she pushed me in, quickly closing the door.

It's been a busy first week in February. First, on the fourth, Italians began evacuating Benghazi, Libya. On the sixth, Australians captured the city, and some Italians couldn't make it out.

Still only seeing Atalia in church. Her English has improved a little, but it would be better if she were in school.
Mrs. Evans looks so pale. She must be stressed. We offer to help, but she refuses. When we see her (usually in church), she quickly answers our questions. "We're fine. I don't need anything. Anne, come.

Girls, no talking." Things like that! Atalia whispered to me once that Mr. Evans sometimes stays in bed for weeks. She looks exhausted, too. The daughters just scowl.

This year is turning out to be as bad as last year, with more bombings, this time in Wales and Portsmouth.
I'm relieved one of the Nazi's bombs hasn't hit us yet. I hope they don't.

Spring should almost be here. The snow started melting. The bad thing about that is the barnyard becomes a swamp. The chickens fly everywhere, and our clothes become covered in mud and droppings in no time, which means extra laundry.

It's a Very Windy March

The twelfth now, and Miss told us that President Roosevelt signed the Lend-Lease Act in America. That means he can send weapons and food to Britain and the other countries helping us. I don't think this war will end anytime soon. England needs all the help it can get.

At school, the bullying has stopped, and for now, parents are relieved. Recess is enjoyable again.

Mum's made spam sandwiches for dinner tonight. They're very salty and disgusting. I wish she'd make baked Reis Kugel for dessert. Oh, wait, that's too Kosher for her. Breakfast was toast this morning.

It's the fifteenth, and more English cities have been bombed. Glad we're not living there.

Whenever I ask Mum or Dad to post this letter, their answers are, "Wait for the snow to clear." So sorry for the delay. And calling you is out of the question. That means not allowed. I asked, but Mum said we can't bother anyone. I'll end this letter now.

Hope to hear from you soon!

Love you always,

Leah

Translating is hard, but here's the next part of the song you included in your letter (of course, I remember it, by the way).

Tis pleasant to sing your praises. There was a copy of the song, in my case!

March 26

Dear Leah,

How exciting! I received your letter! Here's mine.

I'm so happy to write you finally.

It's spring now, and everyone's working in the garden with less complaining. Whenever we're working with the older girls, I stay away from Anna and Susan, the worst of them all. Some still call me the "Charity Girl" when we see each other. One time, they threw dirt, but it missed me and hit Lydia instead. Mother didn't see, but she promised to speak to Mother Matthews when we told her.

When Mother explained, Mother Matthews replied, "Esther must have said something. You know how girls are."

I'm not sure if I told you, but Julia (one of the older girls), is pleasant. She asks how we're doing and doesn't laugh at our games. She has younger siblings, too.

Are all evacuated children bullied at your school? From what you say, Andrew seems to hate everyone.

That letter-writing assignment sounds strange to me. Why write to someone who won't read them? I sort of understand why your teacher's making you all write, but still ... Being a nurse seems dangerous. Maybe, Nora and her friend will tell you more.
We listen to the radio, so we have an idea about the events of this war.

One night in January, we were in our nightdresses when we finished Beauty's story. Mary asked if he was real.

"No, horses can't talk," Catherine said crossly, "You know that."

"Why is the book an autobiography, then?" Mary asked. Mother explained that the author (the woman who wrote it) wanted it told in Beauty's own words.

"I liked the ending, finally a nice family for Beauty!" Kathleen yawned.

"What story will you read next?"

"We'll see.
I'll have to send for another.
Any suggestions?" Mother asked.

I guess suggestions mean to give ideas because everyone called out their favorite stories. Lydia wanted a story about a toad, a mole, and a badger.

Hannah wanted one about a girl who falls down a hole. "Mama read Leah and I a book of stories. There was a wolf, a little girl with a cape, and lots of witches."

"You mean the Grimm fairy tales?" Kathleen's hand accidentally touched my cheek, "I know those!" Everyone else did, too.

"They're in English?" I asked excitedly. Mother said they certainly were.

"You mean they're not English stories?" Hannah made a noise.

"No, German!" I said proudly.

"Why don't you know any English stories?" Mary wasn't sitting. She was jumping around the room. Mother grabbed her hand and made her sit. I told them our parents only read German stories.

The bell rang, and we slowly fell asleep.

It's been a busy first week in April, and still, the war continues. The English sank two German ships. That's good news for them, bad for Hitler. The BBC reported bombings in a place called Ireland. In North Africa, Tobruk was captured by the Germans.

School is getting harder. Mrs. Blake believes I could learn to play more difficult piano pieces. Braille music was difficult to learn since you can't read and play at the same time. When two of us play together, it's like being with you and Fraulein Gerta again.

I like playing with two people, but Lydia can play some pieces one-handed. "The trick is to be really fast," she said.

Miss Pryce wants us to recite English cities alphabetically. If we miss any, our hands get smacked with her ruler. Two mistakes, two smacks. Three mistakes, three smacks. Yes, our hands sting.

Today was a very rainy day, so our walks were canceled. Our exercise with the older girls, and Mother Matthews wanted us to practice ballet. She paired us up; since the older girls are much taller, many toes were stepped on. I was with Anna, and each time I tried to raise my arm for a position, she knocked into it.

On the radio, we heard that the Luftwaffe bombed Belfast, Ireland. Since it's warm, we've been spending more time outside. That's when the skipping ropes appear. It's great learning to turn the rope and skip at the same time.

Counting quickly in English is much faster than writing, and it's still fun to sing English rhymes. Hannah taught me "Ding Dong Dell, Pussy's in the Well." She knows all the rhymes.

It's the twenty-second and Miss Pryce told us German bombs once again hit Plymouth.

I saw William in the garden while writing this letter. He wrote underneath, you'll appreciate it, he said. John will post it.

I'm relieved you have our song. Please don't lose your copy! I can sometimes sing German songs here, but everybody expects me to speak

English, just like the people at your house. Our song will always be sung in German.

Your sister,
Esther
P.S... Let our house of prayer be restored—restoring means to be new again.

Dear Esther,

I can't wait for summer!

The BBC reports there are bombings in Scotland.

In the Atlantic, a British Navy ship was captured by a German U-Boat. Miss Simmons explained that a U-Boat is a vehicle that can go underwater, which uses a special light to watch for other ships.

We haven't read Black Beauty; Sarah has Aesop's Fables, though. She let me borrow Wind in the Willows. That's the story one of your friends suggested.

Please be careful about where you are when you sing those songs. In the music room only is best. If I even said one German word by mistake, I'd never hear the end of it.

You have it easier, just please take care. At least, you have a friend to talk to you. Speaking of music, I'll be sending you a surprise!

Nora's sister described some of her patients in her last letter. Nora explained, "Many soldiers come to the field hospital with missing limbs. Others are sick in their minds, shell shock, it's called. They're so distressed. They hide at loud bangs."

We were silent. It must be challenging for those women and patients, living in those conditions, isolated.

I saw Daniel and his mother in town recently. He said Eva might come over, and he also invited me too. I'll see what Mum says. Three guesses!

We listen to the radio, also, it's a school assignment. I write about news I hear on the radio. Thanks to your friend, I don't have to watch what I

111

say in our letters. And yes, seeing your friend's German in your last letter was a surprise! Tell him thank you. His handwriting is perfect and easy to read. He'll be able to read my letters to you!

I asked Mum about visiting Daniel, and she refused—big sigh.

I wish I'd learned those rhymes at recess; all we play is tag, hopscotch, marbles, or jump rope.

The song's next line is: There, we will offer you our thanks.

All the best,

Leah

June 15

Dear Leah,

Shame about not seeing Daniel. I wouldn't expect your Mum to allow you many visits to friends' houses.

Summer's almost here.
Everyone can't wait to go home!

I can't imagine being a nurse. Those are brave women. Like you said, it must be lonely as well.

For now, Miss Walters says clothes are being rationed. Now we have extra sewing classes; she's been helping us make our old clothes look almost new. Longer hemlines mended socks. "Mum sews our clothes!" Catherine volunteered one day.

"That's good. All of you will be doing more sewing than you're used to," Miss Walters said. Hannah sighed, and Kathleen groaned. "Sewing is a useful skill, so no complaining. Watch those fingers, Amy. Needles can prick if you're not careful!" She scolded.

Lydia started telling a funny story about her little sister when Miss Walters interrupted.

"Lydia, your stitches are crooked, start again."

"Do I have to undo this whole row?" Lydia asked.

"Most of it.
Find where you went wrong. No talking."

We finished silently.
Are Catherine and I the only ones here who like sewing? Mama taught both of us how to sew when we were little, remember?

In Geography, we're still studying English places without looking at the map. Miss Pryce told us about a road being used to connect Burma with China. "I guess for transporting supplies over there. The Japanese want it closed." They're trying to get to INDIA through Burma, she explained.

Another thing to share, we're raising rabbits! They're cute; we named them Fluffy and Long Ears and hope they have babies soon.

Everyone who lives here returned home for the summer. Catherine was excited when her parents picked her up. They said hello to us, then left.

Now, here is some war news I've recently heard. I wonder if you've heard the same thing. It's the twenty-third, and yesterday, Mr. Churchill announced that Germany had invaded the Soviet Union. Hitler and the leader of the Soviet Union, Stalin, had an agreement that they wouldn't fight for ten years, but that's changed since the invasion of Poland. More control for Hitler, I guess.

This summer, I'm staying with Mrs. Blake. I've been learning more piano, practicing Braille music, and anything else she wants to teach me. She lives in a small house with a vegetable garden (every house has one of those) and flower beds. Mr. Blake is in the RAF. "Royal Air Force. He's a pilot. He flies a plane." Mrs. Blake said. I like it here in England very much, but I miss you terribly!

Here's more of our song: When you will have slaughtered the barking foe. Slaughter means to kill. Barking foe is enemies.
Mrs. Blake finished this letter. Don't worry. She didn't ask to read the first part. She'll post this, too.

I can't wait for your next letter!

Love,

Esther

Dear Esther,

I loved getting your letter in German!

Summer with your piano teacher, how wonderful. Remember Mama had us practice for one hour every day? I miss it so much. Even if we had a piano, I doubt Mum would let me play.

Anyway, here's what we did during our first week of summer. I went on a picnic with Sarah, Jane, and some other friends.

The woods were a welcome relief after the stifling attic. We're so relieved we don't have air raids anymore. We stayed through the evening. Atalia came, though how Sarah convinced Mrs. Evans to let her, I don't know. Her girls stayed home.

Atalia didn't say much, but I was glad she could come. We ran races and swam in the stream. Atalia is a good swimmer, but she and Leron kept bumping into each other. Daniel, Helen, and Eva skipped rocks. Eva's went the furthest. It was the most fun we'd had in a long time!

Walking home, Helen, Sarah, Jane, Eva, and I began singing. There was a breeze, finally. Jane and Sarah ran ahead.

In the middle of a verse, a figure leaped down from a tree, showering leaves on our heads. Shrieking, we dropped to the ground.

"Got you!" The boy laughed and fled.

We scrambled to our feet, Helen and I shaking our fists.

"Andrew again!" Helen grabbed Eva's hand and ran off.

I found Sarah and Jane by a tree. Because of our adventure, we returned quite late. I thought we wouldn't be scolded.

"What kept you, girls?" Dad demanded, "I had to do all your chores."

"Eva, Helen, and I were frightened by a boy. Nothing too serious." Leaves were dropped on us!"

"Is Helen all right?" Mum looked concerned. When I replied that she was, Mum smiled with relief, "I've always liked her. Now, to bed, all of you."

"How can Esther read your letters?" Sarah asked the next day.

"Someone reads them to her. And when she writes, she writes in small dots called Braille, and then someone prints the words underneath so I can read them." When Sarah felt the dots, she giggled because they tickled her fingers.

She asked if I could teach her, and I said, unfortunately, no.
I heard something about the Burma Road, as well.
It was reported the road will be closed, for how long, nobody knows.

Dad finally hired two Land Girls to help on the farm. We grow extra crops and now have a couple more cows.

The Land Girls live with us, so Jane and Sarah have to share a room and a bed! They do more squabbling now, but Dad told them to get used to it as the girls are staying.

Their names are Louisa and Martha, and they are friends from a city that has fortunately not been destroyed by Nazis. They miss their cinema, they said. The last film they saw was Goodbye, Mr. Chips; three years ago. For some reason, they think our cinema is boring.

Lately, we all get up earlier than usual, sometimes working until after dark. They've taken to farm life; Martha likes the garden, and Louisa milks the cows. Jane, Sarah, and I plant and do inside chores like always.

They don't talk much, perhaps they're homesick. They don't have to attend church, but they come anyway.

The poor Soviet Union. The Nazis are spread all over that country. In Ukraine, cities are being captured quickly. I guess they didn't see it coming.

It's raining up here today, but it's still daylight. Jane and Sarah were allowed to go to the cinema. This time they saw a funny film about a ghost haunting a school. In the film, everyone hears bagpipes, and the new teacher has to figure out the mystery. Sarah told me about it while we sat on the stairs. I was stuck in the house all day, in the kitchen, baking. It was miserable, not even an open window.

When Sarah and Jane returned, Mum's friends had arrived. They were sewing, as usual. Mum met them at the door. "Leah, go to the barn. Girls, to me!" Mum said to Sarah and Jane. I'll admit I was green with envy when they skipped off to the cool parlor.

I spent the afternoon helping Louisa, Martha, and Dad muck out stalls and doing other disgusting barn chores. Mum brought sandwiches to us. "Jam today!" She said, handing each of us our sandwich. I thought that was strange. We ate quickly, the bacon crumbling into dust in my mouth. Jam! Liar, that wasn't jam in my sandwich.

Meanwhile, the twenty-ninth and, in Ukraine, cities are still falling; there was a four-day battle.
Germany won.

Miserable in my attic, but there's nowhere else to write without slipping outside. Mum is bottling with Sarah and Jane and the Land Girls.

Louisa's calling me.
Big sigh.

Same day, sunset....

I went down to hear Mum say, "Girl, wash your hands. Start labeling!" Labeling and carrying jars to the cellar all afternoon, at least, it was cool down there. When I looked up, the sun was about to set.

I can see the sun go down above the treetops from my attic. The air becomes colder, but you already know that. My window will only open a little, just enough for a breeze.

I wish we raised rabbits like you! They're sweeter and cuddlier than cows. They don't hop or do much of anything, just chew their hay.

Our song's next line is, we will celebrate the song and psalm the altar's dedication.

Your exhausted sister,

Leah

Dear Leah,

Well, these first couple of weeks have been busy. On the eighth, we heard some news. In the battle between the Soviets and the Germans, the Soviets continued to be beaten by the Germans.

One evening, Mary and I were walking by the flower beds again. "My parents took me to a restaurant over the summer for my birthday."

"Where? How does rationing work?"

"Certain foods cost more. And you still have to pay."

"What did you have?" We turned, walking between two flower beds. As she told me, I thought about how people could still be happy, even in the middle of a war.

"Miss Esther and Mary, come here." William and John were standing at the end of the bed we were walking beside. Using my hand, I trailed along until I reached them. I stumbled over a loose rock, but that was it.

They showed us some new flowers just poking up through the ground. All we could feel were little points. John said they were bulbs. It's the fifteenth, in Geography, we discussed a speech Mr. Churchill gave last night.

He and the American president Roosevelt discussed a joint declaration that would give people the right to have their own governments without fear; and be allowed to keep trading with other countries—finally, peace after war.

The U.S. still won't enter this war, she said. "They send goods to us, but so far, Roosevelt won't send any armies."

"They haven't been bombed, either," Kathleen added.

"No, they've been fortunate." She sighed. I thought she seemed angry about something.

In music, Mrs. Blake is teaching us longer pieces. I still play by ear, because Braille music is challenging to read while playing.

Today was a miserable day. Churchill was on the radio, speaking of the Nazis murdering the Soviet people. He spoke about "Scores of thousands of people being executed in cold blood, whole districts being murdered." I ran out of the dormitory crying, but not before I heard him say something like, "A crime without a name." Lydia called after me, "Esther, wait." I ignored her.

I ran into William in the hall outside our dormitories. When I explained, he said, "I didn't hear that one, but I can imagine it's true. I'm sorry you had to hear it."

"How much more killing will be done?" I sniffed. Rubbing my back, he said he didn't know.

When I returned, I apologized to Mother for leaving. "No, you were upset. I should have turned it off when the speech became unpleasant."

"It was a horrible speech, Julia. Just awful!" Julia and I were taking our usual walk the next evening. "People being murdered! Not pleasant!"

"You're right about that. The way this war's going, more murders will follow."

"I agree, I believe those Germans won't give up until they have control everywhere. Not sure if you know, but we're not sure where our parents are."

"Yes, I know. The others keep reminding you." We continued walking, listening to the chirping birds. It was still hot; we longed for a breeze.

Something more cheerful, thank you for the song. William can help me translate now.

Here's the next line; My soul was sated with misery, my strength was spent with grief. Sated means having more than enough, I think. (Let's do a bit every other month or so. That way, it'll last longer.)

Your sister,

Esther

Dear Esther,

Well, autumn has arrived. The leaves are still very colorful, and the harvest is busy, as usual.

Martha and Louisa are more cheerful now. On Saturday, they walked with us to town. "Just to look," they said. There is not much to buy, but we can still imagine what we'd like to have when this is all over. New shoes, handbags, and jewelry are just a few things most girls want.

That day, we were walking past a clothing shop when Martha spoke. "I wish I could dress like the actress in that film!" She gushed.
"She was beautiful.
Remember, Louisa?"

We stepped around a puddle left by that morning's rain. Martha bumped me, so my shoes slipped into it. "Yes, I remember. The man was scary, but the lady was amazing!" Louisa said.

"What was her name?" I asked. We moved aside to let a wagon drive past.

The horses' coats were damp with sweat, and they seemed tired.

"A foreign one!" Martha sniffed. "She had some sort of accent."

"Will your Mum let me copy that dress from my magazine?" Louisa begged, "Could you please ask?" She looked at Jane with pleading eyes. Jane promised she'd try.

"How was the man scary?" I was curious now.

"He becomes two different people. Nice by day, mad by night."

"Mad?" I was puzzled, "Like angry?"

"No, stupid!" Louisa sneered, "Crazy." She tapped her head. Not helpful, I thought.

Sarah cut in, "He isn't himself, kind of like Mr. Evans." That's a little better. Still, I wondered again how English words could sound similar but mean something different when used.

When Sarah asked where they'd seen that film, Louisa winked at Martha and replied, "We don't always do everything with you!"

"So, how was your walk?" Dad asked at dinner.

"Mum, Louisa wants to copy a dress from her magazine!" Jane's eyes sparkled, "Please let her."

Mum laughed, "Of course, love." Turning to Louisa, she continued, "You work here. You may use my machine. You have to buy the material yourself, though." She added.

"Thank you, Miss." Louisa grinned at Jane and Sarah.

Only Dad noticed my half-empty plate, giving Mum a disgusted "not again" look.

I don't blame you for leaving; I also left the room. Mother Anderson couldn't have known what that speech would be about. At least, William and Julia seemed sympathetic.

The Soviet-German battle continues, with the Germans heading toward Kiev. More cities continue to fall.

There's something important you need to know. Mama packed sanitary towels in our cases. Since you're twelve, you will probably start bleeding every month. They're rectangle pads made of cotton. You clip the two ends to a belt under your clothes. That should prevent blood from ruining your undergarments. You still have to be careful, though, because sometimes they slip. Maybe Mother Anderson can explain more since I'm unable to.

Evening writing again.

It's raining now and sort of cooling down. I'm sewing most of the afternoon. We're making socks for the soldiers. A friend will send them in his package when everything's ready.

Dinner was roast beef sandwiches. Louisa and Martha were given two each. I only got bread with gravy. I shouldn't complain, but we can't eat that, anyway.

The rain's pattering softly on the roof. That's one of the nice things about being in the attic: I can see and hear thunder and lightning.

It's the nineteenth, and Kiev is taken. I doubt there's a city in Ukraine left unharmed. Now that's been done, what's next?

Finally, this week, I'm visiting Eva. Her sister Carmela is beautiful, curly-haired, and full of energy. This evening after school, we played games like tag and hopscotch. Her shrill voice can be heard all over the house. When it was bedtime, she wouldn't go. Eva coaxed her, promising two stories. She was still restless when she was in bed, tossing blankets everywhere.

Their Mum sat on their bed, and each girl said part of the Shema. I felt peace, reciting with them. Eventually, we all slept.

It's Friday now.
Shabbat starts tonight. I can't wait.

Same day

Like I anticipated, I spent today after school preparing. Making Challah was wonderful.

Eva's family's recipe is different from Mama's, but I'm sure it'll still taste great. Carmela tried kneading with us, but all she did was make handprints.

While we worked, Eva asked questions. "The people you're staying with celebrate Shabbat?"

"No, they're English.
And not great, like Daniel's family," I said.

"Do you know where your Mama and Papa are? I don't know about mine!" she said. I shook my head sadly in response.

"Does Esther like her school?" she asked. Eva's Mum interrupted, telling her to pay attention.

When it was dinnertime, we gathered around the table. Her Mum lit the candles, just like Mama did. Her Dad said the blessing. Carmela started giggling. Her Dad glared at her and said one word; she behaved after that.

During dinner, a song was sung, each person singing a part. It was one I didn't know, but still beautiful. When it was Carmela's turn, Eva helped her.

Today, Saturday, we took a walk in the woods. For fall, the air was warm, and birds were singing. It was great! And I had no chores to do.

"Catch me, Leah!" Eva yelled and took off, hair held back by a hat her Mum had put on her.

I let her run, then raced after her.

I didn't need to tell her twice. My feet slipped on dry leaves and cracked on sharp sticks as I ran on them. Panting, I stopped to catch my breath. I sank down on a log and looked around-no Eva.

I called, but no answer. I walked around, trying not to make noise. She's probably hiding, I thought. I peered around tree trunks but heard and saw nothing.

"Got you!" Eva leaped down, landing beside me.

"Where did you come from?" I gasped. Grinning, she pointed to a tree. I picked leaves out of her hair.

Her parents and sister joined us. "There you are! What were you doing?"

"Playing!" She said innocently. I nodded in agreement.

"Where's your hat?" Her Mum demanded.

"The wind took it!" She said as she held up her crumpled hat.

We spread a blanket under a tree for a picnic. Munching on cold stuffed grape leaves and Challah, I felt sad. Mama, Papa, or you weren't there!

"Look, the birds are hungry!" Carmela threw some Challah crumbs to some birds singing above our heads.

"No, darling, birds eat worms, not people's food." Her Dad scolded.

After lunch, we rested.
Carmela sat on my lap, and we watched two squirrels chase each other up a tree. Eva gazed at the stream, maybe hoping for a fish to leap out. And their parents just held hands.

122

The silence was broken when Eva's Mum began singing a Shabbat song.

It was beautiful at dinner, but in nature, it gave me chills to hear. She sang it through, accompanied by birdsong. When she finished, there was silence.

While walking back to their house, I thought about how I wished my visit could've lasted longer.
Eva lagged behind us. Carmela was asleep in her Dad's arms. The sun was setting, filling the sky with splashes of orange, gold, and red; but everything felt perfect.

Sunday now, and I must go home. Long sigh.

Eva's Mum walked me home.
We took the long way. Mum answered the door when we arrived.

"Hurry up and change. We're studying now!" She ordered me. Hello to you, too! I thought irritably.

"She's welcome anytime!" Eva's Mum said and smiled. Trying not to look too cheerful, I thanked her. Mum forced a smile. When she had gone, Mum slammed the door. I was given Bible memorization to do all afternoon. By the evening, my head hurt. And I wasn't given any dinner, only milk.

Watching us clean up afterward, Mum snapped at Jane. That is something she almost never does. All she did was rattle dishes. I was very relieved when we finally went to bed.

Earlier, Sarah said that Mum had been angry most of yesterday. "Not sure why, although it was between her and Dad. Let's hope her mood improves tomorrow.

Our song continues with; They embittered my life with hardship...

Love you always,

Leah

Dear Leah,

Your letter was exciting to read! I wish we had Land Girls. Some girls still complain about gardening or inside chores. I do, sometimes.

Do you have a beau yet? We don't talk to boys, ever! I'm not sure if I told you, but blind boys are in a separate school.

And yes, I did find the supplies Mama packed, but nothing's happened yet. Thanks for warning me about them; Mother said she'll be glad to help and for me to tell you not to worry. Lydia calls it her monthlies.

One night she whispered, "When you bleed, it goes on for days."

"What are you talking about?" Catherine whispered back. Her bed is next to Lydia's.

Lydia hissed angrily, "You'll see when you're twelve, now be quiet and go to sleep."

I'm just glad you or Eva weren't hurt when Andrew scared you both. Did Helen ever say it was really Andrew? Your Mum wasn't even concerned for you or Eva! How terrible!

Everyone here wants to return home. Unfortunately, we still must wait for the war to end. If your Mum would just let us talk, we wouldn't have to wait so long for letters. It isn't fair that everyone else receives letters every week.

We're reading Little Women now. It's about four sisters living with their mother while their father's away, fighting. Amy likes the character Amy, though she's nothing like her. Mary likes Jo, which makes some sense since she climbs trees, too.

124

I heard things about the Soviet Union on the radio this week. First, on the twenty-fourth, the city of Kharkov was invaded by the Germans, and now they've taken over.

One evening, Mary told me about going to the cinema. She saw Snow White and the Seven Dwarfs a couple of years ago.

I told them the story Mama and Papa told us. "The ending is different!" Amy cried.

"Yes, it was gentler!" Mother said, sitting by the fire, knitting.

"Can we go again?" Kathleen begged.

Mother said she'd think about it. The last film we saw was The Seven Ravens, remember?

Those stories are in Braille, and I love reading them. They're in English, of course. I think they're the same as the ones Mama reads to us. When I discovered them, I laughed out loud. I told Mother, and she said, "There are several books here, but we don't have much space." So, those stories are my favorite.

There's only one copy, I have to share it, unfortunately.

Your weekend with Eva sounded wonderful. I actually felt like I was there.

The thirtieth, and German armies have entered the city of Sevastopol. We assisted in the kitchen today, washing vegetables, when John entered.

"Here, Mrs. Porter. It's ready!" He said, handing her something that smelled funny.

We could hear it banging when he passed.

"Thank you, put it in the storeroom, please," she said. We heard a door open, then something being set down.

"Would you like some tea?" We eagerly said yes, but Mrs. Porter interrupted. "No, girls. I was asking John." He said he would love one. She quickly put the kettle on.

"What was that?" Hannah demanded, "Tell me."

"You'll see, young lady." "I must speak to you!" John said urgently to Mrs.

Porter.

She excused herself, saying, "When I return, I'd like the potatoes washed and peeled, carrots scrubbed and cut." As soon as she closed the door, we talked.

"What was in that bag?" Mary wanted to know, "Flowers or vegetables?"

"Don't be daft," Lydia snapped, "It's too cold for flowers, and we're doing the vegetables now."

"Stuff from the cellar, maybe?" Catherine's hand brushed against mine at the sink. I pretended to steal her potato. Giggling, we passed them on to Amy and Kathleen at the cutting boards. Hannah, Lydia, and Catherine were washing and cutting carrots. Miss Leigh knitted and supervised.

"Where's William?" I hadn't seen him all day.

"In the garden. He'll be in soon."

"Oh, that's Mrs. Porter's tea!" Amy cried. We stopped talking and listened.

The kettle whistle was shrill, kind of like the trains. "Where are they?"

"The room in the back!" Miss Leigh said and instructed Amy to get a tray down from a cupboard, then Kathleen arranged the teapot and four cups on it. "No, Catherine, the carrots should be cut smaller, and please cut off the ends." Miss Leigh carried the tray in.

"I wanted to carry it!" Hannah pouted. Kathleen said it was probably too heavy.

"Why are you Mrs. Blake's favorite?" Hannah asked suddenly.

"I'm not," I said, "I've always been a good piano player. Papa always wanted us to learn." I'm learning loads here.
Maybe if I see my family again, I can show them."

"Well, we never get to spend the summer with the teachers." Kathleen peeled quickly, her voice lowered, "It's just not right."

"If I had family, I wouldn't need to spend summers with anyone!" I said defensively.

Suddenly, we heard loud laughter coming from the storeroom. I

126

dropped my potato. Crouching, I picked it up, washed it again, and handed it to Amy.

"What's so funny?" Mary used her "I'm curious" voice. She walked around, searching for the door. Of course, she found it.
"No, Mary!" Amy called, "Don't. Do you want to get in trouble?" But Mary ignored her. I heard the knob turn.

Then, the door opened.
"What were you doing?" Mrs. Porter demanded.

Miss Leigh and John were angry, too. "Are the vegetables finished?"

"Yes!" Lydia answered for us. "What are they for?"

"Your dinner." Mrs. Porter walked over, inspecting our work.

She had me cut some missed carrots, and Hannah peeled more potatoes. "That's better." William entered with something banging in his hands. "William, your tea is ready."

"Thank you!" He said while washing his hands.

"Hurry up. I need to wash, too, you know!" Hannah hissed under her breath. When he'd finished, he turned and accidentally bumped her shoulder.

"Sorry, Miss Hannah," he said. We all stifled giggles.

Mrs. Porter sent us back to Mother, all except Mary. As we left, we heard Mary say she just wanted to know what was funny in the storeroom.

"Mary's getting punished!" Hannah sang to Mother, "She was listening in the kitchen." Catherine explained what had happened.

"I see. I'll speak to her." Mother said. We were folding clean clothes when she returned. "There you are! Thank you, William."

"I was told to bring her back!" We couldn't hear what else was said because Mother stepped out.

We were quiet then.
I think we were all waiting for Mother's punishment, but she didn't give one.

It's Monday evening.
We're all in our dormitory except Mary.
She's doing her punishment, Mother said.
"She'll be back."

It's later,

When we entered the washroom this evening, Mary was already there.
"Where were you?" Catherine passed Lydia the soap.

"With us!" Anna laughed. "Learning her lesson." I couldn't hear Mother
Matthew's keys.

"Shouldn't you girls be finished?" Mother asked. "Your dormitory's left.
Now, hurry."

"Mother Anderson, I tried to have her stay with me, but I couldn't
always."

"Thank you, Julia. It's over. Mary, you may return with us." Mary hugged
her.
Here it is, when enslaved under the rule of Egypt.

Your sister,

Esther

November 7

Dear Esther,

This is turning into a busy month. Germans are still trying to attack
Sevastopol, Russia.

Other cities are captured, too, like Kerch.

Snow is falling late this year, Dad says. When it arrives, that's when the
digging begins. My least favorite part about winter is the endless hiking
through snow to the barn. My hands and feet become numb in seconds.

The twenty-sixth and the Soviets are still protecting Sevastopol. They're
trying to prevent the Germans from getting further in, even though the
Russians have lost ships and aircraft.

128

Nice kitchen conversation.

Maybe it was a rabbit in that bag. Just don't tell your friends, in case I'm mistaken.

Your Christmas present may reach you before then. I hope you like it!

I can't wait for our song!

Your waiting sister,

Leah

December 6

Dear Leah,

Well, Christmas will be here soon, I can't wait. We've been decorating rooms with paper chains. Catherine and Mary no longer believe in Father Christmas. Someone told them it was their parents who give presents. I think it was nasty, Anna.

It's December seventh, Night! Today something terrible happened, America has been attacked by Japan.

It seemed to be navy ships that were destroyed. So many lives were lost.

This morning, in our dormitory, there was silence. "Now, they know what we had to go through!!" Lydia burst out.

"What do you mean?" Mother Anderson demanded.

"England's been bombed for months. They've been bombed only once!"

"Now, America must fight in the war with us." That was Hannah.

"They've helped by sending tanks and seeds to us and patrolling the Atlantic. Mrs. Davis and Miss Pryce explained that to you!" Mother Anderson's voice was stern.

"President Roosevelt has been doing everything to help without declaring war. And my brother is now fighting overseas!" She spoke softly, but we all heard. Everyone's involved in this ugly war, I thought.

We somehow made it through the day, trying not to discuss the attack.

129

It's evening now. I see a little light from the window. Mother just closed the curtains.

Before bed, we were all sitting quietly, then Mary asked, "Can we read about the sisters?" Mother asked our opinions.

I wasn't sure, but Amy, Lydia, and Hannah wanted to hear more. Kathleen mumbled, "I don't care." And Catherine said nothing.

"Very well. I'll start," Mother said.

By the time she had read a couple of pages, we were all listening again, so she finished the chapter.

"Will there be bombs in this book?" I asked. Mother replied, no.

Now it's Monday evening, and we listened to the radio tonight. In a new speech, President Roosevelt declared war on Japan.

Now, an American submarine has sunk a Japanese ship.

Christmas is approaching. Even though most of us are unhappy about what America went through, we're still celebrating.
Decorations this year are made with paper and paste. Miss Leigh used the last bit of flour to make it.

It's not good news anywhere. In Sevastopol, the Germans are still there. They tried to damage ships, but they didn't accomplish much damage. Armies from Kerch are trying to help.

It's Christmas evening! Some of us played outside, yes, in the cold. The snow was fresh, which was much easier to walk in and shape into snowballs.
We didn't always hit each other, but we still enjoyed ourselves. The older girls were outside, too, so there was a snowball war between us. Someone hit me in the back of the head. When I threw a snowball behind me, I must have missed whoever I was trying to hit. Lydia hit Susan, I think. Then, Julia joined our side. She's the only one with bells on her shoes. She has some sight in one eye, so could help us aim. Hannah and Anna ended up fighting each other.

Mary and Amy made snow angels. They took their hats off, so they could feel the snow in their hair. When we came back in, Mother scolded us. "Girls, your hair's wet! Go to the washroom at once."

We all had to change before we could open presents. Everyone had received something. (Thanks for the bookmark! Now that I can read, I need something to keep my place.) Catherine squealed when she opened a new dress. "Mum made this! There's buttons in different sizes on the front!" All of us eagerly touched it, the buttons were beautiful! "It doesn't matter if they're used, I like them anyway."

"Where did your Mum find those?" Mother asked.

Catherine didn't know but would write and ask.

As always, Hannah's presents were very expensive, fur coats, dresses, shoes and thick stockings. "My parents buy me anything I want!" She said proudly. "I don't need a used dress."

She touched my arm and said loudly, "You shouldn't get presents. Mum says Jews don't celebrate Christmas." Furiously, I reached out, pulling at her hair. Mother separated us right away.

We were kept apart for the rest of the day and are forbidden to use the piano or sewing rooms for the whole break. Even after I explained to Mother why I pulled her hair, I'm still being punished.

Dinner was potatoes, vegetables, and meat in gravy. (I'm pretty certain they were the vegetables we had chopped). We'd just begun eating when someone whispered loudly, "Mrs. Porter, how did you cook this rabbit?"

Catherine started crying.

"Oh no, we're eating Fluffy and Long Ears!" She screamed. Mother took her out until she calmed down.

Some of the others laughed. "She's such a baby!" Anna snickered, "Didn't she notice their rabbits had disappeared?"

The King broadcast his Christmas speech again. It's been another hard year, but we must do our part and keep faith in G-D.

It's probably much harder for America now that they've entered this war. Mother Matthews complained, "Those Americans should have been fighting with us ages ago. Roosevelt didn't want to get involved."

After we listened, I asked Mother Anderson, "Can I show my bookmark to Miss Leigh?"

"Yes, then come straight back."

Really, I ran into William on the way back. He and I talked about our families. It was wonderful sharing stories. When he was young, he'd leave his shoe out for Saint Nicholaus on his Feast Day. He would find it filled with nuts and chocolate. We had to stop when we heard voices outside the door. It was two older girls. They remained outside for a long time, just talking. We whispered, but the fun was gone. When they'd finally moved on, William looked up and down the hall making sure nobody was around.

When I returned, Mother was assigning us our chores for tomorrow. "There you are. Come and sit down!" She said.

If only William and I could plan our meetings. It's not fair we have to meet secretly, even though I understand why.

And here's more; But G-d with His mighty power brought out His treasured people...

Love you always,

Esther

P.S... Sorry, the decorating is mentioned twice. And yes, Miss Leigh loved the bookmark.

1942
Sunday, January 5

Dear Esther,

Our Christmas was similar to yours. We had chicken instead of rabbit and listened to the King like you did.

Mum cried as she killed, plucked, and scooped out the insides of Henrietta, but what do you do when you go to the butcher for ham and come back empty-handed? The queue was long, and when Mum's turn came, there wasn't much of anything available.

We were expected to prepare for a killing day a few days before Christmas. Dad needed us out in the yard to keep the other chickens from flying around. Naturally, our clothes and hair were covered in feathers and straw. Not to mention us trying not to slip on the frozen droppings. When Henrietta was finally slaughtered, we scurried into the house to change. As you know, blood makes my stomach churn. Now, you can tell your friends that we slaughter and eat our animals, too.

Since Jane's a teenager who doesn't care for dolls, Mum gave her hair ribbons and permission to use the sewing machine by herself. Sarah and I each received our usual oranges and writing paper. More letters for you!

Your present and letter arrived after Christmas. I just blamed the rotten weather. I appreciate the stockings. Jane wanted to read your letter, but Dad said it was private. Good thing, too; I don't believe Mum would be pleased with our secret conversations. She can't read our letters, anyway.

Louisa and Martha got presents from home and gloves from Mum and Dad. Their packages from home were more enjoyable. They included new handbags, hats, and perfume! Sarah and Jane tried some and loved its scent. Their new hats matched their coats.

"Those are summer hats!" Sarah exclaimed, "With flowers on them." Both laughed and said they'd wear them in summer then. Sarah thought it was funny, summer hats at Christmas!

"Ridiculous!" Mum grumbled to Dad later, "Where are they going to use those handbags? And that perfume! Not in my house or barn."

I had to listen to Churchill's speech about Pearl Harbor. He said if the US became involved, Britain would, too. He spoke to Roosevelt when Japan declared war on the US and Britain. Then Churchill's cabinet declared war on Japan.

Hannah's a very spoiled girl. Just be careful from now on; if she upsets you again, walk away. You are right. We're simply trying to fit in. I still have to read the Christmas story and say mealtime prayers in English. When we can be together again, we'll attend synagogue. I'm jealous of Leron; his family attends!

Back to Pearl Harbor. It was horrible, but now the US has joined this war, we'll have another Allie. Some of my classmates were bitter, too. Miss Simmons explained that Japan and America have been having meetings for some time now. They couldn't reach an agreement about trading for things the Japanese army needed.

Daniel's now learning with everyone else and no longer needs English lessons. Miss is proud of all of us for learning English and making friends. Eva is content, too. Andrew hasn't tormented her, thank G-D. Miss still watches at recess when she can.

One afternoon, after reading our Princess Elizabeth letters, she announced, "We don't begin a letter with, "Hello, Elizabeth." Some kids laughed. I glanced around, wondering who had written that one! Our letters were returned marked with corrections. Mine were grammatical suggestions.

I haven't seen Atalia lately. Of course, it's winter, that's how it is. I wish Mrs. Evans would accept food.

The best news is the Americans have arrived. Louisa and Martha have already picked their favorites. And no, I don't have a beau yet. It seems they have a use for perfume, after all. Jane sneaks into their room, and they style their hair together. She's even tried Louisa's lipstick.

January's over, and the Soviet armies are now fighting in Ukraine.

Did you know that during winter months on a farm can be dull? Nowhere to go, you're stuck in the house for weeks. Sarah and I talk in her room, but I can't share anything with her. She wouldn't tell Mum. She wouldn't understand. Her dolls we used to play with are in their corner, gathering dust. We play jacks instead. She offered to take me to Helen's to use their phone to call you, but I couldn't accept. "We'll be discovered. Maybe another time."

Have you read the English New Testament yet? I've finished it. Some of the others told me they still pray quietly in Hebrew when they're alone. If I tried that, who knows what Mum would do?

Louisa and Martha complain about their cold room. Mum just says, "The cold is good for you. Here's another blanket."

February is bone-chilling cold, at least up here in the attic. Extra blankets help a little. The only reason I have any is that Dad or Sarah smuggles them to me, usually at night or early in the morning. When I awake, they're outside my door.

We've been having hot porridge for breakfast when it's available. English tea wakes us up. But without sugar, just milk. If not, eggs are plentiful, at least the ones we keep. I never thought I'd say this, but I'm tired of eggs. And there's sausage. Disgusting.

Dinner has been tinned fish and bread with margarine. Like you, we also eat from the garden. Endless bowls of vegetable soup. At least it's hot.

Still sewing for soldiers, too. Mum's friends gather at a different house every week if the weather cooperates. Like today, we were sewing here. Martha prefers machine work. She says it does the work for her. "Lazy!" Jane hissed. We were making a quilt, and Martha made a full section. Jane, Sarah, and I each made squares to stitch together later.

Hurray, March is here! Today, I decided to ask Dad if I could phone you.

"What is it?" Dad asked. He was sitting in the garden, watching the sunset.

"May I phone Esther?" I held my breath.

"What did Mum say?" He asked.

I let out my breath impatiently. "No, of course." I feel frustrated that he agrees with her again.

"It's expensive, and you know that," he said. I returned inside, closing the door.

Tonight, I returned from the outhouse to hear Mum and Dad arguing.

"She wants to phone that sister of hers. No, she can't!" Mum said.

"You let Jane use Helen's phone. Why can't Leah?" Dad argued.

I stepped on a creaky step, and their voices grew quiet. I slipped back into the house, closing the door silently behind me.

The first free Saturday we had, the five of us walked to town and met up with Louisa and Martha's American beaus. We found ourselves behind a barn, and I began to feel uneasy.
"Why are we here?" Martha asked.

"You found it; you tell us." Her beau, Josh, replied. He put his arm around her and pulled her close.

"Here, Sarah, have one." Louisa pulled cigarettes from her pocket, and Sarah and I refused ours. Smoke filled our noses, making us cough.

Where had she gotten those?

"Do Jews smoke?" Tim, Martha's beau, asked. He was right beside me. I was definitely nervous now. He reached out toward me.

"We must go. Mum needs cloth." Sarah said. We edged away from the others, but Martha grabbed Sarah's hair. "Stay," She coaxed, "Try one." I pulled Sarah away, and we ran. Martha angrily threw her cigarette at the wooden barn.

Outside the dry goods store, we paused to catch our breath. We purchased the cloth and returned home. Immediately, we told Mum.

"Thank you, both." She said and smiled, relieved we weren't seriously hurt.

When Dad found out, he dismissed both girls. They work nearby.

The barn we were standing by belonged to an old farmer but wasn't damaged by the cigarette she threw. Fortunately, it was only one. Sarah, Jane, and I won't ever smoke now.

This is a long letter, I know, but I had to tell you everything.

I'm surprised you and William weren't caught. Why is he working at your school, anyway?

Can't wait to hear your news!

Your anxious sister,

Leah

P.S... While Pharaoh's host and followers Sank like a stone into the deep.

136

Dear Leah,

Thank G-d you weren't hurt near the barn that day. So far, nothing that scary has happened here.

In February, I started my monthlies. They're painful. You didn't mention that! Mother says Kathleen should be next. When Mary asked what they were, Mother answered, "You'll find out when you're a little older." "I already know what they are, my Mum told me," Hannah interrupted, "You bleed every month, then you can have babies."

"Shhh, Hannah. When you're all older, your mothers will explain." Mother said. Is Hannah right? When Lydia and I returned from the washroom, she whispered to me that her mother had told her the same thing. "You have to marry, and then you have babies. My mother wouldn't explain how, though."

We had to end there because Catherine came over, saying she was bored. It was almost bedtime, so we played until everyone else returned. (Sorry, I didn't tell you, Mother gave Lydia, Kathleen, and me permission to leave the washroom by ourselves.) When the younger girls returned, Mother was angry Catherine had left without getting permission.

Kathleen, Lydia, and I have a new subject this year—typing! As Julia explained, you can't correct your mistakes! Mrs. Davis taught us the location of the keys, then handed us sheets of paper. I rolled the paper in, then slowly started typing. My first attempt was horrible; many of the words were left incomplete at the end of a line. The entire page was filled with errors. Afterward, Mrs. Davis explained our paper had been crooked.

We replaced our rabbits; they've been given the same names as our last pair. These should have babies, though. I have a feeling they may become stew this winter.

We haven't seen any Americans, but Lydia's village is full of them, she said. Her sister is courting one; their parents don't know, but they're bound to find out eventually. Lydia explained courting means they see each other like dating. Lydia caught them kissing one evening.

Yes, I'm reading the New Testament now. The Bible takes up so much space on our shelves there's only one copy. We take turns; older girls one month, us the next. It is read so often that the Braille becomes dull, some of the Bible's difficult to read. Still wish the Hebrew Torah was in Braille, though. The first part of the English Bible is the same, did you notice?

In our book, Meg, Jo, Amy, and Beth continue to have adventures. It was unfortunate about their father's illness. Laurie seems to like Jo. Meg and Mr. Brooke sort of have feelings for each other.

We've spent wonderful days outside recently. Somehow, our rabbits escaped this evening, so Mother Anderson, Matthews, John, and William had to chase after them. They were found unharmed in some nearby woods. We were exercising, and Anna whispered to Mary that they might be Christmas dinner.

Of course, later, Susan was disrespectful to John, ordering him, "Hold the door, will you? You see, we're going in!" Mother Matthews didn't even scold her. She just walked past, her keys jangling. Not for the first time. I'm definitely glad we're not friendly.
Julia spoke loudly, "You ought to be more polite." The others just giggled. "You have to obey us," Hannah chimed in, "You're a servant."

"We'll talk later about your tone, Missy," Mother Anderson whispered. In our dormitory, she did. She spoke about respecting the workers here, something most of us already do.

Bitter news: the Luftwaffe bombed England five nights in a row, Exeter on the twenty-fourth and twenty-fifth; Bath, three nights, twenty-sixth through the twenty-eighth.

Even though I know it, I can't wait for more of our song!

Love,

Esther

Dear Esther,

School has almost finished. So far, this has been a slow-going month.

Hitler still won't stop- Exeter was bombed again.

On the eighth, Germany continued to fight in Sevastopol.

Sarah is relieved those Land Girls have departed. "Extra work, but at least they're gone!"

Another battle's ended. This time, it was in the air and sea between the US and Japan. The Japanese had captured most of the Pacific Islands and the Philippines earlier this year. The Americans prevented an Australian port from being attacked.

Endless sewing almost every weekend; I understand it's to aid the war effort, but does it have to be with the same group of women?

This week, the fighting continues, with another battle in Kharkov on the twelfth. Germans and the Soviet army are losing men. More men and supplies arrived for the Germans.

There's a new song, The White Cliffs of Dover, on the radio. Mum cries every time it plays.

Well, the twenty-eighth, and in Kharkov, it's not good. They're surrounded by Germans.

Not sure how we'll spend our summer. Seeing another film, perhaps?

Love you always,

Leah

June 7

Dear Leah,

We have exams this year. Last year, everything was canceled because of the Blitz. The only exams that are not written are music and sewing. I don't think of those classes as exams. They're more practical, Miss Walters says.

Lydia wants me to stay with her for the summer! I can't wait to meet her family. I just hope they're wonderful like she says they are.

The first week of June has ended, and so much has happened. First, exams are over. One of the advantages of being blind is no one can cheat! The hardest ones for me were writing, geography, typing, and arithmetic. Writing sentences and remembering how to solve math problems isn't easy, even with slates. Tracing map outlines, and writing their names, was also difficult.

Typing was still the worst; I know my paper had errors! At lunch, Kathleen remarked, "Will it matter that I ran out of space on one line, but completed the word on the next?" Hearing her distress, Lydia and I moaned about our failed attempts at typing!

Our music exam was just playing and reading Braille music for Mrs. Blake. To me, that was the easiest one. Even in sewing, we had to make something for our exam. I think we all made the same thing—blouses.

Did you hear the terrible news about what the Nazis are doing? The awful part was what I found out in the washroom.

I was coming out of the toilet when the older girls entered with Mother Matthews. I walked toward the sink, hoping to get away. "The little girls should be done here, so there's no need to rush." Mother Matthews said.

"What do you think of the Charity girl?" Susan asked.

140

"She still can't speak properly, still has that German accent."

"Does she know what's been happening? Jews like her were murdered!" Susan said, acting shocked.

I heard the water in the sink, then Mother Matthews replied, "Yes, Jews are dying, by the thousands, according to the BBC. Seven hundred seventy-seven thousand in Poland, I believe." She didn't seem upset or bothered. "She better thank G-D she's here. Oh, hello, Esther!" Mother Matthews said in a cheerful voice. "Didn't see you there."

I just stood there, unmoving. I couldn't breathe.

"Well, what do you think of that?" Another girl close to me demanded, "We want to know. That could be your parents." I opened my mouth, but nothing came out.

"Can't you leave her alone? Mother, I doubt she would've heard that news yet." Julia!

"Well, she's quiet. Can't speak now."

"Do you need a sink, Esther?" Mother Matthews turned on the water, "Here."

"Oh!" I screamed. The scalding water burned my hands! I stepped back, knocking into one of the girls, who tried stepping around me. "Move! We don't have all night."

"Let her through!" Mother Matthews said calmly, "You mustn't be late. Mother Anderson will worry."

Sobbing, I flung open the door, but not before one girl called after me, "This school is nice, isn't it?" I ran, my cane tapping loudly. I could hear their laughter all the way down the hall.

Reaching safety, I burst through the door. "You're late!" Mother Anderson scolded, "What kept you?" Then, she gasped, grabbing my hands. "Poor child, come with me. No talking, please." The others had already started asking questions, whispering among themselves. "We'll be back."

She took me to her room and put something on my hands to stop the stinging. When I stopped crying, I told her everything. She said she would have a word with Mrs. Davis.

That night, I could finally think about what Mother Matthews said. Jews dying? Seven hundred seventy- seven thousand? A day? A week? A month? I can't believe it's taken this long for people to hear about it. I sobbed, thinking about our friends in Berlin. Are they okay? Is our family even alive? And why are the older girls being so cruel about this?

Back to the war; On the sixth, the US defeated Japan in the Battle of Midway.

During one of our conversations, William declared that even though he's German, he hates Hitler. Like me, he's thankful he lives in England. He's written to his aunt in Germany but hasn't received a response. His German mother immigrated here before the previous war. When Britain fought with Germany then, he told me there was violence in the streets. British civilians fought with German civilians. His parents were terrified they'd be next.

That reminded me of the night Mama and Papa told us about when Nazis destroyed Jewish shops. There had been violence in the streets that night too.

Relief, June's over. This week, Germany recaptured Tobruk.

Today, the thirtieth Sevastopol's fallen.

I didn't get a chance to speak to Julia, however. That'll have to wait until we return.

I'm definitely with Lydia this summer, so I'll have more wonderful news to write you next time. So far, this has happened; it's been great, except for one thing: Lydia's parents didn't know I was Jewish.

My first week, everything was going well- until Sunday. We were walking to church when Lydia's Dad asked what church I attended. I replied, I attend a synagogue, he stopped walking. I was holding his arm and almost fell. I explained we all attended church at school, and I was used to it.

Lydia and I didn't mention my praying in Hebrew, though.

After church, Lydia's younger sister questioned me nonstop about being Jewish. She wanted to know about the Tanakh, eating Kosher food, and our writing. I was very relieved when her mother called her for

142

something.

Lydia's older sister, Edith, continues on with her secret love affair, and no, we haven't met him. All we know is she missed church because of a headache. However, when we returned, she was outside. When asked, she said she'd been "Over by the stream." Her Dad spoke to her after we'd gone inside. Lydia's little sister tried to eavesdrop at a window, but their Mum caught her.

Like before, William printed some of it, and Edith completed and will post this.

Here's the next part: He brought me to His holy abode...

Your excited sister,

Esther

P.S One more thing: If people knew William and I are talking, they'd say I'm talking to the enemy, even though I'm German too. He'll continue to print all my letters.

July 10

Dear Esther,

How wonderful you're with Lydia! I'm envious. We had exams, too, and I believe everyone passed.

How dare those girls say and do those evil things to you? I felt sick reading about it in your letter. Once again, I begged Mum to let me call you, but she said, "You don't have the time." Please, let me know what Mother Anderson says. And no, I didn't hear about that.

Reading Little Women sounds exciting. Keep telling me about it. Jane tried to spoil the ending, but I said I'd rather hear it from you.

Meanwhile, there seems to be fighting everywhere. A battle has started in El Alamein, Egypt, between the Germans, British, and Italians.

The Americans and Japanese continue to fight it out. On the eighth, there was fighting on the island of Guadalcanal; Henderson Field was captured by the US.

Here, it's been long and hot; nothing to do but chores, church, and sometimes seeing friends. It's hard to believe I've been here for almost four years; I still don't feel at home, although school and friends make it bearable.

William's family sounds interesting, ask him which part of Germany his family lived in. You're right, to the English, he is the enemy.

Sarah, Jane, and I try to visit Mrs. Evans' children, but she refuses to even open the door. She screams, "Go away! We don't need charity!" You'd think after all this time she'd start to come around to accept help, at least for her family's sake.

Jane's still curious about Mr. Evans. "He's a hermit." She whispered one day outside their house.

I'm always looking for Atalia, but there's no sign of her. It's maddening how a woman treats her family, keeping them hidden.

The Germans have been busy elsewhere, as well. By breaking through the Russian Army protecting southern Russia, they're attempting to capture Stalingrad.
If you read the Torah, don't forget it's in Hebrew. You'd have to learn to read it.

At last, July has ended. The battle in El Alamein is over too. It lasted twenty-seven days. That heat must have been unbearable.

We continue to hear more nursing stories. I guess Nora's sister is still in the desert. She has experience treating tropical diseases and dealing with the endless, dry heat. She wrote about heatstroke among themselves and soldiers that have to be treated with cold water poured over the patient. Besides that, their bodies were covered in ice. Once they warm up, they're given glucose (sugar), so everything else can cool down.

The QA's in the desert fight animal battles, too. They Check their beds for scorpions, mosquito netting around patients' beds, and fight off rats with sticks are just part of their days.

Have you tasted the National Loaf yet? It tastes dry. Mum has tried adding margarine or jam, but nothing helps. I know it's meant to be helpful-it's made with wholemeal flour because there's a shortage of white flour-but I hope she won't use it for anything else, like stuffing the

144

roast at dinnertime.

A new family has moved into a house near the Evans's. They have a little girl, Charlotte. We met her, queuing in line in a shop. Charlotte became angry when there wasn't any chocolate. There hasn't been any chocolate in months! Her mother was embarrassed and paid as quickly as she could.

Charlotte was still fussing when they left.

Love,

Leah
P.S. Sorry, no song. Next time...

August 7

Dear Leah,

A little more about Lydia; after they discovered me being Jewish, her Mum served me vegetarian dishes. Except for my last night when we had fish and chips. An English dish, but still delicious.

We're all back in school, and I have news!

As their punishment for being cruel, Mrs. Davis gave the older girls extra work. Mother explained that Mother Matthews isn't speaking to her, and all the girls were forced to apologize in front of everybody else. So, the girls aren't happy, either. On one of our walks, Kathleen overheard two of them talking. "They hate us," she said.

"That's all you overheard!" Hannah sniffed. "We knew that already."

The bell rang, and everyone fell asleep except me. I lay awake, hoping our fight with the older girls wouldn't last.

The German Armies have advanced into Stalingrad. The Soviets continue to defend the city.
Yes, we eat that horrible bread. "What's in this?" Mary almost choked the first time.

"You don't want to know. We all have to eat it!" Miss Leigh said.

Ever since learning to type, the clattering typewriter is heard most weekends in our dormitory and across the hall in the older girls' dorm. Our lessons with Mrs. Davis are divided between Braille and typing. She times us, checking for speed and accuracy. "Once your speed and accuracy improve, you all can be employed as typists." She explained one day.

"Us?" Lydia paused mid-type, "How?"

"You can Braille the information on a shorthand Braille machine, then type it out." When asked, she explained it's a machine with a long strip of paper at one end. As you type, the paper drops into a basket. It has six keys and a spacebar.
In music, we're learning.

The White Cliffs of Dover. When someone complained about the number of verses, Mrs. Blake remarked that was the whole song. Yes, it's sad but beautiful.

William and I managed to talk yesterday. He said he doesn't have memories of Germany, only stories he's been told.

I asked him if his mother dislikes Hitler as well. "Yes!" He replied. "Very much. She was thinking about returning and helping the resistance, but it's too risky. The resistance is a group of German and Jewish people fighting in their own way, like hiding Jews."

"How do they know who they can help?" I asked curiously.

"Many are their neighbors. Some are hiding children within their own families," he said. We had to end it there because Mother Matthews passed by the room. I waited until I could no longer hear her keys, then hurried to our dormitory.

"Where were you this evening?" Mother demanded. "You weren't out walking. You know the rules." I lied, saying I'd come in earlier, and went to the sewing room. To my relief, she didn't ask any more questions.

Back in Russia, the Luftwaffe bombed Stalingrad. The other German armies are halted by the Soviet army.
My other school news: I met Julia on one of our walks. She slipped away from Mother Matthews, hearing, "You're talking to that Charity girl!" ringing in our ears. "How are you?"
"Still furious. By the way, thank you for sticking up for me."

She took a deep breath. "I almost didn't. When Mother Matthews taunted you with that horrible piece of information, I thought about how to stay silent. You wouldn't have known I was there."

The air was still warm, but the sun was down. My cane bumped her foot lightly. "Well, I'm relieved you did. Did Mother Matthews give you a hard time?"

"What do you think? She certainly said some things. `You shouldn't be so soft. That girl doesn't belong in this country! She mimicked Mother Matthew's voice. Giggling, we continued our walk uninterrupted. Julia tried describing the sunset to me, then changed the subject—still, a pleasant way to end the day.

The thirtieth: And in Africa, Alam Halfa has begun with the German armies trying to make their way past the British armies and out of Egypt.

The British are stronger, so it should be interesting to see who wins. Finally, one hundred thirty-one allied ships had been sunk by U-Boats. Not very cheerful, is it?

Love you always,

Esther

P.S... Finally, here's more: Even there, I found no rest.

September 12

Dear Esther,

I ran into Atalia today- literally. I was in the woods, and we bumped into each other. I suppose I was daydreaming. We sat on the ground under a tree. I noticed with dismay again how thin she was; with her patched, secondhand dress which probably belonged to Mrs. Evans's daughters, and tangled, unwashed hair!

Mixing English and German words, she described horrible stuff! "Mrs. Evans doesn't have enough food. When we eat, it's once a day. Her daughters cry sometimes."

"Well, we're all eating rations," I said. "What about her garden?"

She explained Mrs. Evans doesn't have one. I stared at her in disbelief.

147

How could she not have a garden? Then, she said Mr. Evans was ill.

"In his mind. He has nightmares, shouting in his sleep. He hardly ever leaves his room. I feed him when he doesn't eat himself. Mrs. Evans does the heavy lifting, like changing sheets and bathing him." I knew some of that already but hearing it from Atalia seemed worse. We were silent, looking out at the trees and listening to the gurgling stream. I didn't know what to say.

"I want to paint again!" She said and stood up suddenly, "I enjoyed art in school." We talked about our German families for a little while. Then we said goodbye, leaving together.

I told everyone the next day at lunch about my conversation with Atalia.

"She doesn't have a garden!" Mum exclaimed, "How's that possible?" (The family was eating lunch; I had leftover porridge from breakfast. Cold and lumpy!)

"I don't know, and maybe she's exhausted from caring for Mr. Evans," I said.

"How does she earn her living," Jane asked?

"She still sews for the army. She has a machine. They all sew!" Mum said.

Sarah wanted to give her some of our extra food, but Dad stopped her.

"She won't take it, remember?" Mum sighed, eyes teary.

Sarah tried to slip me some bread with margarine, but Dad caught her. We can't believe he still goes along with Mum. I wonder how they're willing to help their neighbors but treat me like I'm invisible?

On September fifth, the battle at Alam Halfa ended with one thousand seven hundred fifty British soldiers killed or missing, along with sixty-eight tanks and sixty-seven aircraft destroyed.

Charlotte's a joker in school, not in a good way. She's six and has a pet snake! I know this because she brought it to class on her first day. It escaped and slithered under Jane's bench. The girls on that side of the room screamed, and Charlotte just laughed. Sarah returned it to her, Miss scolded her for bringing it, and the day ended with the girls acting jittery until the bell rang. Now, the teacher searches her bag and pockets before class. Andrew even speaks to her. I'm afraid they're planning something together...

On September seventh, Guadalcanal continued. The US attacked the Japanese on the island of Taivu Point. Their supplies were destroyed.

On a lighter note, Carmela started school. There aren't any younger evacuees anymore, but the girls she sits near are pleasant. The trouble is, she won't sit still. The others warn her about time-outs, but she won't listen.

Finally, September's almost over. We're storing fruit, vegetables, and extra milk in the cellar, so we have it for winter. I still don't have any Land Girls.

I think I'll go crazy if I wash another potato.

Well, it has happened. Her first month in school, and Carmela was punished.

She was whispering to her friends one morning when Miss took her hand and put her in the cold corner. Well, she fussed until Miss hit her head with her ruler. She was finally quiet, and we continued with our lessons. When lunchtime came, Miss asked if Carmela could behave now. She nodded, so she joined her class. Miss even had her stay in during recess.

We walked Eva and Carmela home as usual, and she complained the whole way. "I'm telling Mum that Miss hit me!" Eva just shrugged and laughed.

"Carmela was put in the cold corner today!" Sarah announced when we returned home. "She complained, walking home."

"Is she one of your lot?" Mum jabbed her fork at me. As usual, my plate held a smaller portion of dinner.

"What do you mean? An evacuee or Jewish?"

"Both. Is she or not?" I replied she was Jewish. Mum sniffed. "When this war ends, you'll all return to your people!"

The twenty-fifth: and the last couple of weeks have been busy. The Luftwaffe bombed Stalingrad, and in Leningrad, Hitler's paused the fighting.

When Carmela told her parents about her behavior, they remarked, "Good, now you know what happens to naughty girls in school."

Here's my part; The oppressor came and exiled me... An oppressor is someone who forces others to become like them. Sound familiar?

Your relieved sister,

Leah

Dear Leah,

That snake joke of Charlotte's sounds like something Mary might do. The only thing she's done is run and sing in the hall" In the early morning, I might add. Mother gave her extra weeding for disturbing us. I bet Andrew was probably planning more jokes with Charlotte.

Atalia must be so miserable! I suppose she can't leave! Mr. Evans needs a lot of care, it seems.
It's the fourteenth, and in Stalingrad, Germany has halted all fighting for the rest of the year. How will they survive the winter? Just joking; I want those Germans to freeze!

Carmela was naughty. Now, she knows what to expect in school! What is it like in winter if the corner's that cold during fall?

The twenty-third: Now Germany and Britain are fighting in yet another battle in El Alamein.

While practicing typing in the dorm, Mother brought up our letter-writing. "Why don't you type your letters, Esther?" Mother inquired.

"I prefer Braille!" I replied, hoping she'd stop questioning.

"But Leah could read them." Amy pointed out.

So could everyone else! I thought.

Julia and I continue to speak often. She's informed me that Mother Matthews and the others have ceased taunting her.

At last, the twenty-sixth: battles at Guadalcanal have ended, and the

Japanese have too many losses.

One hundred twenty-one Allied ships were sunk. Depressing!

Looking forward to your letter,
Esther

Dear Esther,

It's snowing a bit. At recess, the little kids pretended to ice skate, which was amusing. Leron promised to teach them the basics soon.

Today, the eighth, in Egypt, another battle began called Operation Torch, between Britain under General Montgomery, the US under General Eisenhower, and Germany under Rommel.

Daniel invited me to their house for the weekend. Of course, like last time, Mum refused. Daniel's Mum couldn't change her mind!

The war continues. It's the eleventh, and the Allies (British and American troops) are now being pushed into Tunisia in North Africa.

Your typing seems to be improving. Perhaps Mrs. Davis is right—you could be employed as a typist. For now, stick with Braille.
It's been thirteen days at El Alamein. Germany's overwhelmed because Britain has all the supplies. And, after just eight days, Operation Torch has ended. And a couple of days ago, the allies captured Tobruk. The Axis forces are still there.

Mum and Dad hope this winter won't be so harsh. Not much snow yet.

It's been a busy couple of days fighting elsewhere, too. In Stalingrad, Operation Uranus has started; the Soviet Army now has the Germans surrounded.

Back in Tunisia, Allies captured cities, and the Axis forces made it through the Vichy French line.

More news: walking to school, we passed one of the Evans daughters. I noticed her shoes were stuffed with paper. She looked confused, lost. I called to her, but she appeared not to hear.

"Where's she going? What a dress!" Jane giggled. Sarah furiously

151

scolded her.

For some reason, the girl wouldn't leave my mind all day. She looked so cold, maybe that was why!

The twentieth: In Egypt, the British have now recaptured Benghazi from the Italians. The Germans and Italians tried and failed to attack the British in Tunisia.

School's canceled again. Still studying the Bible and sending packages of clothes to soldiers. The Jews don't believe Jesus is the Messiah. They wanted him crucified.
It's the last day of November, it's been very busy in Tunisia. The last couple of days, the UK has attacked the Germans, and cities have fallen to the Allies. And the US shot down an enemy aircraft.

I can't wait for Christmas,

Leah

Leah's German diary

I didn't have the heart to write this down in my last letter to Esther. It's been a week, and I can now think about it without crying. I'd just picked up my sewing when Dad called from the kitchen, "Leah, we're leaving." Leaving, where?

Dad explained on the way. As we strolled to Helen's, I was puzzled. Why was I invited to help on their farm? The air was cold, and the bright sun appeared as we chatted, Dad asking about Eva.

"One call!" He smiled. I gasped! Really? Ecstatic, I flew inside.

"You're here!" Helen pulled me down the hall.

"We'll be in the barn." Helen's Dad said, "But, as I told you, I really don't need help!"
"Hello, Mrs. Davis is speaking. How may I help you?" The voice was firm but kind. I almost forgot how to speak. My tongue froze. She repeated the question.
"Hello, I'm Leah. May I please speak to my sister, Esther?" I held my breath.

Mrs. Davis laughed. "Certainly, love. I'll fetch her."

152

Clutching the phone in my sweaty hand, I waited, not wanting to miss anything. "Leah?" The voice on the other end was deeper but very recognizable. Fighting back the tears, I answered. We chatted in German and English for several minutes, because "Mrs. Davis wants us to speak English!" Esther says unhappily. Then Dad's hand touched my shoulder. I was in the middle of a sentence and prayed he hadn't heard.

"Time to go, darling." He smiled. We said goodbye, and Esther ended our call first. I stared at the receiver, wishing I was there!
"You did what?" Mum's scowl greeted me a few days later.
"What do you mean?" I tried to be calm, although I was pretty sure I knew why she was angry.

"You phoned your sister. Correct?" When I nodded, she continued, "I found out from Helen's Mum. Is it true that the men were in the barn?" Again, I nodded. "Can anyone confirm your conversation?"
I was puzzled by the word confirm.

"If you mean, can anyone repeat what we said? I'm not sure." I admitted. "Helen and her Mum were in the house."

"How dare you disobey me!" Mum suddenly raised her hand as if to slap me. Fearfully, I stepped back. I'd never seen her this outraged.
"Enough!" Dad appeared as if from nowhere. He stepped between us, placing his hands on my shoulders. "It was my idea; she had nothing to do with it! I couldn't see the harm in allowing her one conversation."

Please, don't tell! I pleaded silently. "Besides, everyone was occupied." Mum breathed heavily and was quiet. Gratitude washed over me then. As Dad led me away, I looked into his eyes. I couldn't speak; he understood, saying, "You're **welcome.**"

December 10

Dear Leah,

I enjoyed our phone call! Shame it was so short! Best present ever!
It's snowing, just not enough for practical jokes. It's fun putting snow in your friends' beds, and then everybody figures out who tricked who. William and John helped Mary and Lydia bring snow into Mother's room one day. She wasn't pleased, and we were all punished because we wouldn't tell on one another.

Our punishment was being on kitchen duty for two weeks. I've never heard Hannah complain more; she hated scrubbing pots and pans, peeling vegetables, or anything else we were told to do.

More girls than usual are staying for Christmas. Why, I don't know. The older ones wonder if they'll still receive presents.

"Yes!" Catherine said.

"You'd know that, wouldn't you! Your family never wants you home for Christmas!" Anna taunted.

"Anna! It's not her fault her family is poor," Julia replied. We couldn't say anything in the halls, but luckily Mrs. Blake heard.

"Anna! Apologize immediately. What class do you have next?" She informed Anna she would have to explain to that teacher why she was late.

Catherine tried not to let the girls' comments bother her. "My parents just can't see me all the time."

She whispered sadly. "Only in the summer."

Meanwhile, our rabbits are huge! Yes, one or both will be eaten, most likely for Christmas.

Most weekends, we're spending more time in the kitchen, doing everything from washing dishes to baking bread. There's less complaining from everyone.
"Can we bake Christmas cookies?" Catherine begged. "We can send them home!"

"We'll see!" Miss Leigh laughed. "That would make a lovely present."

We're preparing for Christmas. This year, we're decorating our dormitories with strings of dried berries; ours are red, and the older girls have blue. Mary wanted a tree, but Kathleen pointed out, "Why? It wouldn't be complete without decorations."

The twelfth: The German-Soviet battle in Stalingrad seems endless. Germany's waiting for an additional army. In Libya, the fighting continues; with a few days till Christmas, most of the Axis forces have evacuated. In North Africa, the US captured German prisoners. However, the German armies have taken back land that the US and UK armies had taken the day before.

We finally finished Little Women. I won't tell you the ending. We were all crying tears of joy and sadness.

It's snowing again, but like I said, no practical jokes. Not on Mother Anderson. She didn't say we couldn't do anything to anyone else!

Christmas Night...,

Will this war ever stop? Operation Uranus still isn't going well for the Germans- they're still waiting for an additional army. That's a relief, I guess.

Catherine got a new coat and gloves for Christmas. Handmade, of course.

Amy was excited when she opened her socks. Mary now has two cardigans.

Kathleen's Mum sent all of us hair ribbons.

Christmas dinner was, of course, rabbit pie. Mrs. Porter commented she's running out of rabbit recipes. Since we used berries for decorating, the pudding was jam tarts with mock cream on top. (Mrs. Porter couldn't find honey. It's just butter and sugar, but it tastes good.) Even Hannah didn't complain about our meal, only remarking, "Our gamekeeper's gone. His assistant took over, which means less meat for us. He's a terrible hunter."

Thanks for the scarf; it's lovely! Mother says it matches my coat. As usual, your present and this letter should arrive next in the New Year.

To round out the day, we gathered around the radio to hear the King's Christmas broadcast. This year, he spoke about America's and our Allies help. The King and the Queen are proud that so many people have taken up their duties in order to help-in the factory or on land.

I'll end with;

Merry Christmas,

Esther

Dear Esther,

It sounds like your Christmas dinner was delicious! I'm jealous! Even if it's a disgusting rabbit, it was an improvement over ours. We had vegetable stew with apple pie. I suppose I should be grateful Mum didn't serve non-Kosher food. I know; I should stop complaining.

Our presents were still practical: material for dresses and one orange apiece. I'm making mine last as long as possible!

Like you, we listened to the King. Thanks so much for the bracelet and necklace. Mum thought they were ugly, but what does she know? "They're from my sister!" I said through clenched teeth, "It might be plain beadwork, but there's a war on." Jane entered then, needing her help with something.

In school, one boy shared a story about his brother, who's in Stalingrad. The boy told us that the Germans aren't exactly winning, either. I suppose they couldn't survive the cold winter. And, in Leningrad, the Soviets broke through the Germans. That's some good news.

Our regular dinners are bland, just vegetable soup or spam. Breakfast is porridge, sausage, or toast. Once, Mum found disgusting bacon. We've experimented with the "dried egg." Horrible! Mum thinks she'll use it the next time she bakes. Hopefully, it doesn't taste as awful in a cake.

It's the seventeenth, and Japanese troops are preparing to leave Guadalcanal. I bet the Americans are anxious to return home. Someone else has a relative in Tunisia. The Germans crushed the French there.

Lydia's sister needs to be more cautious. There's a girl in town who's seeing an American boy, and her parents aren't thrilled. Not sure why since they're helping us. How long before Lydia's parents find out, do

156

you think?

Nora's sister wrote about setting up another tent hospital, still in North Africa. "Makeshift equipment was used because the equipment they'd been waiting for was gone."

Bridget interrupted, "I know. My sister was on the hospital ship that sank." We gasped! She described how the ship was hit, then began to sink. The nurses and troops were pulled onto lifeboats. My sister was one of the fortunate ones. Many nurses and wounded were stuck on the ship as it went down. A passing ship picked up the survivors."

Nora continued her story. "Some American wounded are frightened when they hear guns and dash to the woods."

At last, it's the thirty-first, and all German generals in Stalingrad have surrendered. And in Tunisia, the French were defeated. Will our troops return home?

Well, Mum used the dried egg in cookies she baked. They were delicious!

Try to meet at different times when you and William speak. Ask him what the resistance is doing. Maybe Mama and Papa are involved. It's better than believing they could be dead.

It's February second, and the German armies finally left Stalingrad! And the Japanese have left Guadalcanal, too.

It's really chilly; my attic is as cold as always. Somehow, I'm finding extra blankets outside my door! I'm pretty sure they're Sarah's. I have four now, which I keep in my suitcase.

These last couple of weeks have been action-packed. First, in Tunisia, the Germans captured Americans. They fought but lost tanks. On the sixteenth and back in Kharkov, the Soviets reclaimed the city. On the twenty-fifth, after days of fighting in Tunisia, the Italians and Germans defeated the Americans.

Windy March, and walking to school, Sarah and I talked about some of the girls and their beaus, but we still haven't found ones we like for ourselves. Jane might like someone, but nothing definite yet. She heard us talking and informed us: "You'll know when I've decided, so stop talking about me." (Informed means letting someone know something!)

Eva and Daniel are relieved. No taunts from Andrew.

The battle in Tunisia continues, and Germans are still fighting. Kharkov continues to switch from Germany to the Soviet Union's control and back again. The fourteenth now, and Germany has control.

Charlotte's snake disaster hasn't occurred again, thank goodness. We laugh about it now, but we're not supposed to encourage her.

Still, she misbehaves in other ways. Last week, Miss Simmons sniffed the air.

"What's that awful smell?" She demanded. Of course, we all turned to Charlotte.

"I don't know, Miss," she said innocently. "Ask the boys."

Miss wasn't fooled but decided to play along. The boys denied knowing anything. Daniel helped Miss search the room, and they found the source of the smell: a dead mouse. She calmly threw it out, made Charlotte scrub the floor, then continued with our lessons. Charlotte missed recess and was assigned extra math, in addition to her regular homework, to be completed by Monday.

She whined, "But Agnes invited me to her party on Saturday!" Miss told her she should have thought of that before she played her practical joke. When her parents came, they were told, and they promised to "Punish her again."

Finally, British troops in Tunisia broke through the German line. Then, New Zealand and Indian troops came in to help the British, but the Germans took back some territory they had. Indian troops made it over the German line, though.

I finally went inside the Evanses' house. I brought them extra food. When I knocked, there was no answer. I peered in a window but only saw darkness. I was about to give up and just leave the food on the porch, when the door slowly creaked open a few inches. "Yes?" One of her daughters asked, "Who's there?" I could barely see her face in the gap.

"Leah, your neighbor. We'll see you in church. My Mum has food for you." I said. Silence, was I going to have to stand there all day? I wondered.

The door closed quickly. Sighing with exasperation, I set the basket down.

I decided to look around before leaving. Moving carefully, I edged around the side of the house. All the windows were closed; no lights were on. I saw an outhouse with a partially completed roof. I shivered, imagining the sweltering summers, and the freezing winters spent out there!

"Leah, come here, now!" The girl motioned me to come into the house. Surprised I did. I stepped into a small room without carpet, just wood. The walls were stained, not sure from what. The windows I could see were covered like I thought they were.

"Put it there." She pointed to a chair.

I jumped when a man's voice called, "Now, Lily, get that German girl out!"

Lily grabbed my shoulder and practically threw me out, slamming the door behind her.

"There's no garden," I announced at dinner. "I did hear Mr. Evans, though." I had everyone's attention now. Sarah and Mum had forks halfway to their mouths, Dad and Jane stared. "He shouted at me to leave."

"But she took the food?" Mum leaned forward. I nodded. "How wonderful!" Mum said and smiled, then she frowned. "Will they eat it?" she asked Dad.

"Dear, she won't starve them." They may be poor, but even she has to accept help sometimes," Dad said as his teacup rattled in its saucer.

"I'm surprised I even made it inside!" I admitted, "I thought Lily was going to tell me to leave it outside."

"Where was their mother?" Mum collected dirty plates. I said I only saw Lily.

"Well, you still have dishes, and make sure you don't miss anything," Mum ordered.

It's the last week in March, and the Tunisian fighting is still strong. The British pushed through the German Mareth line, but German soldiers tried to prevent them. The Line runs from east to west through northern Tunisia. The British finally made it over the line, and Axis troops were evacuated and went to Wadi Akarit.

We're growing extra potatoes, so Dad is seriously considering hiring Land Girls again. Hopefully, they're better than the previous ones.

Lengthy letter, but a lot happened!

Leah

Ps. On to our song: Because I served strange gods and drank poisonous wine.

April 9

Dear Leah,

Sounds like you had a hard Christmas. You'd think your Mum would be more understanding about that jewelry, nobody has much money, after all.

We make do with what we have, even if it's just beads and thread.

Those were my cookies! I can't believe your mother did that. Well, I can. I just didn't think she would; I never would've sent them.

It's the eighteenth, the US shot down the Japanese navy bomber aircraft responsible for their Pearl Harbor attack. Miss Pryce explained that a bomber is an aircraft that's made to drop bombs.

We're reading The Secret Garden now. It's hilarious whenever Mother reads the funny English called Yorkshire English. The character Mary reminds me of Hannah. She had an ayah at the beginning of the story. An ayah is an Indian nurse. There's a mystery in this one, but I won't spoil it for you. Can't you borrow books from your neighbors?

Like every subject, typing's more difficult. We're typing out arithmetic problems. Kathleen groaned, "I thought the slate was difficult." Once, my ink ran out; I had to redo the whole assignment!

Christmas wasn't so pleasant for Lydia either. Edith's in the family way. Preparing to have a baby. Now, her parents know about her American beau. He says he wants to marry her, and they'll live in America with his family. Edith cried when she told them, and their Mum shouted.

Thankfully, their little sister was with a friend.

Rainy this week, so exercising with the older girls, like before. Julia continues to help us when she can, teaching Amy or Hannah how to dance on their toes. "We can do ballet, like my sister!" Hannah exclaimed.

Classes are more difficult this year. We're finally working with the sewing machine and playing more difficult pieces in music class. Mrs. Blake plays a piece, and we write the notes! The longer the piece, the more notes to remember and write. Mrs. Davis is still teaching us the difficult way to write Braille. It's faster, just like shorthand. Numbers are still written the same, and now we've learned there's a multiplication sign too.

In Geography, Miss Pryce's teaching us about India. She said there's a famine in Bengal, one of the provinces (big cities.) I asked her if there was anything we could do to help, and she answered, "Nothing. They'll survive somehow."

When we talked (this time before our evening walk), William advised me not to get my hopes up about finding our parents. He's anxious about some of his Jewish neighbors—but it's like they've vanished. All he knows is Jews are being taken to other places, who knows where. I really had to hurry back, and luckily only Lydia noticed I had gone. "Where did you go?" She asked. "Looking for something I lost in the music room!" I replied. "Really, Esther? I don't believe you."

"There you are!" Mother entered, saying, "Esther, we're about to leave. It's actually a pleasant evening. Hurry."

"She was in the music room!" Lydia added. I wonder how long I can keep our meetings a secret. We did our normal routine that night. Still, I wondered why Lydia didn't believe me.

Mary and Catherine are looking forward to the summer; they're visiting Hannah. "Mum and Dad are sending our car!" Hannah announced. "Arthur is our chauffeur." It's my turn, yet scarcely had I gone into exile, ... Exile Forcing someone to flee their country. Sound familiar?

Your worried sister,

Esther

Dear Esther,

Here we are, very rainy. A German plane has bombed a British ship, and seven hundred ninety-nine peo
ple are dead—gloomy news to match gloomy days.

Hannah shouldn't brag about her family like that-some girls are terrible. Let me know what happens with their summers. Lydia's, too.

It continues to pour, so we're inside most of the time. At recess, we've heard endless nurse stories from Nora. "The hardest part is to get the wounded fit for travel. As soon as they're well, it's off to a base hospital. There, the patients receive better treatment and surgery. The beds fill quickly. Sometimes, the overflow of patients sleeps on the floor."

"The Americans invite the QA's to dances on their nights off. They swim in a nearby beach and take walks. I had doubts about that one. With so much socializing, who was tending to the patients? Nora made it sound like they were on holiday. She also described how their tents become a sticky mess because of the rains. Everything's in tents, but they leak. They now wear trousers and boots instead of capes and dresses.

I thought the rain in England was awful! When I go to the barn, my shoes fill with water. School is bearable, with Andrew not taunting as much. Miss is still watchful.

May is drawing to a close, but the news has been cheerful. There was victory in Tunisia, and forty-two U-Boats were sunk. Not good for Germany, but wonderful for the English.

Your bored sister,

Leah

Dear Leah,

Now it's almost summertime. Already, a civilian plane was shot down by the Germans. Tragically, everyone onboard died.

School's almost over; We finished the book. Good thing because I thought Kathleen was going to take it with her. "Nice ending!" Hannah commented. Mother said she'll think about what to read next.

Our typing exam was challenging. Mrs. Davis tested our speed and accuracy: two pages of English sentences and two with arithmetic. I believe we've improved.
It's now the twenty-ninth, and Germany must be worried about an invasion because they've removed their U-Boats from the Atlantic.

This summer, I'm with Amy; I'm not sure if I told you, but her family lives in a cottage by the sea, so we swim almost every day. Amy's Dad will post this letter for me.

Here's more of our song; When Babylon fell, and Zerubbabel took charge; ...

Best wishes,

Esther

Dear Esther,

I can't wait to hear about the rest of your summer by the sea. Just wish I were with you! Perhaps, when this war is over, we'll live there.

The new Land girls are sisters: Dora and Enid. So far, they're hardworking; Dad's given them a trial period. I think that means they work for a while, and then he'll decide whether they'll stay with us. They don't even mind bottling, which is my least favorite house chore.

On the Eastern front of the Soviet Union, another battle has begun. This one is in Kursk. On the fifth, after being attacked, the Germans fought back with their Luftwaffe, tanks, and artillery. The Soviet Army is still stronger, with more tanks and men. And yesterday, in the city of Prokhorovka, Germany was pushed back by the Soviets. After a week of fighting, Germany is now defeated! - In Prokhorovka, anyway.

I borrowed Sarah's copy of The Secret Garden. Mum and Dad approve of my reading English books.

Saturday, Sarah and I went to the woods with friends to escape the heat.

We raced, climbed trees, and just talked. Daniel and Eva, being the youngest, wanted us to play hide-and-seek, so we did. We let them win one game.

Sarah offered to walk Eva home, but she wanted to stay with Daniel. "I'll tell Mum."

So once our English friends left, the rest of us finally spoke in our own language. We don't want to forget our country, even though we can't stand some of our country's people right now. Like the other evacuees, Eva and Daniel are concerned for their families. Like me, Leron has written to his parents but hasn't received a reply.

Helen and I walked Eva home. It was a hot night. Eva said she wished it would rain. The crickets chirped, and the moon was out. We passed by Helen's house. The front garden appeared empty.

"Hey, girl," A voice taunted, "Be careful." Suddenly a rock came out of nowhere, hitting Eva in the head. She cried as a trickle of blood ran down her cheek. When we looked back, the garden was still deserted. Even the night was silent. No crickets.

"I'll carry her," Helen said. I thought I heard a door close.

Helen picked Eva up and carried her home. Eva's mother met us at the door! When we explained what occurred, she demanded an answer, "But who threw it?"

"I think it was Andrew!" Helen looked Eva's Mum in the eye when she spoke, "I'm really sorry!" She looked ashamed.
"It isn't you who should apologize!" Eva's Dad appeared behind them. "Please, come in. There's blood on you." Helen then saw a small spot on her dress.

"It's nothing," She said, "I'll be fine."

Eva threw her arms around her Mum as she was carried inside.

We stood there silently, then walked back to Helen's house.

"See you!" She said, then kicked her gate hard. Looking miserably at each other, we went our separate ways.

Unhappy,

Leah

August 4

Dear Leah,

Summer was amazing! The sea was warm, the smell of salty air, and the sand beneath our feet was fantastic. Much better than the boat ride over here, remember? Building sandcastles with Amy's sister and brother was funny because a wave would always knock it down just as we put the stick flags on top.

Sometimes, a seagull would fly near, usually when we were eating.

Most days, the neighbor foster kids joined us. They'd never been to the sea before-they lived in a crowded flat with another family. The sister shared something strange on the beach one evening, "We don't want to leave. We like it here better! Our Mum writes that she'll come for us when this is over. But we don't want to live with her anymore."

"The air there smells like rotten garbage!" Her brother added, holding his nose. "And out here, you can run and run. I like the seagulls and other creatures out here." They asked about my family. I told them it was my first time away from my parents.

In bed, Amy pointed out that it sometimes smells of rotten fish here. We laughed, but then we wondered if they would return to their parents when the time came.

Why must we Jewish evacuees endure unfair treatment from our schoolmates? He's so evil. Why does Andrew hate Eva and nobody else? He hasn't taunted you, has he? He hurt her, and I wouldn't want the same thing to happen to you!

Finally, on the twenty-third, Kharkov is at last freed by the Soviet Army.

One day, Amy's Dad took us rowing in his boat and taught me how to fish. The smell was awful, but the taste was great when cooked. The water was calm, and the warm sun felt pleasant, not unbearably hot.

He told us about his trip while we were rowing. He was at Dunkirk.

Amy recalled the trip he'd gone on three years previously.

"It was cold, but the boats waited on the water for the soldiers. They rowed them out to us, and we rowed to hospital ships. They came back across the Channel. We had to keep returning for more. As you know, thousands of men were rescued. But many also died."

"How many men rowed their own boats?" I was wondering because Mother hadn't said.

"Not many. The Royal Navy rowed most." We wanted to ask more questions, but we'd reached the shore, and her Mum was calling.

"I wish you'd told us then!" Amy pouted.

"We didn't want you kids to worry," Her Dad sighed, "You were too young."

I was seven!" Amy cried.

I wonder if Bridget's sister was helping that day. She probably was.

Her parents will accompany us on the train to return to school. I wish summer could have lasted longer!

Love you always,

Esther

Dear Esther,

I'm so jealous! How exciting! Meeting those children, playing in the sea! Well, reading the part about Dunkirk was dreadful, but still...
School's started, it's much emptier this year. Some of the older kids left to work in factories or hospitals.

I saw Helen's family in town, and Helen whispered that Andrew isn't being punished. "We don't know if it was him, though!" I sighed, "But it probably was."

"He was the only one who would know we'd be coming that way. How's Eva?" Before I could answer, Mum called me. Disappointed, we

167

returned to our families without finishing our conversation.

In the barn, Sarah asked what Helen had meant. "Andrew not punished for what?"

I scattered hay in a stall while I answered. "Something he might have done to Eva." I leaned on the door. "We think he threw a rock at her. The garden was empty, though." I stared at the wall. I felt frustrated that nothing could be done.

"Mum wants you, Leah!" Jane came in, talking, "Sarah, can you milk tonight?"

"No, that's your chore. And don't bribe the Land Girls, either." Sarah replied, hands on hips. I left them to it. Passing Dad, I told him about their argument. Mum wanted me to set the table. Boring!

Speaking of chores, the Land Girls are working out! They like farm work and aren't planning to have beaus anytime soon. Sarah, Jane, and I still have our chores to do before and after school. Sometimes, Dora swaps (trades) with me, and she feeds the chickens, and I do the milking. Enid cleans the animals' stalls with Jane.

In the evening, it's the same chores as always, except when Mum gives me ironing to do. I like that one. My mind can wander back to memories of our house. Except Jane will interrupt, demanding, "Is that mine? Finish that tonight." I glare but keep silent. When she bosses me, I feel like the girl in that story with the evil stepsisters.

In school, Miss Simmons keeps an eye on Andrew. She found out about the rock-throwing incident and made him apologize in front of everybody! He confessed, but there's still no proof. "You take the word of my sister and a little Jew?" He spat. All this week, he sulked and wouldn't participate.

Now, we walk Eva to school and home, just in case.
Yesterday, we discussed the famine in class. Our morning began with: "Disgraceful!" We were eating breakfast when Dad uttered that word. "Darling, look!" He thrust his newspaper at Mum, who'd just poured more tea.

"What is it?" She asked, slightly irritated, "Can't it wait?" She glanced down at the paper anyway. "Those people can manage without our help." She handed it back to Dad. "Next time, don't fuss over nonsense."

Sarah and I glanced up, puzzled. Whatever the upset was, we weren't going to find out.

In class, Miss answered that question for us. "Did any of your parents see this?" She held up a photo of a line of Indians waiting for food. "In Bengal, there's still reports of famine." There was silence.

"Who cares!" A girl mumbled, "We're fighting a deadly enemy." Kids murmured in agreement. Not again! I sighed, exasperated. Every time Miss tries teaching about other countries, this happens!

"For some, this may not be significant, but India's been aiding Britain since this war began, as you know. Without food, the people are at risk of starvation."

I asked, "Can't the English government help? India's part of their empire, after all."

"I'm not sure, Leah. Britain has an Imperial rule over India."
What? She wrote the new word on the board. "When a country dominates over another by use of military force." She turned back to us, "Like we discussed before, India wants independence. Wouldn't you if our country was ruled by another?"

Silence again. She let that question hang in the air. Not that different from Germany. I wondered if the other evacuees were thinking along those lines. The bell rang, and the silence was broken by chatter. Benches scraped, and kids hurried out the door.

Whenever we go anywhere with Enid and Dora, we report back to Mum and Dad. Enid and Dora think it's ridiculous, but after last time, I don't blame Mum for being cautious. Next time could be worse.

The last part of this long line; Within seventy years, I was saved.

Your anxious sister,

Leah

Dear Leah,

It's business as usual now we've returned to school. We're still making bed linens for the hospital. Writing has become an almost daily habit, but we just want this war to end.

Some war news, Mr. Blake's plane bombed Hannover. Some planes are missing; she doesn't know if his plane was among them.

Back to summer, Mary told us gleefully that, "Hannah's was absolutely splendid. Apparently, Hannah has enough dresses to last for years, and she and her siblings each have their own dressers. The opera was enjoyable. "They have their own private box!" They talked of dining in restaurants and going shopping. The shopgirls were used to Hannah, who still insisted on being dressed by them.

Mary and Catherine couldn't believe it.

"The first time we shopped for dresses, one of the assistants tried to undress me. I told her the only help I'd need would be with the pinning. When I finished trying on a dress, she remarked, "I didn't know blind people could dress themselves, and thank you for being polite," Mary said.

"Hannah was rude to all the staff!" Catherine whispered on a walk one evening, "She pinched her maid when she accidentally missed a button."

Lydia's been quiet since returning. She and Mother talk in private sometimes; Mother has been sleeping in our dormitory now to be nearby.

Whenever we ask, we're told sharply, "Lydia will explain when she's ready, and we're to leave her be."
One day, we were assisting in the kitchen when Lydia burst out, "Do the

older girls have to do this work?" She slammed down a pot as she spoke.

"Certainly," John replied cheerfully.
"I wasn't speaking to you!" She snapped.
"Enough, back to work this instant!" Mrs. Porter commanded.
Will Lydia be punished? I wondered.
She was assigned extra sewing. The hospital requested more pillowcases, that task has become Lydia's.
"Sewing's not a punishment!" She grumbled.
How long will she continue like this?

Confused,

Esther

Dear Esther,

I'm furious with Jane! On our way to school last week, we spotted Atalia with one of the Evans's children. Both were thinly clothed, walking quickly. Jane managed to sneak up behind them and push the Evans girl into a tree.

"Jane, don't." Sarah and I followed, but Atalia and the girl were already fleeing. "Why on earth did you do that?" Sarah rounded on her sister, hands on hips.

"Because they were walking past." Jane replied calmly, "Now, we need to hurry. The bell's about to ring."

It's turning into a busy month for the Germans. First, on the eighteenth, Britain used their bombers to bomb Berlin, then three days bombing, with ships sinking in the Atlantic.

I believe something happened to Lydia's sister. You said she was expecting. Lydia will probably continue to snap at everyone.

Your friends seemed to enjoy themselves. Good of Catherine and Mary for setting the record straight: not all blind people are helpless.

When I told Mum and Dad about Jane's mischief, Mum responded, "She wouldn't do that! She knows how I feel." When Dad asked Sarah, she backed up my story.

171

Jane's punishment is similar to Lydia's; she has extra sewing as well! I'm relieved Dad believed us.

Finally, the twenty-second and the RAF bombed Berlin again, and two more U-Boats sank.

Love you always,

Leah

Dear Leah,

So far, US and UK leaders met for a conference yesterday to discuss an invasion of Normandy, France, in May.

So relieved Jane's being punished. Have you spoken to Atalia?

Meanwhile, it's the usual bustle around Christmas, with preparations and paper decorations. The packages are arriving, and dinner is being bought. Mrs. Porter and Miss Leigh have gone to the shops for months, purchasing meat, sugar, and dried fruit, like every year.

William says that with all this bombing in Berlin and elsewhere last month, he fears our parents or anyone else we know aren't even alive. I cried when he told me, but that night, I thought about it. We haven't heard from Mama and Papa, and Jews are disappearing more rapidly!

Other news here is Hannah's sister's getting married. Hannah's going to be a bridesmaid-their seamstress is making her dress. Her Mum promised she'll phone when it's ready.

Lydia finally told us about her troubling summer. Her sister Edith lost her baby. It happened in July. Edith woke up screaming, and Lydia woke their parents, who tried to phone their doctor. He was away, so their Mum helped. Lydia and their sister waited downstairs, so they only found out what happened afterward. The doctor finally came in the early morning. Lydia doesn't know what happened. Only her little sister said, "There was blood on her sheets and nightdress." She saw them in the washing basket.

Through the rest of July, Edith sobbed every night. She barely ate. Their

172

Mum said, "There will always be others. Stop feeling sorry for yourself."

To make matters worse, her American beau didn't visit or phone her. Their parents agreed it was for the best. Whenever friends or her sisters tried speaking to her, Edith threw pillows, screaming for everyone to "Go away, LEAVE ME ALONE!"

It's the week before Christmas! Yesterday, William told me there's no news from our parents. He's written to his friends in Berlin but has heard nothing.

I miserably returned to our dormitory. I couldn't even go in. Mother stopped me in the hall. "Esther, come with me." I'd only been in her room once. That's where she took me. I stood there, dreading the questions I thought were coming.

"You missed your evening chores. Lydia said you'd be along, but you never came." "I know, Mother. I was in the sewing room, finishing Leah's present."

"I see. You can clean the dormitory windows for the next two weeks." My least favorite chore!" Could I do something with William or John?" I begged, "Please?" "Absolutely not. You'll stay in the dormitory, where I can see you. Now, go."

Christmas Night...

Everything was ordinary today. The King's message was about the brotherhood of many nations fighting against our common enemy. He once again spoke of our brave men and women and allies fighting abroad. He went on to say we all need to hope for victory.

My punishment is almost over, but Hannah's enjoyed gloating ever since it began. "You're being punished!" She taunts. Mother keeps stopping her, so she only does it when we're alone. Even Susan said something like, "Finally, the Charity Girl's no longer their favorite." Somehow, everybody seems to know about everything. Well, almost everything.

As always,

Esther

Dear Esther,

You had a wonderful Christmas! Mine was, as it's always been, dull and practical.

We all got the same thing, oranges, more writing paper, and dress material.

What I wouldn't give for some chocolate and Babka. Enid and Dora stayed for Christmas. They received presents from home and from Mum and Dad. They continue to meet with Dad and Mum's approval. They adore sewing, which means less for us to do. I always wonder how Atalia spends her Christmases-she never says. And no, we haven't spoken.

Italy is being attacked by the Allies. It's the eleventh, and an Abbey is under threat in Monte Cassino. The Allies believe it's being used as a German base. Now, the eighteenth, it appears the US and the British are fighting. Berlin continues to be bombed by the RAF. I guess the British are getting revenge for the bombings Hitler ordered to be done to them.

You had a horrible time after your talk with William. Perhaps, mother Anderson's getting suspicious. Too bad she wouldn't let you do your punishment with him. At the same time, you were almost discovered.

At least Hannah has some cheerful news. I'm sure you'll hear all about the wedding afterward.

Sorry about Mr. Blake. How horrible for all their families! When will she return?

February eleventh, and it's not looking good for the Allies at Monte

Cassino. The Indian and US armies have suffered losses.

Jane fell this morning. She was in the henhouse and slipped on ice. Her foot's been propped up on the sofa, and Mum and Dad are fussing over her.

Sarah and I have been told to be quiet and help her. She was served lunch and dinner on a tray.

"Now, Leah, you have extra chores until she's better!" Dad told me over lunch. What extra chores? I thought.

Later the same night. I was helping Enid and Dora spread straw in the cows' stalls. Dora said, "We'll help. We all do much of the same work, anyway."

After dinner, Sarah and I had to read to Jane, "Because I'm bored!" We were in the middle of The Strange Adventures of Dr. Jekyll and Mr. Hyde when Mum interrupted. She begged us to read Shakespeare.

So, we started act one of A Midsummer Night's Dream. Jane was laughing as we struggled with the difficult English. Mum commented, "It's like the Bible. You should be used to that." Pointing at me, she left us. We plodded on.

"Stop!" Dad said, coming in, warming his hands by the fire. I glanced at the clock-we'd been reading for an hour and a half. "Mum's made hot chocolate."

We raced to the kitchen, Enid and Dora were already at the table.

My heart sank when I saw six cups. "Sit, Sarah. Leah, this one's for Jane." Then, to bed with you." When I asked Dad if he wanted any, he shook his head. Then, I hopefully asked Mum if I could have his, and she said no. "I thought I told you to go to bed!" She yelled.

"She can have mine!" Enid offered.

"No, but thanks anyway." Scowling, she motioned toward the stairs. Dragging my feet, I reluctantly climbed to my cold attic. I buried my head in the pillow and cried.

It's now the end of February, and the Germans are still at Monte Cassino. The Abbey was destroyed on the fifteenth by the British, and a nearby town was taken by the Indian Army. The allies are apparently running out of supplies, so they wait.

It's the seventeenth, and at dinner, Sarah asked how long Jane would have to sit with her foot propped up like that. "Until it's healed!" Mum's sharp words and the glare made everyone keep silent.

How terrible for Lydia's family. What do I say? I can't imagine going through that.

You're right. It's very unfair about Eva. When we asked why he taunts her, Andrew just growled, "Because she's there!" Not a good explanation, is it? The other day, at recess, he shoved Daniel, who fell face-first in the snow.

Helen and Leron pulled Daniel up. His parents collected him after school, and they glared furiously at Andrew.
"Not me, honest!" Andrew said.

"We saw you!" Several kids called out. Miss promised she'd speak to his parents. Helen and I exchanged skeptical looks. They won't do anything.

Finally, March is here, with the Germans still not surrendering. On the fifteenth, the Indian Army gained control. It's the twenty-first, and after days of intense fighting, Monte Cassino is taken by the British.

On Saturday, Atalia, Daniel, Eva, Leron, and I got together. Atalia says she wants to leave the Evanses as soon as she can. Daniel hopes to stay with his family for a little while after the war, at least until he's older. He really wants to find his German family, too. He's starting to forget them. Leron and I might want to stay in England, but first, we all need to finish school. Eva says if she can't contact her parents, she wants to live with her English family. She'll miss Carmela if she leaves.

Berlin is still being bombed, but this time by the Americans. If all goes well, Hitler will surrender, haha. We'll be together by Christmas! Truly though, I pray this war ends quickly; everyone's exhausted and fed up with family separations and everything else in between.

Who will you stay with this summer? It's good you're not alone at school when everyone leaves. I wish I could meet everyone!

Love you always,

Leah

Dear Leah,

This summer, I'm staying with Kathleen. She says her family has acquired (somehow gotten) extra food.

It's the middle of April, and an American named General Eisenhower is commander of the Allied Expeditionary Forces. He has control of all parts of the military in England. In Monte Cassino, there haven't been any further attacks yet.

I cried when I read about that horrible night. Can't you leave? Perhaps it's too late. Jane's foot seems to be healing slowly, she's enjoying all the attention.

Thanks for your concern about Mr. Blake. Mrs. Blake returned in March. She was very quiet and would sometimes snap at us more than usual.

One evening, in our dormitory, we were discussing our future plans after we finish here. Everyone knows mine. "To find your sister, we know!" Hannah sniffed. Kathleen wants to be a teacher. (Mrs. Davis told us about a place for blind teenagers and adults. Subjects like dictation, telephone operating, and how to live independently in a home are taught.)
Hannah believes she'll be married, like her sister.

As you know, her sister's wedding is approaching. The cake sounds amazing, with many layers and flowered icing. Her Mum said they had to save their sugar ration for months to buy it. Mary wants to work in a dress shop if anyone would hire her.

Contented,

Esther

Dear Esther,

Glad Mrs. Blake has returned. Be patient with her; she's been through a lot.

We've heard about that Monte Casino battle as well. On the eleventh, we heard that the Germans came back stronger than before. For the fourth time, they were still fighting.

Our first week back to school, Jane walked with a limp. However, Miss wasn't fooled. "Your leg is fine, Missy. Now sit down." You're right, she's enjoying the attention.

Back to this terrible war! A few days ago, the allies were finally evacuated. Progress.
I agree, we've been many years in England, too. I have no idea where we'll live once this war ends! If our parents are alive, obviously we'd return home. Or, wherever they're living!

Yesterday was a sad day for the Americans: the twenty-eighth and seven hundred fifty soldiers were killed after their ships were attacked by German torpedo boats.

Can't wait for your news!

Love,

Leah

P.S. The Agagite, son of Hammedatha, plotted to cut down the lofty fire. Agagite Jewish enemy.

Dear Leah,

Everyone's enthusiastic about summer. I'll be with Kathleen.
We're learning lessons, as usual. I still have to take a breath sometimes.
I can't believe I've been here six years. Some of us are like teachers to
the younger girls, helping them with lessons.

Geography is still difficult. We're now studying the map of America.
There are many states that are similarly shaped. That's the same with all
our maps.

Anyway, it's wonderful teaching them English songs we learned here and
the German songs you and I sang. They mispronounce words; it's just
for fun, anyway. Hannah refuses to learn German songs. She's become
an excellent pianist; she reads Braille music with ease. I'm not just
complimenting her.
Sewing is still my favorite- even though we're still making those blankets.

In case you somehow missed it, June sixth was D-day. British, Canadian,
and American troops landed on five beaches in Normandy, France.
Americans landed on Utah and Omaha, and the English and Canadians
landed on Gold, Sword, and Juno. Amy's father described in a letter
how five thousand ships left the day before carrying supplies and troops
across the Channel. He said he went to the cliff along the beach and saw
the ships sailing past.

School's over now. Exams were the same. Practical, like baking bread
and using the machine independently. Who knew you could make a
test out of that? Miss Pryce had us write the states in the order they
appeared on the map; that was difficult! Braille was the usual English
with math problems.
Typing was still challenging. As Mrs. Davis said words rapidly, we
attempted to type them.

I wish Normandy was going as well. Germany beat the Canadians, and seven hundred American ships were sunk during a storm. Can their situation get any worse?

Love you always,

Esther

Dear Esther,

The battle of Normandy continues with a French city being liberated. Germany stopped the Allies from reaching cities in the South.

Our yearly cinema film was about people in Africa trying to escape the fighting. There's a woman who falls in love with an officer, and he convinces her to go with the first man she met, not him. Mum and Dad went with us. They thought the ending was romantic. Jane pretended to limp all day. People asked her if she was okay. Still pretending.

Saw Nora in town. She shared this story of her sister: "My sister was sent to Normandy." Nora announced. "It was top secret. They didn't know until they landed!"

"The hospital was set up with the usual conditions." The soldiers came in right away, some needing amputation to prevent gangrene. The limb was removed. Morphia was given for pain relief. Each soldier had a label around his neck, so the nurses knew which treatment he needed. Others had shell shock. Whenever they heard guns, they tried scratching through canvas floors to hide underground." Sheets are used for surgery only. Everyone still has scratchy Army blankets."

Not seeing much of the Evans family. Just our usual meetings.
Strange way to end a letter. More next time.

Love,

Leah

Dear Leah,

Kathleen's house was terrific! Remember Mama's flower garden?

Kathleen's Mum has the same flowers-it was like being home! They don't have a farm, just a vegetable garden. Like at school, vegetables were our main meal. Except once, her mother somehow made a chicken pie for Kathleen's brother's birthday. All we know is the meat was tender, and there was plenty for other meals. She also seemed to have a lot of dried fruit and chocolate, so we had great desserts. When Kathleen asked, "Where did you purchase everything?"

Her Mum replied, "Shopkeepers like our turnips." I guess she traded or was given them.

Their neighbors have a swing in their back garden, and all of us kids play on it. The one real annoying thing was that some of the farmers' kids didn't know Kathleen and I could read. When a girl came inside to give her mother something, she was fascinated by our Braille books. She didn't get to see us read because, thankfully, her brother told the girl firmly to leave. I guess he thought we would be showing off. I agree with him; the only difference is we read with our fingers.

While Normandy was happening, Kathleen's father taught us an easy way to remember the beaches. Gus and Jo. Not exactly the way the beaches were invaded, but still a clever trick.

August thirtieth: Finally, Normandy is free. Kathleen's Mum thinks the war won't last much longer.

Your contented sister,

Esther

Dear Esther,

Well, the leaves are changing colors, and vegetables are being stored.

School has started, and so far, Charlotte hasn't played any more practical jokes. I guess her parents got through to her. Miss hasn't searched her, so no cold corner either.

Andrew is becoming more vicious. He tormented Leron and me yesterday.

We were passing our homework to the front of the class when notes were passed to us.

"Your parents don't want you!" The note said. Same taunts that you get. At lunch, Leron showed me the note he had received. It was a drawing of a swastika!

Will this continue after the war? Like I said, I hope to be far away by then. I told Dad, and he said, "Ignore it." Not helpful.

On to your other news: Gus and Jo! Very clever of Kathleen's Dad; I wish Miss Simmons had thought of the same trick. Even though it's over, we had to write their names on the board and look at the map. I don't think we'll ever forget that!

Dutch cities are being liberated, and the first US Army had just entered Nazi Germany.

"When this war's over, where will you go?" Jane asked Dora while taking clothes from the line.

She smiled. "Where every stranger wants to be, home. It's not over yet though." Dora's hands flew as she unpinned a bedsheet, "Germany's still holding on."

Enid added, "We can phone our parents. Some still can't." She glanced

182

at me.

It's now the end of September, Dutch cities are still being freed, and an operation by the Allies to capture bridges in Germany failed.

From your irritated sister,

Leah

Dear Leah,

The weather is turning chilly. On our walks, we try not to fall when our canes become stuck in leaf piles. When the wind blows a little stronger; we sometimes have to run.

One Saturday, William told me about a battle in Aaken, Germany. It was short, just two weeks. The Germans defended the city, but the Americans tried to surround the city and fight their way to the center. Once there, both sides fought hard, and the Americans won. Of course, there were casualties on both sides. William hopes Hitler will think about surrendering.

He also told me his family is safe. I didn't ask about ours. We both think we know the answer anyway. Then, we stepped out of the room at the same time.

"There you are!" Mother Anderson's voice rang out, "Come with me. William, go to the kitchen. Someone will speak with you shortly." And tell John to send Mrs. Davis to my room."

"But Mother Anderson," He began, "It's not what you think." She didn't say anything more. She just marched down the halls and into her room, pulling me with her.

"Now, what was that conversation?" Mother demanded, placing her hands on my shoulders. "First, sit!" She ordered, pushing me into a chair. I just sat there, unable to speak. She repeated the question.

"We were just talking." I finally managed. My mouth wouldn't work properly; my tongue felt stuck.

"How long have these conversations been going on? By the sound of it, it's been years," she said. I replied, yes. They had been going on a long time.

"Did it occur to you that we might have allowed you two to talk if you had told us," She asked?

"No," I breathed a sigh, "That's why I kept it a secret. William didn't tell me to. I just did!"

"I see. Starting tonight, no more conversations with him in English or German," she said.

"Mother, how did you know about us meeting anyway?" I asked.

"Lydia!" Mother said, then stood up and walked to the window.

"Something you left in a letter that was almost overlooked!"

I was confused. "What letter?"

"Lydia's sister wrote underneath part of a letter to your sister, then posted it. Remember?"

I had to think for a minute, but I couldn't remember anything.

"Well, do you remember that letter?" She repeated. I said no. "Well, you wrote that if people knew about William, they'd say he was the enemy. Correct?"

Suddenly I remembered. Lydia's sister had written that. "Yes!" I replied softly, "I do remember."

"Good! For now, you'll stay in the dormitory after lessons until Mrs. Davis, and I decide what to do!" I sat silently. I could feel my heart beating.

We heard a knock at the door, and I turned toward it. Who was that? Mother went to the door and stepped into the hall. I waited but couldn't hear anything. Only the ticking clock. She came back.

"Mrs. Davis is coming. You will wait here!" I said nothing.

Mother sighed. "Who knew about this?" She asked.

"No one!" I answered, not looking at her. I hesitated. Will Leah be punished by her mother? I took a deep breath, then let it out. "Except

184

Leah."

"She knew. So, that explains why William was the only one reading your letters. She wrote to you in German, am I right?" Or did you teach her Braille secretly?" I replied the letter was written in German.

"Who printed yours?"

"Lydia's sister, John, Mrs. Blake, William, another parent. They never asked to read the rest."

Another knock. It was Mrs. Davis. When she entered, she walked straight to me, her shoes tapping.

"Mother Anderson, you may leave," she said.

"Well, Missy, explain!" She actually raised her voice. She seemed really tall just then. I explained to her how William and I began meeting, about your letters, and the discovered mistake in mine. When I finished, she was silent. She sat stiffly beside me.

"I'm curious, how long were you going to keep that secret?" I said I didn't know. "Well, if it weren't for Lydia, you wouldn't be here, would you? You and William would still be talking?" She asked.

"Probably!" I replied, not looking up. She raised my chin, so I had to face her. "Is talking all that happened?"

"Yes!" I answered, "
"He's never done anything else, never taken advantage of you." When I replied he hadn't, I felt her body relax a little.

"What will happen now? Will Leah's Mum have to know?" I asked.

"I don't know. First, Mother Anderson and I will speak to William and John. Without you." Now, let's go to your dormitory. And don't tell the others, understand?"

"Yes!" I answered softly. We walked quickly, arriving just as everyone was returning from the washroom.

"Good, you're here!" Mother opened the door and pushed me in. "No talking, any of you. I'll join you in a minute."

"Esther, what happened? You missed dinner!" Amy inquired.

"She said no talking!" Mary interrupted, "So, be quiet." Mother returned, and we continued with our evening.

Finally, this week's over. I had to be escorted everywhere by teachers.

Hannah thought it was hilarious. "Finally, the Charity Girl's in trouble!" she taunted. I'm relieved they still don't know the reason yet. William and John are still working here. That's a good thing. Has Mrs. Davis written to you?

Back to news on the war: on the twenty-third, the Japanese and the Americans fought in another battle as well, this time in the Gulf of Leyte. The Japanese are trying to stop the Americans from capturing an island in the Philippines. So far, a cruiser sank, and Japanese planes were shot down. It's been three days, and the Americans won. They had more powerful torpedoes.

I'll feel horrible if you get punished for knowing about our meetings too. You didn't know anything more.

Your miserable sister,

Esther

P.S... Mother Anderson will print my letters now.

November 3

Dear Esther,

What a horrible thing that happened to you and William! What made Edith remember that part of the letter? I was right about our secret conversations. Yours were discovered. I don't blame Mother Anderson for being angry. At least he's still employed there. But for how long?

War news now: more cities are freed by the Allies, and Mr. Roosevelt was elected for a fourth term. No need to worry. I haven't received a letter or phone call regarding our letters. My part's still unknown to everyone.
Anxiously waiting,

Leah

December 6

Dear Leah,

The first week of December, and if the Germans, British, and Americans hadn't started fighting in Belgium, everything would be all right.

Many more girls will be going home for Christmas. And I overheard Mother Anderson telling John her news yesterday. She received a letter from her sister, saying the family's well, but still nothing from her brother.

Mrs. Porter and Miss Leigh have a surprise for us this year, Mary has tried to get them to reveal it, but they won't. Speaking of surprises, yours should arrive soon! I just wish we could talk; it's been years!

December tenth!: Mrs. Davis sent for me today, with Mrs. Blake escorting me.

She knocked. "Enter!" Mrs. Davis called. "Sit!" She commanded. I sat on a hard wooden chair and waited. "It's about William. Did you know his real name?"

"No, what do you mean?" I looked towards her.

"Wilhelm. That's it. You're sure he never mentioned it?" I replied that he hadn't. "I knew his mother was German, and his father was English," I said and waited, hands clenched in my lap. "I'm German. What's the difference?"

"We knew your history. He deceived us."

"What?"

"Tricked, Esther. He gave us a false name," she answered. I felt sick, my stomach dropped.

"Why?" I asked.

187

"He said using an English name would be better than his German one, especially now. It's Wilhelm." She took a breath. "His English name, you know!"

Yes, but I was still shocked. A different name? "Did he think he couldn't work here with a German name?" I asked.

"Yes, Esther. As I explained, he needed an English name when he came here. So, he chose William. He fooled us because he doesn't have an accent." I said nothing. "Did he tell you anything else about his parents?" I told her what I knew. "Well, you may go. Don't mention this to anyone." I promised I wouldn't.

I couldn't sleep last night. I felt angry at William (or whatever his name is) for lying to us. At the same time, I understood why he did it. To be employed in England, he needed a new name. All day, I was distracted, still in shock. None of the other girls knew anything. They went on chatting about home and how soon this war will be over.

It's been a month since William and my secret were discovered.
And, finally, the girls are talking. "Mother Anderson says William's German!" In Mrs. Davis's class, Amy said, "He had a false name. Esther, is it true you and he have been meeting?"
I was about to answer when Mrs. Davis told us to get back to work. "It's none of your business!"

"William's German, too?" Anna asked us at lunch, "Esther, you two talked?" I admitted we had. However, I refused to say what we talked about.

Night, another Christmas is over, and no tree again this year. Catherine, Amy, and Mary stayed in our dormitory; the older girls who stayed were Susan, Anna, and Julia. After breakfast and Bible reading, we played in the snow. Making snowballs with slushy snow isn't very easy, but we tried, anyway. Of course, the snowballs melted into slushy water.

Our surprise was a turkey! "Where did you get that?" Miss Walters gasped.

"I traded with the butcher!" Miss Leigh said. The pudding was a strawberry tart. Around the table the conversation was about ending the war: "So my Dad will come home!"

We didn't miss the King's Christmas message. This time he began by

188

wishing a happy Christmas to the doctors, nurses, and men fighting overseas. He spoke about the loneliness of separation. He went on to say two things could end the war: First, defeat the Japanese and Germans, then all people could be free. He ended his speech by wishing for peace next year.

If the Allies continue like they have been, families can be reunited soon.

This was a long letter, but I had to tell you everything.

Very confused,

Esther

P.S... Here's something more cheerful- But it proved a snare to him, and his insolence was silenced.

1945
Thursday, January 7

Dear Esther,

I'm very jealous of your Christmas dinner! Ours was ham, without gravy or pepper. Mum should know by now I can't eat that, but she served it anyway, saying, "No wasting, girls!" I ate everything to show her I wasn't wasteful.

Thank you for the pretty gloves! Mine are Jane's old ones that's worn through.

Enid and Dora stayed with us again, so Christmas wasn't as gloomy as it could've been. They opened presents from home, as well as from Mum and Dad. We didn't have presents, because we went to the cinema a couple of weeks earlier as a Christmas treat.

The film was a funny story about women hiding in a house in Germany. The comedy begins when British soldiers have to hide from the Nazis when their plane crashes. Of course, people fall in love. While watching, I thought about how different the war could be if it happened like that.

We went out with friends the other day, having fun until Leron told us shocking news.

He described a concentration camp called Auschwitz. He heard there were dead bodies everywhere because Nazis were murdering Jewish people and thousands of sick prisoners, too. He said that it was liberated by the Soviets! Thank G-D. I hate to think what other horrors will be discovered before this is all over. It makes me sick to think how that kind of evil has been happening all this time. How did we not hear about this?

A German name, unbelievable! William could have deceived many people since his father was English. He surprised everybody, not in a good way.

February eleventh now, Roosevelt, Stalin, and Churchill had a conference to discuss the ending of the war. They agreed that Germany shouldn't have a military, should have free elections in countries no longer under Nazi control, and talked about forming something called the United Nations.

It's the nineteenth, and America's attacked the island of Iwo Jima, Japan. Dad said they don't want the Japanese to use it as an airfield.

The twenty-sixth, after six more weeks of fighting, the Germans retreated from Belgium. The Americans have lost many soldiers, and some are missing. Finally, the US bombed Berlin.

Mum and Dad said I can stay with them as long as I needed to after the war is over. That's very generous of them. I would have thought they'd want me to leave as soon as possible.

It's a very windy March. The UK and US troops have crossed the Rhine River into Germany, and perhaps they won't fight for much longer.

School was interesting last week. "How long do we have to keep doing this assignment?" Andrew complained toward the end of our history lesson. "It's pointless. The war's nearly over."

"Not much longer. Andrew, this exercise isn't pointless. Like I said, writing about your experiences may help later."

"She won't read them. If she did, what could she do?" He said, speaking of Princess Elizabeth.

"She'd know other children are going through similar experiences."
"She's doing plenty to help the war effort. She's a mechanic, repairing engines and learning to drive."

"She's still a lot safer than most people." Another boy spoke out.

"Enough. Let's get back to history, please." Miss looked sternly at us, "For better or worse, we are all in this war together. The King didn't leave when the Blitz occured, remember?"

Several kids nodded. "The Palace was hit." A girl added.

I personally felt that my classmates had a point. No matter what Miss said, Princess Elizabeth would always be protected behind those walls. She might be a mechanic, but to me, that doesn't change who she is.

The twenty-sixth, the fighting ended on Iwo Jima. America won, and as usual, there was death on both sides.

Three days of bombing in Dresden and one day in Berlin this month, more innocent people were killed. Depressing and dreary.

Your sister,

Leah

April 6

Dear Leah,

It's been horrible. Throughout January, Lydia was silent, speaking to me only when necessary. Something happened One evening, on our walk. "How could you?" she burst out, "You used my sister!" I tried telling her I didn't mean to get Edith involved, but Lydia wouldn't listen. "I told you our secret! You kept it, right?" Guiltily, I admitted I'd told you.

She sighed angrily and walked beside me but purposely kept a lot of space between us. I had almost to shout to be heard.

"Lydia, Edith didn't know. She didn't question me when she printed the last part; she just posted it!" I explained. There was silence. "When did she remember?"

"After our disastrous summer. I told her about all the times you sneaked away. She said, "It's just her and someone named William.'` She didn't realize who William was, and I didn't tell her." The day Mother discovered you, I told her I might know who you were meeting. I didn't know where you two met. I suppose she figured it out." She walked on

191

ahead and, understandably, wouldn't say another word. I tried changing the subject, but she still refused to speak.

Like other times, I went quietly to bed. Only Amy inquired how I was. When Lydia ordered her not to talk to me, she replied, "It wasn't my sister who posted that letter."

The Americans and Japanese are fighting on the island of Okinawa. So far, Japanese aircraft have destroyed American ships.

William departed for good. John handed me a letter from him, saying, "It's in German."

Mrs. Davis explained to everyone that he left because he "Told a horrible lie so he couldn't work here any longer." She didn't need to say more. I'm sure by that time, everyone knew the whole story.

Canadians are still liberating Dutch cities. More concentration camps are being freed as well, thank G-d. Some by Americans, others by the English.

It's horrifying listening to reports about Jews and other people being tortured by the Nazis in those places. Even their names sound evil, names like Buchenwald, Colditz Castle, and Bergen-Belsen. Some of those reports are so horrible I can't listen; I leave when they begin.

One report I managed to listen to was from Bergen-Belsen. The man reported that forty thousand men, women, and children were imprisoned behind barbed wire. When he drove through the gate, he saw bony faces at the barrack windows. In one of the huts, he found a girl who was alive and asking for medicine. Some children were sharing food next to a pile of bodies. A man fell and was dragged to the side of the road. The reporter had come to a hut and looked at each person to see if they were alive or dead. His report ended with discovering a pit filled with dead bodies lying on top of one another. The starving prisoners were eating them.

During the report, I wanted to say, "Turn it off." But I couldn't. I just sat there, unable to breathe. I think everyone was shocked. I heard crying and sniffling while we listened.

I'm more grateful now that our parents put us on that train to safety. I thank G-d we're here instead of dead in one of those camps!

Here's more cheerful news, Germany's finally stopped resisting, so total surrender can't be far away. I bet Hitler's vision of victory has been crushed.

I don't know who I'll be with this summer, maybe you?

I hope your news is better than mine,

Esther

May 10

Dear Esther,

Such joyful news: Hitler's dead! We don't know how, only that it happened a couple of days ago.

On Tuesday, Miss announced, "Eva would like to read one of her letters aloud. Please, start."

Gripping her papers, Eva turned to face us. She took a deep breath, and began:

Your Royal Highness;

My name is Eva. I am eleven years old. I came here because Germany is dangerous. My parents wanted me to be safe, so they sent me here.

When I first arrived, I was terrified! I couldn't speak, read, or write English. Would I fit in and make friends? What kind of family would I have?
(Miss held up her hand, and Eva looked up. "No interruptions!" Miss glared sternly at some English girls who'd been whispering. She nodded for Eva to continue):
My foster family is Jewish, like me. I also have a younger sister to play with, too! (At home, I'm an only child.)
The English teacher assisted us with English when we arrived. She could be strict, like when my English foster sister was put in the cold corner when she misbehaved.

I've made many friends; one is an English girl named Helen. Once, we skipped stones at our local pond, and she always walks me to and from school.

Our first year here, we celebrated Hanukkah at Daniel's. That's an eight-day celebration, a bit like Christmas.

I miss my German family; I pray for them often. I hope to be reunited when this is over. I live with a wonderful family and am fortunate to be in this country. If I can't be reunited with my family, I'd like to remain here.

Sincerely, Eva

There was silence when Eva finished. I glanced around and noticed two of the English kids wiping their eyes. Miss blinked, then took Eva's letter from her. We couldn't see what was written on it, but Eva grinned. Before she reached her seat, Carmela rushed over and hugged her.

Did you hear the King's V.E. speech? He honored the servicemen who gave their lives and once again praised the civilians who fought on land. Our faith kept us strong, he said. Now, England and the world have to be restored. He ended by thanking G-d for his mercies during the war and for the peaceful guidance of that same strong hand.

Love you,

Leah!

June 12

Dear Leah,

Finally, people are starting to speak to me again. Miss Leigh talked about her summer plans. John asked me how you are. Lydia played a piano piece with me, and Catherine and I walked together.

Exams were odd this year. Mrs. Davis wanted an essay on Oliver Twist, which Mother had to read to us because Mrs. Davis was unable to find a Braille copy. Dismal story, except when Oliver finds his family.

Sewing was making blankets on the machine. Not exactly hard, in my opinion. Even Geography was fun. We had a contest to see who could name the most English places. Hannah won. The prize was chocolate. Of course, she didn't share!

Eva's letter was beautiful, she expressed my feelings about England, as well.

It's the twenty-second, and I'm with Mary this summer! So more exciting stories to share with you. The only war news is Okinawa has surrendered to the Americans. Perhaps, Japan will surrender now?

Esther

July 5

Dear Esther,

The conversation in class about Hitler's suicide was pretty... well... cheerful. Kids are relieved he's dead.

They talked of their siblings returning home now. They want things to return to normal, but I don't think anything will ever be normal again.

Everything's still rationed; when will that end? Jane can't wait to taste chocolate. Mum wants to plant onions. Everybody wants to wear fashionable clothes.

Yes, those reports about those evil concentration camps were terrible listening. I left the room in the middle of a report about Buchenwald. There were twenty-one thousand prisoners in all, liberated by the Americans. I also thank G-d we're here. My family was just as shocked as everybody else about those camps. It's like the world woke up to what we suspected was happening over there all along. Why it had to happen, we'll never understand.
Winston Churchill resigned as Prime Minister. He was defeated by Clement Attlee.

On to something lighter like summer, Enid and Dora are still with us. They have beaus, but they're not American. We haven't met them, and I don't suppose we ever will. They went to a dance, returning bright-eyed and giggling.

Prisoners of war camps are being liberated as well. Wherever they were held, the prisoners were housed in barracks and fed very little. Many became ill and died. The survivors were treated in hospitals or aboard hospital ships. They were described as skeletal and starved.

195

I'm not surprised you're having such a horrible time with this William business. Glad they came around in the end, though. Has the school replaced him?

America and Japan are still fighting. Speaking of Japan, there was a meeting between the leaders of China, America, and Britain, where they demanded Japan to surrender, but they refused.

Leron and I took Atalia to the cinema, her first time going in a long while. This film was about a supposedly haunted house. This couple moves in, and the companion who lives with them sees the ghost of the previous owner. The husband hires a man to play the dead husband. Confusing, I know.

Excited
Leah

Dear Leah,

Busy week so far. America's new President, Truman, Mr. Churchill, and Stalin met again. This time they agreed that the Nazis should be punished, and Germany should be split into four zones controlled by France, the US, Britain, and the Soviet Union.

I can't believe how awful Mary's parents were! Concerning our family, anyway.

One night over dinner, her Mum casually asked, "Have they found your parents' bodies? I read those camps are crawling with the dead."

Mary and I stopped eating; I sat there, unmoving. I tried to speak but couldn't. I felt angry all over again, like that night in the washroom. Jumping up, I angrily shoved my chair back. Mary and I fled the kitchen.

"Dad, how dare you?" Mary shouted. We heard both parents chuckling. Her siblings continued eating silently.

In her room, I couldn't stop shaking and crying. Mary apologized, promising me, "They've never been this horrible to other friends I've brought home. You don't have to come back again." I didn't speak to her at all the next day. I ignored her parents as much as possible until we returned.

Her siblings were sweet. Her brother taught me to play marbles. I didn't win, but it was a nice distraction. Her sisters ran around, singing.

The seventh, America bombed Hiroshima, Japan! The ninth, and Nagasaki was bombed. It's a shame all those innocent people had to die! Will Japan finally surrender?

We've returned, and something unusual occurred. Anna found me in the music room on Saturday. "Do you know where your family is?" She inquired. I stopped playing.

"No, why?"

"Two teachers want you to live with them once you finish school. Will you?" She demanded. I was silent. When had this been discussed? I wondered.

"Which one will you choose?" Her voice was loud, almost shouting. "You've gotten special treatment ever since you arrived!"

"Anna, I don't know anything about that!" I said.

"Miss Walters and Mrs. Blake were talking just now. I overheard them discussing you. They both want you to live with them. They've never had favorites with any of us, only you!"

"Anna, please," I interrupted, "Stop. I honestly haven't a clue about that. I don't want to live with them. They're wonderful teachers, but I think you know who I want to live with?"

"That sister of yours? How do you know she'll have you?"

"She's my sister! We've been separated too long!" I cried.

Anna laughed mockingly. "So has everybody else. The only difference is we'll probably see our families. Your parents could be dead, like those other Jews we've heard about."

I was speechless. I knew she was saying those words to upset me.

"Anna, Esther, stop this minute. You're both almost grown women. What's this about?"

I turned at Mother Anderson's voice.

"Mother, she's the teachers' favorite!" Anna said over my shoulder.

Mother asked for my side, and I explained I knew nothing about that conversation. Anna repeated what she'd heard. Mother said she'd speak to the teachers and sent us on our way. I found out we both received kitchen chores that evening and didn't get our free music period on Sunday.

Love, Esther

Leah's German Diary
September 20

For some reason, Jane and Sarah were allowed to go to the cinema. I had chores, as always. Sarah filled me in when they returned.

"It was a short documentary about Burma. By 1942, the Japanese had cut off the road, China was blocked from reaching their allies, and Japan could invade India. The Indians and British became the Southeast Asian army. By 1943, the province of Kohima was attacked, supply routes were cut. Americans supplied tons of supplies by air. The wounded had little medical aid. The road was reopened, and the Americans invaded Burma by air and planned to attack Japanese railways. When they reached it, they were able to carry out their plan. After that, the Americans captured a Japanese airfield. Then the narrator read soldiers' diaries, detailing their jungle march over the mountains to reach a river. Malaria and other diseases kept them exhausted, and the weather didn't improve. Malaria tablets weren't useful. They used elephants to transport everything. By October, they'd came out the other side and had to build a bridge to cross another river. In 1945, the two armies fought in Mandalay. There was a sea battle to prevent the Japanese from bringing reinforcements, and the Ledo-Burma Road was complete. They built boats and ships to cross the river and brought back supplies for the Allies. To the West, English and Indian armies fought the Japanese and pushed them back. By March, Mandalay was freed. The film ended with the Nagasaki bombings.

On the third, in class, Miss Simmons announced that Japan had surrendered! I'm not sure how anyone concentrated. We talked of nothing else.

Well, there was excitement on the playground yesterday. "Girls, stop this instant!" Miss ran on to the schoolyard, where we were playing. I was with Eva and Daniel, so I didn't see them at first. "You two, enough!" Miss shouted. There was silence as Miss ran to Nora and Bridget! I saw Nora had a cut lip and blood on her forehead; Bridget's dress was torn. Both were crying as Miss separated them. Jane heard they had to stay inside for the rest of the year.

"No wonder! Nora's grieving for her sister." Mum looked sympathetic, "She's heartbroken!"

"Bridget's relatives came home," Sarah said softly.

"I think there won't be a family anywhere who won't be grieving for someone they love," Dad added. Jane just stared at the table. Enid and Dora came in then, and Dad prayed, asking G-d to give strength to the families grieving for loved ones. We ate silently. Dora and Enid looked curiously at us but asked nothing. Didn't they have relatives in the war, too?

It's very sad. Soldiers and nurses are returning, and many are injured in some way. But there are many families without loved ones. Funeral services have been held, with more to come. Miss canceled school for a while.

(Tuesday, December 18, Morning

I'm so overjoyed that I couldn't sleep last night! Esther's coming. Mother Anderson's bringing her today. She can stay with us for Christmas and the New Year!

"She seems like a lovely girl!" Dad commented. Sarah can't wait to meet her. She'll probably pester her with questions. Dad's calling me. I think she's here!)

The car is driven by a woman in a pretty dress and coat: Mother Anderson. I rush out of the house and run to meet it. Her door opens, she climbs out, then opens the door for Esther.

I stare, my mouth open. She's so tall, I think, not my little sister, but a beautiful girl with long braided hair.

I reach out to her, and we hug for a long time, crying and laughing. We run our hands through each other's hair, not speaking. Esther's thick braid comes midway down her back, the end tied with a ribbon; she strokes my long straight hair. Babbling in German, we begin to talk at once.

"Well, I know who you are!"

We break apart, and Esther gasps. Then, turning, she answers, "I'm Esther. Nice to meet you. You must be Leah's Mum." I guess she hadn't heard her coming. She holds out her hand, but Mum refuses to take it. How dare you! I scream silently.

Mother Anderson comes around the car and introduces herself. "I'll come for you soon after the New Year. Now, have fun, and Merry Christmas!" She hands Esther her case and drives away.

"You sit there!" Mum shouts at Esther. She points, but of course, Esther can't see.

"Over here, by me," I say. She touches each chair until she finds the empty one between Jane and me. We pray, then Mum serves us. "It's in front of you!" Mum says, exasperated, "See, right there."

Esther finds her plate. "I can use cutlery, Miss." Everyone stops eating. I look over and see a slice of bread, cheese, and a piece of chicken.

"You'll only make a mess." Mum snaps. "Just eat!"

"Dear, perhaps she can manage!" Dad says.

"Yes, I can. If we made messes in school, we cleaned them up." Esther explains impatiently.

"Show me!" Mum slams down a fresh plate with our dinner and the meal continues; no spills and no food on her clothes or floor.

Esther tries to have a conversation with Jane to her left, but she's not talking. Dad eventually asks her something about Mother Anderson but nothing else. Only Sarah keeps the conversation going. She and I tell her stories about Eva and Charlotte. Some of it Esther knew from letters, but she laughs anyway. I catch Jane smiling a little. Mum eats silently, cutlery scraping her plate.

"Leah, if she's finished, tell her the plate goes over there!" Mum says.

200

"I can hear. The sink?" Esther asks, "Where is it?"

"Stand up, walk past my chair. The sink's straight ahead." She finds the sink without a problem.

"No, girl. Leah, tell her you do the washing up here. She'll break the dishes if she does!" Mum orders. I want to slap her.

"Miss, I can speak English. I may not know where things are, but at least let me help wash up!" Esther says, answering for herself.

"Mum, since Esther's here, I'll take over!" Sarah offers. Thank you, Sarah.

"Sarah, Jane, dishes!" Dad cuts in. Finally!

We're alone now in my dismal attic. Wrapped in worn thin blankets, we finish singing the song we've been translating. Then, we talk in German.

"Is she always that horrible?" Esther asks.

"If you mean Mum, yes! You've read my letters!" I say.

"I thought perhaps she'd be civil to me. Jane, she didn't say much."

"No, she and Dad were both quiet!" I reply.

"He wasn't very helpful, either," Esther says angrily.

"That's how they are!" I sigh, "I can't wait until I leave with you, just not sure where yet." Laughing, we embrace for a long time.

"I was hoping you'd say that!" She says. We talk about Mama and Papa for a while, wishing they were here.

She fills me in on her friends' party. Still no word from Wilhelm. "On September third, there was so much joy! The war was over.

In the dining hall, the whole school celebrated.

The celebrations would have been complete if Wilhelm had been there. I'm still furious he was dismissed. He was my friend, the one person I could talk to about our family. Just because he's half German, they had to dismiss him. Yes, I realize he lied. John doesn't even know where he is.

I bumped into Anna in the hall after our party. She put her hand on my arm, saying, "It's over!!"

"Yes," I replied, "Now, families who've been apart can be reunited."

"What's your plan now?" She asked.

"To see Leah and then finish school." Esther finishes.

"Oh, here." Esther hands me his last letter.

Dear Esther,

It was a pleasure to know you. I enjoyed our conversations very much, even though they were a secret. Please forgive me for not sharing my true name with you. I didn't want you to be burdened with my lie. I apologize for how things ended the way they did. Mrs. Davis felt it best that I leave.

I wish you the best in school and hope you find your sister someday.

Your friend,

Wilhelm

We're both crying as I finish. Esther slips it in her case.

To change the subject, I show her my German diaries.

"Leah, do you think anyone will want to read these?" She asks, inspecting the diaries. "There's so many here."

"I don't know," I reply quietly, "Maybe they're only meant for us." Now, before bed, we say the Shema, thanking G-d we're finally together.

Esther

Holding my cane, I stand at the corner, waiting to cross. The button's pressed, traffic stops, and I cross the street to the bakery. We've been employed there since a couple of years after the war ended. I open the door, and the bell tinkles pleasantly. The aroma of warm bread fills my nose.

"Esther, is that you?"

"Yes, Atalia," I call. I make my way to the kitchen, where she's rolling out dough.

"Leah's picking up supplies." She says. Placing my cane in the corner, I put on an apron and join her at the baking counter. "Did Mrs. C. enjoy her basket?" She asks.

"She thanks you for the cake and wants the recipe," I answer.

The bell tinkles, and wiping her hands on her apron, Atalia heads to the front of the shop. I turn my attention to the dough. Where's Elizabeth? (She's an Englishwoman we hired when we first opened.)

When Atalia returns, I ask about her. "Sick today!" She says. We continue working in silence for a while. The soft dough taking shape in our hands.

The bell tinkles again, and Leah enters with bags. I know it's her; I recognize the old German song she's singing.

I Finish with the dough, we unpack. We wait on customers until closing time. Most of them speak English, but some speak German or other languages. If Atalia or Leah can't communicate, they use gestures. Me, it's either guesswork or asking someone for assistance.

"The dough's risen," Atalia calls. We clean up; the dough's placed in the

203

freezer. Then, we lock up.

Our house isn't far, so walking home isn't bad, except when it's cold.

The street is crowded with people speaking many languages. The sun is setting now, and a cool breeze blows. I smell flowers in the air. Someone's car radio is playing a Petula Clarke song; kids play on the sidewalk.

"Teacher!" A girl calls.

"Yes?" Leah and I answer in unison.

"Is my lesson Sunday?" She asks.

"Yes," Leah turns toward her, answering sternly, "And bring your music."

We turn onto our street; the noise seems to fade into the background.

Reaching our house, Leah unlocks the door. We're home.

It's taken a long time to arrive here. After Leah and I finished school, Leah, Atalia, and I couldn't find employment in the countryside, so we moved to the city. (Atalia and I were introduced during my Christmas visit. We couldn't speak much because, as Leah described in her letters, Mrs. Evans was always nearby. We had a brief conversation on the street. She was thrilled when the war ended. Not surprisingly, she hasn't heard from her family, either.)

She joined us when Mrs. Evans informed her she was no longer needed. "No warning, no "good luck!" Atalia was both furious and relieved. Since she still wasn't comfortable speaking English with strangers, we agreed she could live with us.

Many people weren't comfortable hiring Jews or a blind woman. It was a constant struggle for us to find employment at all, even domestic work. Whenever I applied for a typist position, I was told, "The position has been filled." Along the way, we met many people looking for a place to call home- wherever that was.

Leah and I couldn't bear to return to Berlin. We learned that our parents had been killed in a concentration camp, along with many others. To honor our loved ones, we wore black ribbons in our hair. Returning to our old house was difficult, but we decided to see for ourselves. Utterly destroyed, burnt buildings scattered everywhere! Our neighbors, places we knew, and family were gone. Nothing remains now except memories. Heartbroken, we returned to England. We barely said a word the whole journey back.

Atalia didn't want to see her town. She pointed out, "Why see a dead city?"

When Hitler committed suicide because Germany was losing, I don't know anyone who mourned. He caused too much suffering for millions of people.

Leah told me something fascinating. He wrote a book called Mein Kampf.

One of my friends said it has six Braille volumes.

That's not on my bookshelves, but the Tanakh is. Yes, it's taken years, but it is at long last available in Braille.

When we were finally settled, Mrs. Davis wrote me about an institute that produces Jewish literature in Braille. Of course, I wrote to them, inquiring about the Tanakh. They had it, but I had to learn to read Hebrew Braille first. That was great, except for one problem. Hebrew Braille was more complicated to learn than English because of how the letters are formed. Many different combinations of dots make up the Hebrew alphabet. At least I don't have to read it backward. I wish I could take the book to our synagogue; it's too bulky.

In our relaxing room, on a small table, sits my Brailler. It's louder but much easier to use than the slate and stylus. The piano stands in another corner by a window, and under the bench seat is Braille and print sheet music. Leah plays whenever she wants. (She and I teach on weekends.) Atalia prefers her paintings. Her easel stands underneath a window, where she has a view of the park; she says, in winter, the snow-covered trees are beautiful.

Meanwhile, Winston Churchill and King George the sixth are dead, replaced by Anthony Eden as Prime Minister and Princess Elizabeth as Queen. I still remember her speech, telling us to have courage. We watched her coronation on our neighbor's television. It's like radio, accompanied by a black-and-white picture. The ceremony was beautiful, held in the Abbey where her father was crowned. Many attended, and when she appeared on the balcony, crowds lining the streets cheered. Last year, she gave birth to a son, Prince Edward.

India gained its independence in 1947. It's partitioned into two nations, India and Pakistan. The centuries under British rule weren't exactly kind to the Indian people. Many fought and lost their lives for their independence.

During partition, there was violence, millions of people were displaced or killed.

Gandhi was assassinated in 1948. Thousands attended the funeral, where his body was cremated. Many laid flowers around him. Mourners lining the streets wept as his body was driven past.

Nehru became the Prime Minister of India after India gained independence. His new laws included allowing women to inherit property and free education for the people. Jinnah became the first governor of Pakistan after partition.

In America, General Eisenhower became President and was replaced by John F. Kennedy, who was later assassinated. Now Lyndon Johnson is President.

We discovered the Americans weren't so great after all. Their government interned thousands of Japanese Americans after Pearl Harbor. Those camps weren't quite like the Nazi sites, but Roosevelt shouldn't have imprisoned innocent people. I suppose Americans believed they were the enemy, just like the English thought we Germans were (and to some still are!)

It's Friday, we open the bakery early. Leah and Elizabeth work up front while Atalia and I begin working in the kitchen. It's time to bake our special Challah for Shabbat.

The End

Acknowledgments

I began researching this book four years ago. I discovered the word Kindertransport by chance while researching evacuated children. That took me down a path of research I didn't expect to go down.

The Internet is fantastic! Some websites provided inspiration for my imaginary school. For their archived documentaries on Chorleywood College and Royal broadcasts, thanks to YouTube! Stumbling across a diary written by evacuated blind girls was very exciting; after reading it, my imagination did the rest! Other websites were useful when I researched rationing, fashion, and entertainment.

Books were beneficial; some were for research, and others were inspirational. For nurses' experiences, I turned to Sisters In Arms by Nicola Tyrer. Worth Saving, Disabled Children During the Second World War, described the evacuation and education of disabled British children. Churchill's Secret War was a great help when researching the famine in India. For Judaism facts, there was The Everything Judaism Book and How to Keep Kosher. Hitler's Forgotten Victims was a horrifying look at disabled children who the Nazis killed. Inferno, The World At War looked at wartime life for the people and countries involved. Never Give In are audio versions of Churchill's speeches.

People assisted me with this project, as well. I had great editors who provided helpful feedback on the characters, plot, and historical accuracy.

Certain creative parts of the story are my own. The blind girls using canes are my invention since Orientation and Mobility teachers weren't trained until the 1960s. I didn't read any memoirs written by evacuated children; I wanted my characters to come out of my own imagination. That's why this novel is historical fiction. It's taken multiple drafts to complete Esther and Leah's journey. Every single character was exciting to create.

Bibliography

1. Sept. 7- Berlin because of Hitler and his Nazi soldiers---
www.bbc.com

2. Sept. 5- Berlin, before Hitler's violence---www.annefrank.org

3. September 17- Winston Churchill, whose speeches talk about being
against Hitler.
September 3rd, Britain declared war on Germany---www.gov.uk,
history.com

4. Prime Minister, Neville Chamberlain met with Hitler
www.nationalarchives.gov.uk

5. Sept. 18-Hitler's Nazis took over https://encyclopedia.ushmm.org

6. Winston Churchill spoke to Britain about the Soviet Union's
invasion of Poland. www.winstonchurchill.org

7. Soviet Union is trying to stay out of this war.) German submarines
are being attacked by British www.history.com

8. October 13- BBC (British Broadcasting Corporation.)—
www.britannica.com

9. October 16- German bomb that destroyed three Royal Navy ships--
-www.royalnavy.mod.uk

10. October 30 Mr. Churchill and others were on a warship that didn't
explode when it was attacked by the Germans yesterday—
www.history.co.uk

11. December 25- Mr. Churchill was right-, it's going to be a long war
for everyone. www.winstonchurchill.org

12. Germans are fighting with Poland, and Britain. www.bbc.com

13. The war is in Europe Brave men and women are helping to fighting Hitler—www.nationalww2museum.org

14. President Roosevelt wasn't sending his Armies? Churchill pleaded for America to fight against the Nazis www.nationalgeographic.com and https://nationalarchives.gov.uk (America offered to take up to 200.000 children as evacuees

15. Prince Albert died, her grief lasted the rest of her life. She was named Empress of India in 1868 www.britannica.com https://royalcentral.co.uk-she became Empress of India in 1876

16. British men were on board a German tanker and they were rescued by a British Navy ship in Norwegian waters, Hitler's planes was shot down over Scotland. Hitler's Nazis invaded Denmark and Norway— https://www.warhistoryonline.com, www.smithsonianmag.com(there was no reference that the plane was shot down. The plane was found ablaze by a Scottish farmer in his field), www.annefrank.org

17. Indians died of that sickness-the Spanish Flu!"— www.washingtonpost.com

18. Britain taxed farmers for their crops—www.britannica.com

19. India powerless? Because it's under British rule?---www.gktoday.in

20. April 4-"Isn't India part of Britain?" British are superior www.britannica.com India Independence Day from British rule was 1947—not verified that English government felt India's people couldn't govern on their own and that British were superior.

21. English Empire are powerful (www.newyorker.com).

22. Government formed the North India Company in 1630, (The English-www.britannica.com)

23. Merchants were hoping to become wealthy (www.history.com)

24. The actual assassination of Viceroy Lord Mayo (www.outlookindia.com)

25. Religious blokes couldn't agree on whether India should be split (www.pewresearch.org)

26. Winston Churchill formed a new administration with a war cabinet, and Parliament (www.nationalchurchillmuseum.org).

27. Victory at all costs. speech ended by saying Britain must be united against Hitler. (www.nationalchurchillmuseum.org)

28. Armies have invaded Holland,Belgium, and France.(annefrank.org)

29. "We must go forward together." (https://winstonchurchill.org)

30. Churchill sympathizes with the Jews (https://jcpa.org)

31. Many ships were destroyed in the battle of Norway (www.theguardian.com)

32. The British, Germans, and French are now fighting in Operation Dynamo, in a place called Dunkirk, France Operation Dynamo is over (www.iwm.org.uk)

33. Mr. Churchill spoke about the English troops being rescued by boats (winstonchurchill.org)

34. Ships made trip after trip, bringing back men they'd rescued (www.nationalww2museum.org).

35. The Royal Air Force. (www.raf.mod.uk)

36. British planes attacked German bombers. (www.britannica.com)

37. Threatened by Nazi bombs. (www.history.com)

38. France and Belgium have now surrendered (https://enclyclopedia.ushmm.org)

39. Italy has declared war on France and England. (www.history.com)

40. Norway is now under Nazi control (www.history.com).

41. "Factory   work's   dangerous,   too.
    (https://www.payerandassociates.com)

42. You have to wear special equipment (www.osha.gov)

43. July 10, the Battle of Britain's begun (www.history.com)

44. August 21- British pilots bomb Germany night after night.
    (Unverifiable information)

45. Hitler's plan to attack Britain the British Air Force bombed Berlin
    (www.historyextra.com)

46. Bombs over London September 8th (www.britannica.com)

47. There was fighting in West Africa September 26 British, French, and
    Australian (www.worldnavalships.com)

48. London continues to be bombed (www.britannica.com)

49. Liverpool was bombed November 30 (www.iwm.org.uk)

50. October 14 Children's Hour Princess Elizabeth. (www.royal.uk)
    wartime-broadcast-1940

51. Queen Alexandra founded a nursing school (www.nam.ac.uk).

52. A   Matron   (head   nurse),   is   in   charge
    (https://museumofmilitarymedicine.org.uk)

53. December   9   a   battle   began   in   Libya   Egypt
    (https://encyclopedia.ushmm.org,

54. The British and Indian armies are trying to push the Italians out.
    (www.iwm.org.uk)

55. Italians are out of Egypt. (www.iwm.org.uk)

56. Battle of The British and Indian armies prevented from reaching
    Tobruk, (www.iwm.org.uk)

57. Three nights in a row of bombing in Sheffield December 15 (www.ancestry.co.uk)

58. Christmas is devastating for people in Liverpool and Manchester! (www.manchestereveningnews.co.uk)

59. Men were trapped on the beaches of a place called Dunkirk, France, and many died (www.britannica.com)

60. In the battle in the skies many aircrafts were also shot down, but the English still won. (www.britannica.com)

61. September's begun with bombs dropping on London 1940 (www.history.com)

62. December 1940 Besides snow, bombs are falling, in London, and other cities, too (www.history.com)

63. January 1941 the English bombed airfields in Tobruk, North Africa. (Britannica.com)

64. It's the twenty-fourth, and the English, Italians, and Australians had a battle (www.history.com)

65. Bombings, this time in Wales and Portsmouth. 1941 (www.iwm.org.uk)

66. March. President Roosevelt signed the Lend-Lease Act. (www.archives.gov).

67. It's the fifteenth, and more English cities have been bombed 1941(historicengland.org.uk)

68. Two German ships were sunk by the English. (www.history.com-- the Bismarck was sunk by the British navy).

69. The BBC reported of bombings in a place called Ireland. (www.bbc.com)

70. In North Africa, Tobruk was captured by the Germans. (www.iwm.org.uk)

71. Belfast, Ireland was bombed by the Luftwaffe. (www.bbc.com)

72. Plymouth was once again hit by German bombs. (www.plymouth.gov.uk)

73. The BBC reports there's bombings in Scotland. (www.bbc.com)

74. Definition by Wikipedia naval submarine operated by Germany).

75. Twenty-third, Mr. Churchill announced that Germany has invaded the Soviet Union. (www.iwm.org.uk)

76. Hitler and the leader of the Soviet Union, Stalin, had an agreement to fight for ten years, (www.history.com)

77. That's changed since the invasion of Poland (www.history.com)

78. The Nazis are spread all over that country in the Ukraine, (www.iwm.org.uk)

79. Twenty-ninth and, in the Ukraine, cities are falling; a four-day battle. Germany won. (www.history.com)

80. He and the American President Roosevelt discussed a joint declaration. (www.history.com)

81. Peace after war. (history.state.gov)

82. The Soviet-German battle with the Germans heading toward Kiev. (www.britannica.com)

83. The nineteenth, Kiev is taken. The Ukraine left unharmed. (www.britannica.com)

84. Twenty-fourth, City of Kharkov was invaded by the Germans, (www.iwm.org.uk)

85. The twenty-sixth, the Soviets protected Sevastopol (82 states the German armies are in Sevastopol)

86. America's been attacked by Japan. Many lives were lost. (census.gov)

87. President Roosevelt declared war on Japan. (www.archives.gov)

88. Now, Germany has declared war on Japan, (Germany was an ally of Japan;Hitler declared war on America because of the attack on Japan;Germany and Japan never fought against each other (annefrank.org) and an American submarine has sunk a Japanese ship. (Unverifiable information) In Sevastopol, the Germans are still there.(www.history.com--also called the battle at Crimea) They tried to damage ships, but they didn't accomplish much damage.

89. Churchill's speech about Pearl Harbor. He said if the US became involved, Britain would, too. He spoke to Roosevelt when Japan declared war on the US and Britain. Then Churchill's cabinet declared war on Japan (www.nationalww2museum.org) Back to Pearl Harbor. It was horrible, but now the US has joined this war (www.loc.gov), we'll have another Allie; Japan and America have been having meetings for some time now. They couldn't reach an agreement about trading for things the Japanese army needed. (www.history.com)

90. Soviet armies are now fighting in the Ukraine. (Britannica.com)

91. Operation Barbarossa ended; the Soviets won this one. (www.britannica.com)

92. Germany is fighting in Sevastopol. (www.nationalww2museum.org)

93. Battle in Kharkov on the twelfth. More supplies arrived for the Germans. (www.encyclopedia.com)

94. Jews are dying, by the thousands in Poland, according to the BBC. (www.nationalww2museums.org)

95. Japan was defeated in the Battle of Midway by the US. (www.britannica.com)

96. Page 97-- A battle at El Alamein, Egypt. (www.iwm.org.uk).

97. Fight on the island of Guadalcanal; Henderson Field, captured by the US. (www.britannica.com)

98. Africa, Alam Halfa with the German attempted to past British armies out of Egypt. (www.iwm.org.uk)

99. Stalingrad bombed by the Luftwaffe, (www.britannica.com)

Leningrad, Hitler's paused the fighting. (www.history.com)
Stalingrad, Germany has halted all fighting for the rest of the year,

(www.history.com) o

Germany and Britain are fighting a battle in El Alamein. (www.britannica.com)

Battles at Guadalcanal have ended, (www.brittanica.com)

It's the eighth, and in Egypt, another battle's begun called Operation Torch, between Britain under General Montgomery, the US under General Eisenhower, and Germany under Rommel.(www.britannica.com November 8, 1942, to November 16,1942)

Printed in the USA
CPSIA information can be obtained
at www.ICGtesting.com
LVHW020904300923
759722LV00009B/1279